THE BOOK YOU'VE BEEN WAITING FOR!

Twenty-five men and one beautiful woman got together to produce the most sensational bestseller of the year.

Naked Came the Stranger

Naked Came The Stranger

PENELOPE ASHE

A DELL BOOK

To Daddy

Published by
DELL PUBLISHING CO., INC.
750 Third Avenue
New York, New York 10017
Dell ® TM 681510, Dell Publishing Co., Inc.
Reprinted by arrangement with
Lyle Stuart, Inc.
239 Park Avenue South
New York, New York 10003
Printed in Canada
First Dell printing—March 1970

CONTENTS

Naked
Came
The
Stranger

BILLY AND GILLY

Screwed. It was, Gillian realized, an obscene word. But it was the word that came to mind. Screwed. It had been, after all, an obscene act. She tried not to think about it. She was driving, floating actually, toward her new house, floating past the freshly butchered lawns dotted with the twisted golden butts that were the year's first fallen leaves, past the homes built low and the swimming pools and the kempt hedges and all the trappings that went into the unincorporated village of King's Neck.

Screwed. The word kept coming back to Gillian Blake. Small wonder. For on that bright first Friday morning of October, Gillian had discovered through relatively traditional methods—specifically through the good offices of the Ace-High Private Investigators, Inc. —that her husband had been spending his every week-day afternoon in an apartment leased by one Phyllis Sammis, a twenty-two-year-old Vassar graduate with stringy hair, gapped teeth, horn-rimmed glasses and peculiarly upright breasts. Gillian Blake had paid the Ace-High people six hundred and seventy-five dollars (including expenses) to learn that William—or Billy, as he was known to the rest of the world, or at least that portion of the world described in certain circles as the Metropolitan Listening Area—had been leaving his office every afternoon at 2:45, taking a taxicab to the northeast corner of Seventh Avenue and 23rd Street, walking a half block south, climbing two flights of stairs and entering the apartment rented by Phyllis Sammis, recently hired production assistant on *The Billy & Gilly Show*.

Now Gillian was floating slowly past the road signs (*Stop* and *Hidden Driveway* and *Slow Children* and *Yield* and *Stop* again). Floating. It was this floating feeling that had drawn her to King's Neck in the first place. King's Neck, a boomerang of land twisting out from the mainland into the waters of Long Island Sound. Floating, floating toward the three-bedroom, two-bath, two-car house that was, as the man said, within easy commuting distance (forty-one minutes) of Manhattan and within sight (nine miles, through leaves) of the Connecticut shoreline.

Screwed. It was not so much that William Blake had cheated on Gillian Blake. Nor even that Billy had cheated on Gilly. In a sense, a quite real sense, he had cheated on that portion of the world known as the Metropolitan Listening Area. For William Blake was half of *The Billy & Gilly Show,* fifty per cent of "New York's Sweethearts of the Air," part of a radio team that five times a week dispensed a blend of controversy, information and . . . love. The show, so the announcer said every weekday morning at five seconds past nine, provided "a frank and open look into the reality of marriage in the crucible of modern living."

What held the show together (every poll indicated) was the quality of the marriage, the fact that this was a meeting of minds as well as bodies. The fact that every woman listening (the listenership was eighty-four per cent female) sensed that this was the way marriage should be. In cheating on Gilly, Billy had cheated on an audience that regularly numbered over eight hundred thousand—or at least he had cheated on eighty-four per cent of that audience. It was, when you considered it, an act of breathtaking infidelity.

Floating then into the circular driveway, mashed gravel, one and a half acres, imitation Tudor, water view, $85,000. There were several possibilities. She could, and the thought seemed strangely appealing at the moment, put arsenic in William's morning coffee. She could sue for divorce in any state in the Union and get it, along with a fair share of William Blake's not inconsiderable inheritance. These alternatives were considered, savored, ultimately discarded. The difficulty was that either course of action would mean the demise of *The Billy & Gilly Show*. And the show was what kept Gilly alive.

The car was parked. The keys were in her purse. Still, Gillian Blake did not move. There was yet another possibility. Gillian Blake could even the score. Absurd? Well, why not? King's Neck could be her laboratory, her testing ground. She could, with the cool detachment of a scientist, gather all the raw data necessary to determine how other marriages were faring "in the crucible of modern living." In the process, Billy would be screwed. Good and screwed.

She stepped from the car then, walked over fresh slate to the front door, past the bogus pillars, through the twin front doors. The clock showed it to be three in the afternoon. William was, if the pattern of the past week held true, mounting the down elevator from his office, mounting the downtown taxi, mounting a mousy twenty-two-year-old girl with remarkable breasts.

Damn Billy! Damn him anyway! But why all this outrage? Gillian realized it was not simply that William Blake had made a mockery of her marriage. Even worse he had made a mockery of her radio show. The show had started as a cliché, patterned after a formula that was perfected in the thirties. The thing that had kept it alive was Gillian Blake. And vice versa. It was what defined her, fulfilled her. It was what had saved her marriage this long, and it had quite possibly saved her life.

Gillian did not take full credit for the success of the show, even in her thoughts. It was, after all, a smooth division of labor. Gillian had proved adept at dragooning the squadrons of sociologists, the marriage counselors, the new authors, the broad spectrum of human engineers, onto the show. A few of the guests were clients of William's youthful public relations firm. Billy clarified, condensed, summed up—seldom departing from the role of straight man. Gilly stimulated, interpreted, played devil's advocate.

It had become so much more than a radio program. It had become, in time, an ideal marriage placed on display every morning for eight years, a model marriage that had been celebrated in three national magazines (one cover), a sophisticated blend of two disparate personalities.

Marriage . . . show—it had been a curious relationship. When the show had begun, marriage was new. As the show took on a life of its own, the marriage became somehow less alive. Now, Gillian reflected, it was almost as though the relationship had been parasitic, as though the show had begun to suck the life juices from the marriage it honored. It was the show that ate up long hours with a new book; it was the show that had at first determined there would be no children (until William's sterility had been medically established); it was the show that had required the presence of the twenty-two-year-old recent graduate of Vassar. It was the show that prevented Gillian from contemplating such eminently logical solutions as murder or divorce.

Screwed. Gillian let her clothes fall on the dressing-room carpet and studied the mirrored full-length portrait of herself. She understood her value to men, had felt their reaction often enough. Guests on the show, construction workers, taxi drivers—they all reacted. And why shouldn't they?

Her skin, the color of India tea at summer's end, flowed nicely over a slender frame. The breasts were small but she wore them well at age twenty-nine. Her legs were superbly designed. The hips, though trim, were deceptively full. Gillian advanced on the mirror, appraised the close-up image. Her long hair was light and now sun-streaked, gathered in a mist around her shoulders. If her lips were a trifle small, they none-

theless served to accentuate the perfectly straight line
of her nose. The total effect was a blend of the aristocratic and the sensual.

Gillian turned from the mirror. The mirror, after
all, couldn't reflect the most essential attribute of them
all. Gillian walked to the bar, made herself a pitcher
of martinis, sat drinking, naked in the Eames chair—
cold leather against skin, nice. The major quality was
something reactive, a chameleon quality that somehow enabled her to transform herself in the eyes of
any man. She could become—and she had felt the
process often enough to know its validity—pale of skin,
full-breasted, intellectual, sexy, aloof. She could be
whatever the man happened to be looking for at the
moment. She could become any man's dream woman,
and somehow accomplish it without relinquishing her
own identity.

William had noticed this, had noticed it but never
understood it. He had somehow confused it with
coquettishness. Whenever a male guest would challenge Gillian, would display an intellectual vigor or
simple male virility, Gillian would, as William put it
so inadequately, "flutter her fan." William claimed
to have developed an emotional radar to his wife's
vibrations, but William so often missed the point, mis-
labeled the process. It was a process of *becoming*. It
existed not in mechanical tricks but in acute sensitiv-
ity; it took place not in her physical alterations but in
the eye of the beholder.

Hers was a talent that ought to be intensively ex-
ploited, thought Gillian, before she fell asleep. It was
a deep but disturbed sleep, a heavy buzzing sleep that
ended shortly after eight o'clock with the arrival of an
unfaithful husband.

"For chrissake, look at yourself," he said. "It's past
eight for chrissake."

"That's cute," she said. "Do you do the weather
too?"

"I mean it, it's eight-damn-o'clock."

"So it's eight o'clock," she said. "So what?"

"Don't tell me you don't remember. The damn party begins at 8:30. Oh no you don't, don't give me one of *those* looks. This wasn't *my* idea. You were the one who told me about it, an end-of-summer blast, remember? Two houses over and one down. The wops. Remember now?"

The details returned to Gillian—of course, the party —and she stood up. Not until that instant did she realize she was still naked. She walked over to William, brushed meaningfully against him, then noticed the fresh lipstick prints on his collar. Those slight red smudges—was it carelessness, stupidity, a Freudian reflection of guilt?—irritated her almost as much as the thought of his infidelity. That bastard.

"We don't have to go to the party," she teased. "We could stay home and . . . oh . . . christen the new house properly. It's been a long time, Billy."

"We've got to get a move on. . . ."

"But isn't there anything you'd rather do?" she said. "Any little thing I might do for you?"

"Yes, as a matter of fact there is," he said. "One little thing you could do for me is hurry-the-hell-up and get into something decent. It's bad enough we've got to go through this thing. Let's not make it any more complicated than we have to."

But it was complicated, extremely complicated. For at that moment Gillian was settling finally on her plan of action. As she selected her dress for the party— emerald green, high in front, low in back—Gillian found herself shivering. In anticipation.

The only uncomfortable moment of the evening came when their hosts—Mario and Donna Marie Vella —greeted them at the door. Donna Marie was short, stout and faintly mustachioed; she looked as though she might faint dead away at the thought of having *the* Billy and Gilly in her home. And Mario's introductory act, his welcoming gesture, was to hand

William his business card, embossed, indicating that he was the executive officer of both the Bella Mia Olive Oil Company and the Fort Sorrento Construction Company.

"Charmed, I'm sure," William said, as only he could say it.

"We certainly appreciate," Gillian said, stepping on his line, "your inviting us newcomers to your home."

After that, needless to say, matters improved. There was, as Gillian had anticipated, a wide selection of men. Fat, thin, short, tall, introverted, extroverted, dumpy, dashing—the full assortment. She mentally resolved not to rush things. At first she contented herself with remaining beside William, allowing him to squeeze her hand and pat her cheek—doing what he had always done, putting the model marriage on public display. Oh, you electronic lovebird, she thought. William was, in fact, the first subject, the first of the adult males residing in King's Neck to come under Gillian's scrutiny that evening.

He was, she decided, the best looking man in the room. Best looking, in the conventional sense. William had been told in his youth that some day he would be able to serve as a stand-in for Prince Philip. Now, approaching his middle years, he more closely resembled the well-dressed dummies in the Brooks Brothers windows. Bland. But he was still trim (regular workouts at the New York Athletic Club), polished (Princeton), at ease with the mighty (scion of the banking Blakes) and an asset to any gathering. The one apparent flaw was a jawline that lacked definition. Oh, say it—a weak chin.

Before beginning his second drink, William had managed to surround himself with those few people of King's Neck who might qualify as resident intellectuals—such people as Rabbi Joshua Turnbull and lawyer Melvin Corby. There was, too, an outer concentric circle of women, the kind of women who always basked in that invisible light cast by certifiable celebrities.

"And I'll maintain," William was saying, "that without parties such as these, suburbia, per se, would disintegrate before our eyes. These are, after all, not merely social gatherings. They are, in the psychological sense, encounters—they're what we have instead of group therapy. It's my sincere feeling that if everyone in the country would go to just one suburban party a week, psychoanalysis would soon go out of vogue."

Gillian's shrug turned into a shudder. William was doing his Hugh Downs imitation—locating his conversation on the right side of pompous and the wrong side of stuffy. His voice—a narcissistic and mellifluent instrument of torture—was professionally resonant, overwhelmingly smooth, always able to intimidate lesser voices and superior intellects in any gathering. The immediate conversation was more than passingly familiar to Gillian; it was a replay of last Tuesday's radio show. Gillian edged slowly away from the group and her space was filled by a plump and matronly woman with eyes that were devouring William.

Working her way toward the bar in an adjacent room, Gillian paused to take note of the décor. Fake beams that had been scarred by an ineptly wielded claw hammer; tapestried walls; lampshades with fringes; gaudy oil paintings of watery sunsets and Italian hill villages; everything overstuffed and red and silk. Expensive and atrocious.

On her way she met the Goodmans—Marvin and Helene. She walked unannounced into what seemed to be a family quarrel of some duration. Marvin Goodman's voice was raised, and tiny bubbles of perspiration were bursting on his forehead: "Ernie Miklos's wife says she can get by on thirty-five dollars a week— thirty-five dollars a week for food *and* car." By way of response, Helene Goodman calmly and methodically unbuttoned the top two buttons of her blouse. Gillian noted a strange phenomenon—as her husband's voice rose, so did her bustline. It led to a lowering of his eyes, a lowering of his voice and finally an end to the discussion.

Then she encountered her next-door neighbors, the Earbrows—Morton and Gloria. Morton's fingernails carried the residue of his day's labors, a colorful mixture of green paint and grease. He was sound asleep. His young wife, Gloria, was holding the attention of a small male audience by explaining precisely how one scraped paint from cement walls, the proper way of cleaning a paint brush, the relative advantages of a Black and Decker five-eighths-inch drill, what steps should be taken to prepare a lawn for a fall seeding— all of this while her husband snored his way into an ever-deepening sleep.

Gillian turned to meet Willoughby Martin and his friend, Hank. Willoughby was saying, "We really must take a drive soon; the foliage in Maine is already changing and before too long it will all just be . . . oh . . . a riot of color."

And Hank said, "Yes, in a few weeks it should be simply breathtaking."

Then Gillian was introduced to the Madigans— Agnes and Paddy. "Paddy Madigan, the fighter?" she said.

"That's right, dear," Agnes said. "Many think the finest left-handed fighter ever to contend for the light-heavyweight championship of the world."

Gillian then complimented Paddy Madigan on his remarkable physical condition. Paddy said nothing and Agnes did the responding: "Thank you, dear, we still manage to do our morning workouts, summer or winter, makes no difference." Gillian then asked Paddy what business he had entered since his retirement. Again Agnes answered for her husband: "Oh, we just putter around the house these days, doing the gardening and so forth."

At this point, what Gillian wanted was another

drink. Before she could reach the bar, Mario Vella, the host for the evening, was standing up on a stool, calling for everyone's attention.

"Quiet, please," Mario said. "Please now, ladies and gentlemen, quiet down now. Tonight, by way of a little entertainment, we have a very special surprise for our neighbors at King's Neck. I have persuaded my very good friend, Johnny Alonga, to come here and favor us with a few of his hit songs."

Gillian was momentarily surprised. Johnny Alonga was a rising young singing star, reportedly Mafia-sponsored, who had sung a song, "A Dying Love," that had been on the charts for over a year. There had not yet been a second hit record. Possibly because Johnny Alonga's syrupy voice made Jerry Vale's seem crisp by comparison.

As all the lights except one were extinguished, two men in tuxedos entered from the bedroom. The black man sat at the piano and quickly picked out the opening notes of Johnny Alonga's one hit record. And the singer began to sing.

> You come to me in all my dreams,
> You touch my lips, or so it seems,
> Your love is but a kiss away
> If only I could make you stay
> A dying love,
> A dying love is what we share. . . .

In the darkened room, now thirstier than ever, Gillian was suddenly aware of the presence beside her of Mario Vella. He had allowed his left elbow to brush gently against her. In any other surroundings, in any other circumstances, Gillian Blake would have gracefully withdrawn. She didn't. She held her ground and his elbow became more persistent.

"You like?" he said.

"Very much," she said in return. "That's quite a thing, having Johnny Alonga come to your house to sing."

"I own him," he said.

"You own him?"

"Forty per cent," Mario said. "That's how much I own. And you want to know what I think about that song?"

"What's that?"

"It makes me sick to my stomach," he said. "It makes me want to puke."

"Oh?" she said, silently agreeing.

There might be something there, she thought. There was an appealing unreal quality to Mario Vella; he was a fabrication, the creation of someone or something else. Beneath the razor cut and the tailored clothes and the scent of expensive cologne there was something threatening to break out of the mold. It was, carried to the extreme, as though someone had put Brooks Brothers clothes on a gorilla.

Then the song ended and Mario disengaged his elbow and walked back up to the piano.

Before Johnny Alonga could launch his next number—"Be My Love," no less—Gillian slipped into the adjoining room, the den, the bar, the oasis. It was all but deserted in honor of Johnny Alonga.

It was then that she met the Franhops—Arthur and Raina. Arthur, the boy, was wearing his hair twisted and curled in the style popularized by Bob Dylan. Beneath his gold-buttoned, double-breasted blazer he wore no shirt. Raina, the girl, was seated in a far corner of the room staring at an unblemished white wall with wide-open Little Orphan Annie eyes.

"Don't mind her," Arthur said. "She's on acid."

"LSD?" Gillian said.

"Yeah, like acid," Arthur said. "We were all set to play a new game tonight and then she has to go and suck on a cube and ruin it all."

"What kind of game?" Gillian asked.

"Time Machine," Arthur said. "We thought we'd go back in time, all the way back here to the seventeenth century, and see what the cats were doing back then. Then she goes and sucks a cube and ruins the game."

"You mean you think most of the people here live in the seventeenth century?"

"Where else?" he said. "Not you, though, you're something else. Outasight. Hey, do you groove?"

"I'm not sure," Gillian said. "Do you speak English?"

"Hey, later," he said.

That was Arthur Franhop's exit line. Without another word he was gone. He paused just long enough to take his blind-eyed Raina with him, and moments later the quiet suburban night was rent by the sound of a Harley-Davidson motorcycle being fired up.

"Shit!" The expletive came from the last man in the room, the bartender. This was Ernie Miklos, a man who had once tended bar in his youth and willingly played the role at most of the King's Neck parties. For one thing, it gave him an excuse to stay away from his wife Laverne.

"I beg your pardon," Gillian said.

"Shit," he repeated. "That kid, he's shit. What're you drinking?"

"Martini-very-dry."

"That's shit too," Ernie Miklos said. "Burn your guts out."

"That's the way I started the day," Gillian said. "And I guess that's the way I better end it."

There was something about Ernie Miklos that Gillian found vaguely intimidating. Possibly his eyes. Ernie's eyes met her own head-on and then insolently surveyed her from top to bottom. Possibly it was the hair on the back of his hands—so thick and luxurious a growth of hair that it seemed more like fur than hair, more like a paw than a hand. The two open shirt buttons above the loosely knotted tie revealed still another thick stand of hair.

"Where's your wife?" Gillian asked.

"The last time I saw Laverne," Ernie said, "she was

drooling all over your husband. Not that I personally give a shit. How do you like it?"

"Very good," Gillian said. "You make a nice martini."

She took another sip. It *was* a nice martini. A nice martini and an odd moment. They stood there, the only people in the room, and they didn't say a word for three, maybe four moments. What to say anyway? Gillian knew that she had nothing at all to say to Ernie Miklos, and quite probably he had nothing at all to say to her. But was she sure? She had, after all, spent twenty-nine years on this planet without ever attempting a conversation with an Ernie Miklos or anyone, for that matter, who remotely resembled him. Finally it was Ernie Miklos who broke the silence with an eminently logical question.

"What are you doing here anyway?" he said. "Why is a broad like you wasting time with someone like me?"

"Maybe it's because you make a nice martini."

"Yeah and maybe it's because I look like Richard Burton," he said. "But that ain't the reason either."

"Maybe you can figure it out for yourself."

"I am doing that," Ernie said. "That is exactly what I am doing. I am figuring it out for myself and about the only way I can figure it is that you want something from me."

"What would I want from you?" Gillian said.

"Maybe you would want to step outside for a while and find out," Ernie said.

"Maybe," Gillian said.

"You want to step outside for some fresh air or what?" he said.

"Yes," she said.

Yes—Gillian heard herself saying the word. It seemed so unnatural, so contrived, that she had the feeling she had shouted it through a megaphone. Ernie Miklos didn't say any more. He dried his hands on his bartender's apron, took off the apron and walked over

to the plate glass doors that opened onto the patio. He
had clearly had too much to drink, and the latch
give him a moment's difficulty. Wordlessly, floating
again, Gillian followed Ernie Miklos out beyond the
reach of the patio lights. A strange feeling. Gillian
had the eerie sensation that she was not actually a
participant in the small silent tableau. She was an
observer, audience for an unreal drama, a spectator
at the theater of the absurd.

Gillian offered no resistance. She allowed herself to
be coaxed down onto the lawn beside a stranger
named Ernie Miklos. She felt removed, alienated,
singularly unexcited. Through the nearby living-room
windows she could see the silhouetted figure of
Johnny Alonga as he sang to all the other strangers.
She could feel the softness of the still warm grass beneath her. And she could feel the lips of Ernie Miklos
against her throat, feel the lips and then the hand as
it reached through the side of her low-backed dress
and snared her left breast.

Gillian didn't move, didn't dare breathe. His lips
had now moved up to her own and his hand had for
some unknown reason switched breasts. She could feel
all of him leaning against her now—his teeth against
her lips, his hands on her breasts, his body thrusting
hard against her own. There was at first fear, fear and
revulsion, but she refused to protest, fought the impulse to pull away from him.

And then she began to feel the beginning of a response. The feeling was foreign to her and quite in-
voluntary. But it was there and it soothed her. Gillian
moved her weight slightly to accommodate Ernie Miklos and then she reached out to him and pulled him
closer against her. And from the far reaches of her
throat she felt the start of a low pleading moan.

Thus was the matter decided. It would be Ernie
Miklos. Yes, it would be a stranger and neighbor
named Ernie Miklos. For starters.

Billy: Wasn't it lovely driving in today, Gilly?

Gilly: It certainly was, Billy. You know, I've always thought that October is the loveliest month. And that's especially true in the suburbs. It's the whole marvelous cliché of Indian summer.

Billy: The golden autumn.

Gilly: The tang in the air.

Billy: The falling leaves.

Gilly: The ripening pumpkins.

Billy: The fresh apple cider.

Gilly: The grand finale of the chrysanthemums.

Billy: The Saturday afternoons in front of the television set.

Gilly: The what?

Billy: The Saturday afternoons in front of the television set.

Gilly: I guess it's my slow day.

Billy: I'm surprised at you, dear. Football. The college football games on Saturday afternoons.

Gilly: I am slow, today. Of course, . . . football. The game with all the numbers. I just love those announcers. "Now the Giants are in a three-four-five with an X-Y-Z and a split disc." Ridiculous!

Billy: A split end.

Gilly: Come again?

Billy: A split end, not a split disc.

Gilly: Well, I knew something was split.

Billy: A can of beer, a color TV, and Army against Notre Dame. Like tomorrow. Now that's living!

Gilly: It's stupid, wasting a Saturday afternoon that way.

Billy: Oh come on. What's wrong with sports?

Gilly: I think games are for playing. I mean there's something so absolutely dreary about a man lying around in an old T-shirt or something, watching a football game all day.

Billy: He works hard, he deserves a little rest.

Gilly: Sure. But what women hate is that everything has to stop while his highness watches the quarterback go in the whatchamacallit.

Billy: In the pocket.

Gilly: Well, whatever he goes in. I mean, it's all supposed to be so important.

Billy: It is. You just don't disturb a man when he's watching football.

Gilly: Phooey.

Billy: No, really.

Gilly: I think the best thing you can do for a man is disturb him.

Billy: Ouch.

Gilly: Okay girls, let's all get out there tomorrow afternoon and make him pay attention to us.

Billy: Hold fast to your couches, men—your way of life is at stake.

ERNIE MIKLOS

The old champ on the TV was telling the rookie to steer clear of the greasy kid stuff. Ernie Miklos sat back and pressed his chunky fingers against his forehead. Oh. For Ernie it was a small hangover, a band of numbness stretched across the temples, and that wasn't bad, not for Ernie. Usually he bombed himself out at those neighborhood bashes. Last night, for some reason, the bar wasn't the center of attraction for him. He kept thinking about the way she had moved inside that dress.

He turned again to the TV and put the cold can of beer against his forehead. A former football "great" on the pregame show was employing stop-action to demonstrate how the guard pulled out of the line to block for the halfback.

"Another great effort by an all-time great," the former great said. "That's why Fuzzy's so . . . great."

Ernie glanced around the room, his room, done in cherrywood paneling that had run 45 cents a foot. He started at the pictures—his high school football team and the photo of seventeen men wearing Marine Corps uniforms. "Iron Man Ernie Miklos" was what he was called in those days, and to Ernie things had never changed. He was the same man despite forty-one years, thinning hair and expanding girth. Beside him were the weights and the exercise bench. He'd spend thirty minutes lying on the bench pushing metal in the morning. The thought of it today, though, forced him to rest his head back on the head rest and prop both feet on the red leather ottoman. The pregame show was ending, and it seemed pretty certain now that the rookie had switched from the greasy kid stuff.

Ernie had reached that point in life where his Saturday afternoon football game was more than welcome respite, it was his raison d'être. This Saturday afternoon there was a small bonus. Laverne had packed up the kids and retreated to her mother's apartment in the city. He was left alone with his six-pack, his Fritos, his memories. The garbage—the lawn, the leaves, the yelling, the kids—that was locked out on this Saturday afternoon. And for the moment he forgot about that woman in the dress and concentrated on the game.

The phone rang. It took only one ring, mainly because Ernie's head couldn't take more.

"Hello there."

Ernie waited for the voice to give him the weather— it was that kind of voice, soft but mechanically so.

"Huh?"

"It's Gillian, remember?"

"You'll have to do better than that."

"You must have been more smashed than I thought," she said. "And that doesn't seem possible. The party last night. You said you wanted to drink beer from my . . . bra."

Oh yes. The one in the dress. Gillian? All he could remember at the moment was that he had seen her at the Plaza West with some woman, and that she had a sweet-working rump, and he hoped he'd see her again, but didn't until he saw her at the party.

"Yeah," Ernie said, chewing off the rest of a mouthful of Fritos. Army had just kicked off. "What's—"

"I have your cuff links," the voice said. "Or one of them anyway, the one you lost outside."

"Cuff links?"

"In the *garden*," she said. "Remember? You were doing a lot of talking. I think you were complimenting me in a sort of, well, basic way."

"If the old man is upset," Ernie said, "tell him I was bombed out, smashed, you know. . . ."

"It's not that." Gillian looked across the room at Bill. He was reading. "It's just I thought you might want it back. I mean it looks like it might be something special, as though it were made specially for you."

Ernie wished the lady would get to the point. Notre Dame was on Army's fourteen-yard line and he had no idea how they got there.

"If you want to know the truth," he said, "I took it off a dead nigger in Hempstead."

"That's just fine," Gillian said—a wince her only reaction. "When would you like me to bring it over? I mean when would be the best time?"

"My wife's in New York now," Ernie said.

"Now it is then," she said.

Bill hadn't looked up from his reading. Gillian brought her fingertips to her mouth, blocked a manufactured yawn, went upstairs to change. The pink slacks, the halter with the white ruffles, yes. The pony tail as is. When she left, Bill was making a gimlet in what he would probably always call the rumpus room. And while all this was happening, Ernie Miklos was looking into a dead telephone receiver. He didn't even see Notre Dame make the game's first extra point.

"Aren't you going to offer a good Samaritan a drink?" Gillan was saying.

"It's over there."

On any other occasion the tailored pink slacks would have been at least distracting. But Ernie had the head. And the Irish were leading ten-zip. The bar was done in Early American. Laverne liked it and Ernie hated it. The only bar in the Western Hemisphere that Ernie couldn't stand. Who ever heard of an Early American bar? Ernie often thought he would like to take an Early American match and destroy it. Right up to the Early American refrigerator with the golden eagle.

"You could drink it up here," Ernie said. Ernie sighted in on the sweet-working rump. "That is, if you like football."

"Only football players," she said, thinking, even as she said it, that it was almost as trite as it was untrue.

"You could bring the olives with you," Ernie said. "Or do you take onions?"

"A twist ordinarily," she said, "but an olive will do."

Ernie did the mixing. He spilled the Vermouth when Harvey Jones dropped the pass deep in Notre Dame territory. *That son of a bitch.* Gillian accepted the dripping glass and dropped into the overstuffed chair. She pulled her legs up under her, tucked them in. Army was punting and Ernie slammed his fist into the armrest of her chair.

Laverne would never have come into the room while he was watching a big game. Maybe it was that.

Maybe it was the hangover. Whatever the reason, Ernie was having trouble focusing on the set. It was like that time one of the curtains was flapping in the wind—it was a distraction without being an interruption. He could feel her eyes. What in the hell was she up to anyway? The first commercial he turned quickly to meet her look. Too quickly. The pain came back.

"Oh God," he said.

Gillian went to the ice bucket and picked up an ice cube. She walked back to Ernie and held it against his forehead. Ernie began to feel his breath quickening. That damn ice cube. Had he said anything about ice cubes last night? No. He couldn't have. The cube in Gillian's hand was melting, sending small rivulets of water into the edges of his eyes. Ernie's pulse was throbbing now, and what happened next was more instinct than design.

Army was driving and Ernie was too. His eyes went to the TV and then back to Gillian. A Christian Scientist with appendicitis. Gillian watched it as it happened. She knew she had aroused the creature in the torn paint-spattered T-shirt. Well, she told herself, that's what you wanted, wasn't it? That's what you wanted. She saw the Marine Corps tattoo barely visible beneath the sleeve on his right arm. So what did you expect, she asked herself, candlelight?

Ernie didn't bother to talk. He merely grabbed out for Gillian, pulled her across the armrest into his lap and bit into her neck.

"No marks," she squealed. "Don't leave marks."

"Don't give me any of that shit," Ernie said.

"All right, armchair quarterbacks," the voice on the television was saying, "what would you do? Go through that same hole again or try for the end?"

Gillian began to fight back, stiffly, ineffectually. She felt her fingernails gouge through the flesh of his back. He didn't seem to feel it. If he did, it only increased his ardor. Her body went limp then, and as their mouths met and then their tongues she gave it up and began to play the game Ernie's way.

"He's in there; he's in there!" The voice from the TV seemed to come from another world. "And, fans, it's all knotted up."

Sixty-eight thousand fans were screaming in the stadium. But on Barnacle Drive in King's Neck at the home of Ernie Miklos there was only quiet. Gillian had disengaged herself, risen. She looked at Ernie and reached down to touch him gently. He didn't stir. So that's it, Gillian thought. It's over in less than a minute and already it is as though nothing had happened. Ernie didn't acknowledge her presence in any way. He was watching the set again, watching Army kick off to Notre Dame.

Ernie was dozing when Laverne called from downstairs.

"Isn't it over yet?" she said.

Ernie rubbed his eyes, and all he could see was the face of Walter Cronkite. His hangover was gone and so was Gillian. He could hear kids running across the kitchen floor and the sound of the dishwasher being activated.

"You couldn't even wash the goddam dishes." Laverne was yelling.

He came downstairs then and she asked him whether the game had gone into extra innings. Laverne never knew when the baseball season ended and the football season began and Ernie never bothered to explain it to her. What was the use? What in goddam hell was the use? He returned to complete consciousness as he went back upstairs, and wondered vaguely what had happened to Gillian. His T-shirt was on the floor. The only trace of his visitor was the empty cocktail glass. He shoved it into his desk drawer and went into the bathroom. His eyes were puffy. He turned around to look at Gillian's brand on his back.

Goddam broads who scratch. They should all be declawed.

"I'll be right down," he shouted from the bathroom door. He turned on the shower.

When Ernie finally crawled into bed, he was played out. Still, sleep came hard. Laverne was suspicious when he put on pajama tops. Ernie never wore pajama tops, even in winter. In fact, the only reason he wore pajama bottoms was that Laverne had made it a condition for sharing the same bed. Sometimes now he wondered why he had ever wanted to share the same bed. They'd been married fifteen years but sometimes, on nights like this one, Ernie felt he had been born married. Born married. He remembered his father used to say something like that—exactly that, as a matter of fact, whenever he got high on boilermakers. That had been his father's salvation, those boilermakers on payday at the bar across the street from the paymaster's shack at the zinc works. Ernie sometimes thought about Donita, Pennsylvania, and how far he had come from that. It was only four hundred miles but it was a whole other world.

Donita was one of those mill towns that edge the Monongahela River on its flow to Pittsburgh. Like all those towns, it was dirty and its people were poor, not so much in money as in spirit. The mill did it to the town. Its people were a potpourri of Polish immigrants, Irish and Negroes. The parents worked, got drunk, reproduced, died young, figured on the same life for their children, only hoping it might happen somewhere else than Donita.

The Donita football teams were the terror of the state, and Ernie Miklos was the terror of the team and this was his salvation. Lying there late at night, listening to the snores of the stranger who shared his bed, Ernie liked to think back and remember those days, the days of his escape. It was about the only time all day anyone would let him think.

Ernie's father had liked to sing; he had never forgotten his father's voice, especially when he'd had one or two. He had the soul of a poet, Ernie felt. But the mill in those days was the beginning and the end. The town was built around the mill and had never been broken up into sections for slums or ethnic groups. The money people, the mill owners, lived eighteen miles beyond town limits and everyone else lived in town. Ernie's house was just a spot somewhere midway between abject poverty and blind hope. There were nine children in that house and Ernie had always been the favorite. He was the second of two sons; the older boy had died of consumption.

Ernie never disappointed his father, and that was important to him. Those days after the football games and his father hitting him across his back and the girls waiting for him to come by. Ernie had gotten laid when he was thirteen, by Sonia, who fucked for three cents. Three cents. God, what she would have done for a dime. The boys used to save milk bottles for the refunds and it was always a big day when you could carry three of them over to Jake Rubenstein's. Everybody hated old Jake. Not because he always kidded about them bringing in *three* milk bottles. But because he was a Jew. Ernie delighted in tormenting Jake's son, Harvey, but Ernie never started a fight. It would have been no fight and Ernie was never that much of a bully when he was in high school.

Ernie had picked the University of Indiana. It had been a tough choice because there were forty-six schools competing for the pleasure of educating him. He picked Indiana for a simple reason: They paid more than anyone else. Still, Ernie would have flunked out after that last season if he hadn't joined the Marines before exams.

The war was the best thing that ever happened to Ernie Miklos. Better than the football games and better than getting laid by a cheerleader named Donah. Once, knee-deep in mud at Cape Gloucester, sharing his foxhole with six dead land crabs, he said to himself—and Ernie always spoke the truth when he spoke to himself—"There are days when I'm sorry this war has to end."

Ernie loved that war and he loved what his drill instructor at Parris Island had told him: "Boy, I'm gonna make a paid fucking killer out of you." And the sergeant would have been proud. Ernie won the Silver Star at Bougainville by wiping out three Japanese strong points with a handful of grenades and a BAR. He was wounded twice and his face still bore the scar of a Jap bayonet. But when Ernie was telling war stories, that wasn't the one he liked to tell. He liked to tell about the time he broke into a hut and found a Japanese lieutenant about to commit hara-kiri. Ernie helped him along, but he performed the ceremony by inserting the knife eleven inches into the lieutenant's rectum.

Ernie's wounds on Bougainville got him returned to Honolulu—something he considered worse than a Section 8. It was in Honolulu that Ernie got the scar that no one saw, the scar he carried on his brain. It was in a slop jar off Hotel Street that Ernie found his absolution. The whores had been thick along Hotel Street that night; but they always were. It was like Piccadilly in London or Pigalle in Paris except that the women sat in bars instead of under street lamps or in doorways. Whores, Ernie discovered, were wonderful when you felt the need of dying quickly with the reasonable assurance you'd rise again from a quick grave. Ernie didn't actually survive that night, not wholly. He had really been buried, and so he still felt, forever. And his executioner was a half-caste little girl with bad teeth, a girl who couldn't have been more than eighteen. In a way Ernie felt it was retribution for what he had done to the Jap lieutenant. He'd known that was wrong, but he couldn't help himself. And while the lieutenant had been fortunate enough to look forward to his Imperial Heaven, Ernie would spend the rest of his life looking forward to absolutely nothing.

Even now he sometimes woke up screaming. Laverne assumed it was the sound of guns and the calls of dying men that echoed through his sleep. But Ernie heard only his own screams—his screams and the sound of water falling on a bare wooden floor in a dingy room in Honolulu.

The perspiration even now was rolling off Ernie's forehead. He hoped his shuddering there in the dark night would not awaken Laverne. Laverne. Ernie had married her because she was one of the few women he could remember saying no to him. Maybe, he reflected, it was because she was one of the few women he had ever bothered to ask. "Not until you marry me," she had said. Ernie didn't believe her, not at first, but he soon learned that Laverne was a threshold girl, able to stop repeatedly just this side of fulfillment. He couldn't stand it any more and, out of curiosity, agreed to marry her.

She wasn't bad looking then and not much worse now. She had maintained through two births a pair of breasts that Ernie counted among the finest in Christendom. She was an Italian-Irish mixture who had somehow managed to capture the worst characteristics of both nationalities. She didn't like to drink and she didn't like to stay up late and she always chastised Ernie when he did either.

The best thing about Laverne had been a father old-fashioned enough to believe in a dowry, which meant a partnership in a construction company specializing in swimming pools. And when suburbanites found they could dig themselves even deeper into debt with a pool, Ernie and his father-in-law were there to help with the digging. Ernie was vice president in charge of pools, which had made him affluent enough to settle in King's Neck rather than Levittown or Huntington. Ernie had been happy in a Bayside apartment with a breakfast balcony. But Laverne wanted to become part of a community—to have roots, as she put it. So Ernie bought a waterfront lot with a seven-bedroom, split-level ranch. They still had no roots, but now they had a mortgage that would grow old with them. The one thing they owned free and clear was the pool.

From the beginning Laverne had never been anything less than a dutiful wife. And not much more. Ernie realized, of course, that Honolulu was a tough act to follow. It could be said of Ernie and Laverne that their marriage started off in low gear and then bogged down.

Ernie's feelings about most of his neighbors were generally expressed in simple terms. "Pushy goddam Jews"—that was one of his favorite appraisals. He took great delight in padding his neighbors' bills when they came to him for a pool on the erroneous assumption that geographical proximity might save them a few dollars.

The Civic Association, the Save Our Schools Committee, the Republican Club, the Young Americans for Freedom—the only thing that meant a good goddam to Ernie was a party. Last night's blast was one of the best. Gillian had been standing beside the pool when he first saw her. She was wearing that low-backed green dress with high heels to match. He was talking to someone, Melvin Corby it was, and he'd just said, "Show me the guy who doesn't eat it and I'll steal his girl," when Gillian walked across his line of vision. Corby had told him that everyone on King's Neck wanted a slice of that butt—only those weren't the words Corby had used (pushy goddam Jew)—Ernie could understand why. Then, later, she had come on with him at the bar.

It was hard for Ernie to believe he had scored with her so quickly. She was class. But it all confirmed what he had always maintained, a broad is a broad.

Ernie fell asleep then. And less than an hour later Laverne woke up to hear him screaming. He woke up screaming something about ice cubes, and when she tried to wipe the perspiration from his brow he begged her not to touch him.

Ernie didn't see Gillian until the following Friday. He was at the Plaza having a sandwich and Gillian was having a late afternoon martini. Apparently she was not having her husband because Bill was sitting at another table talking to several men in business suits. The Plaza was next to the King's Neck Railroad Station and, unlike most restaurants near railroad stations, it was reasonably sanguine. At night there was a darky piano player, and it was known as the launching pad for those who planned to swap mates for the evening. This, to Ernie, made excellent sense, but it also made excellent sense never to broach the subject to Laverne. In the afternoon it was reasonably quiet and Ernie, a man who always looked out of place in a white collar, would sometimes stop off between checks on his work crews. He had been scoring for eight months with one of the waitresses who had to quit when her husband changed jobs.

"Hello there." Gillian carried her martini to the bar and took the stool to his left. Her hair was up. Ernie put his notebook away and took a long look.

"Like another one?" he said.

"Why not?"

Ernie had been debating which stop to make next. Seeing Gillian again, he knew which one he wanted to make. He excused himself and telephoned his foreman. He said there would be no need to check the Freeport job unless there were problems. No sweat, no sweat at all. He went back to Gillian. She was at the table again. Her husband hadn't seemed to notice anything. Ernie had once played against a quarterback who looked like Bill—no chin at all—Michigan, it was

—and he got hit once and that was it for the afternoon.

"Would you join me in one?" Gillian was asking.

Ernie didn't like martinis. He didn't trust them. Anything that looks like water and tastes like fire—he knew he couldn't handle them. But that was the challenge and he nodded assent. He watched the new waitress as she walked away. Maybe there was something there, too, he thought as he watched her posterior stretching the white nylon skirt. Ernie was always working on the next one, even when he was in the middle of drumming up action. He had never discovered that man has relatively little to say about it.

"We just got in from New York," Gillian was saying. "Do you ever listen to our show? I don't blame you—it's basically for women anyway."

When the martinis arrived they were on the rocks. Gillian jiggled the glass and noticed the expression in Ernie's eyes. She jiggled the glass again and again it happened. It was as though his eyes had turned to ice. It was the same look she had seen Saturday before he turned into a raging animal. Gillian had minored in psychology at Bard, but the psychology she relied on now was something she had been born with.

"The ice cubes look nice, don't they?" she said. "Nice, just floating in the glass."

Ernie could feel the dampness on his forehead. He reached for his glass and took it in a single burning swallow. Better, better now. Gillian watched the small scene with mounting academic interest, as though once again she were observing from a concealed vantage point. She said that it might be wise to go slow on the martinis, particularly if he were not used to them.

"I'll drink what I fucking please," Ernie snarled at her. "I was drinking when you were still using candles on yourself."

Gillian knew then she should get up and leave. She looked over at her husband's table—the men had all disappeared. She felt uneasy then, but didn't protest when Ernie ordered the last round of martinis.

"Do you want to tell me about it?" she said.

"Where's your husband?" Ernie said. "Where's old shithead off to now?"

"Is there anything you want to tell me, Ernie?"

"Why did you marry a shithead like that?" Ernie said. "You've got to have a screw loose, marrying a shithead like that."

"Go ahead," Gillian said.

"Broads," he said. "I've fucked more broads than the sultan of Baghdad or somewhere. And I've fucked your kind before. You broads who think your ass is made of gold because you went to college."

Gillian took a drink from the fresh martini. She opened her compact and studied her lips. She knew it was time to go but, even as she thought it, she chided herself. Chicken. What can happen now?

"I've had things with broads," Ernie was saying, "things you wouldn't believe."

"How do you know, Ernie?" Gentle now. "How do you know unless you tell me?"

"I had a thing with a broad in Honolulu. . . ." He stopped and looked around. The main room of the Plaza was all but deserted. The waitress with the nice ass was polishing glasses at the bar, laughing at something Benny the bartender was saying.

"You were telling me about Honolulu," she said.

"Mind your own fucking business," Ernie said. "You want to know what they're gonna put on my tombstone. Here lies Ernie Miklos, yes sir, here lies Ernie Miklos, he got his in Honolulu."

"Tell me about the ice cubes, Ernie," she said.

"Up my ass," he said. "That's right. That little cunt shoved it right up my ass just as I was blowing my load. She took a chunk of ice and jammed it there. She took me, all of me, and I came for it seemed like three days. I thought my teeth were going to be sucked right through my prick. Oh God. . . ."

Ernie slammed his head down against the table.

The bartender and the waitress stopped the giggling and looked around as Ernie screamed again, "Oh my sweet God!" His head fell back against the wall and his eyes were closed tight. Gillian was unprepared for this display and her purse slipped off her lap onto the floor. She reached down, and the dregs of her drink spilled down the front of her gray suit.

"Right up my ass," Ernie said softly. "What do you think of that, huh, bitch? Right up my ass with the ice cube."

"Are you all right, Ernie?" she said.

"Are you all right, Mr. Miklos?" the bartender called. "You want someone should take you home?"

"Is he some kind of a nut?" the waitress whispered.

"It's all right, Benny," Gillian called back. "I live near Mr. Miklos and I'll see him home."

Ernie felt her hand on his arm, felt himself being led toward the door.

"Yeah," he was saying, "right up my ass."

It was a patio but it wasn't his patio. Next to him there was a cold Bud and he reached for the can. He could see the Sound through the trees. He could see the umbrella. He could see Gillian sitting in the next chaise.

"Drink it," she said, "you'll feel better."

"Why did you let me drink that shit at the Plaza?" he said.

"I didn't know what would happen," she said.

"Well, aren't you the hot shit," he said, drinking the beer. "You know it all now."

"Yes," she said, "even about the Japanese lieutenant."

"Fuck you," he said.

Ernie threw the empty beer can onto the patio and listened to it clatter. Gillian moved over toward him and sat on the ground beside the chaise.

"It might be more comfortable in the bedroom," she said.

"I'm too smashed," he said. "I'm bombed out."

"Not for me," she said. "Not for what's waiting for you."

Ernie felt himself coming apart. He could feel the martinis in his stomach like hot coals. He followed her through the plate glass doors to the poolside bedroom. Unglued. He fell onto the bed and managed to reach up for her. Her hair was still up. Like some goddam Egyptian princess. Like Liz Taylor in that movie. She wasn't even looking at him as she reached down and began stroking him. He could feel it happening again, even this drunk, goddam!

Ernie Miklos was beyond effort and he made no effort. He just lay there and let it happen to him. And as it was happening, it was different, lazy. He didn't know it could be that way, goddam.

"I'm going to come," he said.

"Come on," she said. "Come on all the way home, Ernie."

"Oh, God, no, no," he was screaming again.

He knew what was happening, knew somehow that it was going to happen. And then Ernie felt it. She shoved the ice in, the big rock candy mountain, the fucking iceberg, and then his scream died and his whole being oozed forth and he felt he would drown in what was happening.

"Oh my God!"

Together, like garden snakes, they contorted, moaned, gasped, clenched and throbbed. Fucking eternity, Ernie thought, fucking–A eternity! Ernie found what Cervantes and Milton had only sought. He thought the fillings in his teeth would melt. And even afterward, the throbbing went on.

"Are you all right?"

"God, God, God," he said.

"Ernie. . . ."

"Get me home," he pleaded. "Get me home."

"Are you sure you're all right?"

"Home," he said.

Gillian managed to dress both of them, managed to half-carry him to the car. It was only three blocks. Ernie felt the fire burning from his stomach to his head. He stumbled from the car and watched Gillian pull away. He staggered to the back of the house, fell blindly against the portable bar. He heard the bottles crack against the brickwork and the sound of the ice bucket hitting. The fire burned in his chest and he felt he was falling.

Laverne heard the splash and turned on the pool lights. She saw the bar turned over and the broken glass, and then she saw Ernie floating face down in the deep end of the pool. From that distance she didn't notice the ice cubes floating in the water beside him.

Billy: Later today, Gilly, we'll be talking to an especially interesting guest, Creighton Schwartz, the editor of Hammer and Nail. That's the country's leading do-it-yourself magazine.

Gilly: It should be fascinating, Billy. Especially to all our listeners in suburbia.

Billy: No question about it.

Gilly: I know that our neighborhood is an absolute beehive of home projects.

Billy: When you think of it, it's incredible the way do-it-yourself has taken hold in this country in the last few years. And it's not just the men. There are lots of women who can paint and hammer with the best of them.

Gilly: I know. Some of my best friends do it themselves.

Billy: Of course, lots of couples do it together.

Gilly: That's true, Billy. Actually, that's part of the American tradition.

Billy: Yes, it's genuine togetherness. Not pseudo togetherness but the real thing.

Gilly: Right. Doing it together can be a family affair.

Billy: Precisely. A do-it-yourself project represents a way of building something together. Not just the project itself, but a foundation for living.

Gilly: Eloquently said, Billy.

Billy: In other words, it's a way of cementing your marriage.

Gilly: Ummm. Scraping paint side by side.

Billy: Putting up wallpaper together.

Gilly: Pairing on the paneling.

Billy: Laying tile in unison.

Gilly: That does sound like fun.

Billy: When you're working together, you're building together.

Gilly: And that's the solid kind of value that results in a successful marriage.

MORTON EARBROW

Morton Earbrow waited for the sweat to dry. He lay on rancid sheets, too tired to pull off his boxer shorts and grope in the darkness for his pajamas. And there, in the dark, he could hear the clicking, the familiar clicking, the clicking which would continue until sleep dulled his senses.

"What time is it?" he called out. "What time is it anyway?"

"One-fifteen," his wife answered.

But the clicking didn't stop. The pattern of sound didn't even change. She was down at the foot of the stairs scraping paint. She was down there with her can of McBry's paint remover and a scraper. She was down there wearing rubber gloves. She was down there scraping paint and it was Saturday night.

"Why don't you quit for the night?" Morton asked.

"Quit now?" she said. *Click-click-click.* "When I'm almost finished? Few more minutes."

He knew the clicking would go on and he would fall asleep and in the morning Gloria, she of the golden hair and honeydew breasts, would be draped over the other side of the bed. She'd still be wearing slacks and sweatshirt, too exhausted to undress.

All this he knew, but he had to give it one more shot. Pulling his tortured body from the bed, straightening out his crippled body—crippled from having painted ceilings in eleven different rooms—he limped from the bedroom and down the stairs.

"Thought you were going to sleep," Gloria said, never turning her head from her work.

"Couldn't sleep," he said. "Gloria. . . ."

"Mmmmm," she said.

He had nothing to say and they both knew it. He tried to deliver the message in another language, a language they had both understood so long ago. He put his arms around her waist and rubbed his weekend beard into the dampness of her sweatshirt. He raised his hands until they touched the honeydew melons that were her breasts.

"Morton! For God's sake!"

"For my sake, Gloria," he said. "It's been so long."

"Soon we'll be caught up," *click, click, click.* "Soon we'll be caught up with the house. Then we'll have the time."

"Soon is too late," he said. "Gloria. . . ."

"Think of the house," she said, pointing her index finger at the woodwork that was finally showing through the layers of paint. "Think of what we're building, the home our children will have."

"Children," he said. "To have children you've got to. . . ."

"Mor-ton." It was a warning.

He knew when he was defeated. He slunk back up the stairs, crawled into the rancid sheets, waited for sleep to hammer him into unconsciousness. As he sank, he cursed the old house they had purchased, the structure that was once the carriage house of a prominent American millionaire. He cursed the suburban community, cursed the neighbors, cursed the crabgrass, cursed the ceilings he had scraped and painted, cursed the Long Island Expressway and finally, just before going under, cursed the rancid sheets. He must remember to ask Gloria to change the sheets.

In the morning he was better. He was always better in the morning. The great ache in his groin was subdued and the stiffness in his muscles seemed gone. He wished he were older. He wished his recuperative powers were less good. If only he could be fifty and have the excuse of being tired. But no. He and Gloria were both twenty-five. They were able to work eighteen hours a day. They did.

Gloria had left a list on the bureau. "Mow the grass," the note said. "Prepare for fall seeding." Unquestioning, he pushed the old mower over the crabgrass. It was automatic labor and he welcomed it. For he was a dreamer, and he liked tasks that allowed his mind to wander. There were dreams of coolness and cleanliness, dreams of clean sheets and women fresh from hot showers, dreams of hands without blisters and breasts free of sweatshirts. He dreamed of air-conditioned apartments overlooking urban rivers, of stereo sets and soft lights. Horny was the word.

Gloria was deep in the bowels of the house, scraping paint that had been applied at the turn of the century. He was alone with his dreams and his hand mower. He was thinking of high-rise bachelor apartments, of building superintendents and professional repairmen, of plumbers and electricians. Finally he heard the voice.

"Mr. Earbrow," the voice said. "Oh, Mr. Earbrow."

It was a woman's voice, *the* woman's voice. Gillian Blake was leaning against the back fence that separated their properties. The only other time Morton had seen Gillian was at the party. He had congratulated her on something. What was it? Yes. On being the only woman in the neighborhood who didn't hang over back fences and offer advice to neighbors. And here she was hanging over the back fence, with that soft, frilly housecoat.

"You seem to be working so hard," Gillian said. "Wouldn't you rather use our power mower? We're not using it today."

Morton Earbrow found himself staring. Staring hard
at her slim, exciting face. Then staring hard at her
slim, exciting body. Her arms were slim and exciting,
too. Lightly tanned arms and a fine coating of sun-
bleached hair. Those arms, he decided, had never
lifted anything heavier than a champagne glass. Maybe
a tennis racquet—but that just for effect. She was,
he suddenly realized, part and parcel of his most glorious dreams.

"Thank you, Mrs. Blake," he said, "but. . . ."

"You're welcome to it," Gillian said.

"To it?" He hadn't wanted to say that. He knew he
was a fool. He knew she was talking about the power
mower. Despite the phrasing, the way she talked, the
way she looked. Despite all that, she was talking about
a power mower.

In point of fact, Gillian was not talking about a
power mower. If there was anything in the world that
held less interest than a power mower, she couldn't
imagine what it might be. It was just that, on the evidence, the quickest way to Morton Earbrow's heart
would probably be astride a power mower.

"The mower is in the garage," she said.

"Well, thank you, Mrs. Blake," he said.

Morton vaulted the fence easily, and walked beside
her to the garage. It was cool in the garage, cool and
dark. He could see through an open door what must
be a den. Cooler and darker. There was a couch in the
den. Gillian leaned in the doorway and looked at him.
He could feel that aching sensation in his groin, and
he turned away and looked at the power mower.

"You work very hard," Gillian said. "I hear you
working at night, too."

"Well, the house needs a lot of . . . work," he said.

"Don't you ever just sit around and relax?"

"Not very often," he said. "It's an old house."

"My husband doesn't sit around and relax either,"
Gillian said. She wondered whether she was going too
fast. "But our house is a new house. It's just that he's

never home any more. He has work in the city."

"You both work in the city," Morton said. "I mean I've heard the show."

"I'm surprised," Gillian said. "Very few men listen to us."

"Well, I, uh, better be going," Morton said. "Lots of mowing to do today. We're going to be seeding later on."

"Really?" Gillian said. "How interesting."

Morton thought that was delivered in an ambiguous manner, but decided against pursuing it.

"Maybe you had better test the mower before you go," Gillian said. "It hasn't been used in some time."

Morton Earbrow took the machine out into the sunlight beside the swimming pool. He looked at the water, at the small waves stirred up by the wind off the Sound, and he looked at the mower. He realized it was a fine machine, a self-propelled rotary, with a 3½-horsepower, 4-cycle engine, not to mention an automatic starter, a push-button hydraulic fuel pumper, an automatic compression release and a die-cast magnesium alloy housing unit. A beautiful machine, actually, and Morton Earbrow wondered why he couldn't drum up more enthusiasm. He flicked the switch, the machine came alive, purred for a full minute and died.

"Something seems to be wrong," he observed.

"Oh, I hope it's nothing serious," Gillian said.

"We'll have it fixed in a jiffy," Morton said.

He spoke with confidence. And there was, in truth, no reason why Morton Earbrow should have doubts. He had in the past few months repaired chain saws and drills and sanding machines and hand saws and hammers and lathes and he had never yet encountered the machine that could resist his skillful touch.

As he began testing the ignition system, the spark plugs, the distributor, the carburetor, Gillian disappeared. When she came back she carried a cold beer for him. When she came back she was wearing a bathing suit. It was a strange bathing suit, Morton decided, a bathing suit with openings in unexpected places—a bathing suit that seemed to be held together by shoelaces. He accepted the beer and turned back to the lawn mower.

"You mean you'll be able to put all those pieces back again?" she asked.

"Oh, it's not too complicated, actually," Morton said. "But I can't seem to isolate the trouble."

"But that's wonderful," Gillian said. "When something goes wrong we always have to call in a man."

Morton Earbrow returned home for his wrenches and screwdrivers. When he came back, Gillian was in the pool. She swam nicely, especially when one considered the slimness of her arms, which was precisely what Morton was considering. He returned his attention to the machine slowly, regretfully and, for once in his life, to a machine that seemed to be getting the better of him. Of course, Morton Earbrow had no way of knowing that Gillian had emptied a shaker of salt into the gas tank earlier in the day.

His wife appeared but once. Precisely at noon, wearing Bermuda shorts and sweatshirt, she came over and handed him a liverwurst sandwich. No mustard. She disappeared again into the bowels of the house.

Gillian spent the afternoon stretched out on the striped chaise lounge. She thought briefly about Ernie Miklos and felt a twinge of sorrow. She hadn't wanted it to end that way, nothing quite so violent as that. It was sorrow tempered with relief, though; she might not have gotten him home. And how would she have explained that?

The sun was striking her full force now, and she shifted from her stomach to her back. She was aware also of the heat of Morton Earbrow's gaze every time she twitched a muscle. At that moment she inhaled— just for effect, just to see what would be the reaction of her little home handyman. Before exhaling, she had the satisfaction of hearing a wrench drop.

The sense of challenge was already waning. And

Gillian Blake, warm and rested, allowed her mind to speculate on the next candidate. Someone a trifle harder, she mused, someone who would put up more of a . . . struggle.

Melvin Corby—he was so frightened by his wife; he would surely be a challenge. Or maybe Paddy Madigan, the retired prize fighter, but there was something missing there, something about him she didn't quite understand. Marvin Goodman, the skinflint. . . . Willoughby Martin, if he even cared about girls. The possibilities seemed endless. But a challenge, who would be a challenge? There was Mario Vella; everyone said he was a member of the Cosa Nostra. No, not him, not yet.

Rabbi Joshua Turnbull, a man of God. That would surely be a challenge. Well, why not?

"You must be so tired," she said to Morton Earbrow. "Wouldn't you like to take time for a drink?"

"I think I've found the problem," Morton said. "Something seems to be clogging the fuel line."

Gillian reached down and let her uncalloused, satiny hand stroke the back of his neck. He jumped to his feet immediately.

"Come on in and have a drink," she said. "Come on, you deserve it."

"A little break wouldn't hurt, I suppose," he said.

From the garage to the den, darker and cooler. He sat on the couch and let the air conditioning unit strike him directly.

"I'm going to get your slipcovers all . . . ," he started and stopped.

"A Tom Collins this time?" she said. "Change your luck?"

"It wouldn't hurt," he said.

She carried the drinks to him, sat down beside him. That bathing suit; he couldn't imagine how it was held together. The stresses. . . .

"What's next?" Gillian said.

"Excuse me?"

"On the house," she said. "What's your next project?"

"Who knows? Gloria makes lists. She doesn't let me see them until the weekend. But there's lots to do. Lots of work on an old house. Never ends. Sometimes I wish we hadn't bought it."

"What does your wife think about it all?"

"She likes it," he said. "She says it keeps her busy. That's what I can't understand . . . you must hear this kind of thing all the time. I guess you know almost everything about marriage."

"Everything," she said. It sounded cynical. It was cynical.

Her eyes were amber in the dark. "Everyone has problems. People don't seem able to reach out to each other any more."

"I know what you mean," he said. "I know exactly what you mean. But what do you do when that happens?"

"I could tell you what I say on the radio," Gillian said. "Reason, patience, share mutual interests—but what I say when the microphone is off is something else. I don't think the people out there in radioland are ready for what I really think."

She was reaching out her right arm to emphasize the point, and Morton Earbrow looked through one side of her net bathing suit and received a clear vision of her right breast. It seemed both soft and firm. Not like a melon perhaps, more like a pear. But then he had nothing against pears.

"The important thing"—she was still talking—"and this is what I wish I could say on the radio, is that you communicate, communicate with someone, anyone. Reach out and touch another soul. Love someone, that's the important thing. Love and be loved."

"But how?" Morton said. "Who?"

"Use your imagination," she said.

Morton timidly reached out and touched Gillian's knee. His fingers, his fingers would surely leave dust marks on her. But there was no stopping now. He slid his hardened fingers above her knee, to the flesh of her thigh. Slim but soft. He could feel her skin quiver beneath his fingers. He could feel her hand on his knee, feel her hand tightening, moving. His hand slid higher on her thigh and she moved toward him, made it easier for him.

It was then that Morton Earbrow's mechanical genius paid dividends. Without stopping to think about it, without ever having seen a blueprint, acting on instinct alone, he found the string that held her bathing suit together. It came off in three sections. Then they were touching each other in the deepest, most secret places, reaching out. Yes, by God, communicate with someone. Morton bent her beneath him and she was beyond resistance.

"I'm going to soil your couch," he remembered. "My knees and elbows, they're. . . ."

"Kindly shut up," she said.

She had removed the belt to his Bermuda shorts and was pulling them down, down and off. And then, without more words, they merged. In the dark, in the cool darkness, they communicated. Faster and faster they communicated, harder and harder, in dozens of places, in countless ways. Fingers and nails on skin, teeth on skin, then great shudders of total communication. There were explosions of understanding, and the long-drawn-out paroxysm of being as together as two people can be.

"You see," she whispered later. "That's what I meant. That's what I was trying to tell you."

"It seemed so easy. . . ."

They came apart then and rested in the dark. Morton began to laugh and he couldn't stop.

"I'd forgotten about this," he said. "I'd forgotten there was more to life than mowing a lawn."

"There are lawns to mow and lawns to mow," she said.

"A lawn is a lawn is a lawn"—and he was laughing again. Laughing and reaching for his shorts.

"What's your hurry?" Gillian said. "The lawn can wait. That lawn can wait."

"My wife," he said. "It's afternoon and I should have started the seeding by now."

"I think you just did," Gillian said. "I'll let you go, but only if you promise to come back."

"When?"

"Almost any time," she said. "My husband hasn't been coming home much lately. Just check the driveway. If the car is here, he'll be here. If the car's away, then we can . . . play."

"I'm sorry about the dirt on the couch," he said.

"Never apologize," Gillian said.

There were other visits that week. There were Tuesday and Thursday and Saturday afternoon and Sunday morning. And that following Sunday afternoon, with his wife out shopping for spreading junipers, Morton lay down in his uncut crabgrass and rolled over like a puppy and felt happy to feel the cushion that was growing beneath him.

It wasn't just that the lawn never got mowed. Everything fell behind. He painted one window and didn't do the one beside it. He ordered the ceramic tile for the kitchen counter but never ordered the adhesive. He constructed half of a redwood deck and threw his hammer into Mario Vella's yard. The lawn became a field and the house was winning the fight and Morton Earbrow enjoyed the luxury of a world disintegrating around the core of his happiness.

Gloria, meanwhile, scraped the woodwork and stained it and covered it with liquid plastic. She peeled the wallpaper from the hall and put up some more. And, unsurprisingly, she could not help but notice that Morton was no longer keeping pace. She stopped making her lists because she suspected they were not even being read.

On Monday there was an argument.

"I think you owe me an explanation," she said. "You go out to Modell's for paint and it keeps you three hours—"

"You know those crowds at Modell's," he said.

"And you come home without any paint. And that smile—I don't see anything so funny. Then on Thursday you have the office softball game and you say you're so tired you can't do a thing around here."

"Well, I do work during the week," he suggested.

"Sit at a desk," she said. "While I'm here trying to make us a nice home, a good life. And you're sitting there at that desk and you don't care how we live."

"I care," he said. "I *care*. But not twenty-four hours a day. It's inhuman to slave around this house all day. There's no time for anything else. God, when I think of what it was like when we were first married—"

"That's all you ever do think about," Gloria said. "I'm beginning to think I married some kind of a sex maniac. That may have been all right before we had responsibilities. We've finally got a home. Soon we'll have children. We've got to start getting organized."

"*Children!*" Morton was shouting now. "How in the hell can two people have children when they don't even sleep together?"

"Sex maniac!" she screamed.

"Damn right!"

"If that's all that being married means to you," she said, "then we have one beautiful relationship."

"Oh, shit!"

"All you want is my body," she went on. "What about building a life together, a home for our . . . ?"

"Shit, shit, shit!" The deep end. "Screw a life together. Screw the home. Screw your body."

"I'm not listening to you," she said.

"Goodbye," he said.

The dream returned then. The neat, always tidy bachelor apartment. The predecorated, regularly cleaned, air-conditioned, bachelor apartment. The stereo set, the sleep-in guests, Gillian Blake. And Morton Earbrow knew what must be done. He walked up the freshly finished stairs, entered the recently papered bedroom, shoved aside his work clothes, jammed his suits and shirts into two suitcases. And left.

A week later he made the phone call.

"Gillian?"

"Morton," she said.

"What's doing?"

"What's doing with you?" she said. "Where are you?"

"I've got this great new pad," Morton said, "here on 66th Street. You can see the East River right behind the smokestacks."

"That sounds great," Gillian said. "Where's Gloria?"

"Gloria who?" he said. "Hey, you've got to drop up here after the show. I'll show you the East River. I'll show you my etchings."

"You mean it's all over with Gloria?" she said.

"It never was with Gloria," he said. "How about . . . ?"

"Goodbye," she said.

"What do you mean?"

"Goodbye," she said.

Click. Morton Earbrow felt the phone go dead in his hand. He stood there, looking beyond the smokestacks at the East River. He was aware of the mechanical hum of the air conditioner, and the room seemed suddenly cold. Morton Earbrow, a do-it-yourselfer with nothing to do, spent the next hour listening to his new FM radio. He mixed himself two martinis. He changed the linen on his new bed. And it was not until late that night that he began constructing a small and somewhat crude wine rack out of coat hangers and an orange crate. It was hard going, mainly because he didn't have the proper tools.

Before retiring for the night he wrote himself a note: "Buy new drill on way to work."

Gilly: Say, Billy, did you see the newspaper stories about the special religious service that's planned for our own King's Neck?

Billy: You mean at the Jewish temple?

Gilly: Yes, where they're going to feature a rock 'n' roll group.

Billy: Wild.

Gilly: I know, it's too fascinating. I've heard about using jazz as part of the liturgy, but rock 'n' roll! To say the least, that's a bit different.

Billy: Of course, the rabbi there, Rabbi Joshua Turnbull, is well known as an innovator.

Gilly: He's a comparatively young man, too.

Billy: You know, he might make an interesting guest.

Gilly: Yes, I think he would be extremely interesting. I've never drawn out a rabbi before.

JOSHUA TURNBULL

It was too simple, too easy. Ernie Miklos . . . Morton Earbrow. . . . Gillian, weary of automatic conquests, was tempted to abandon her plan. What was needed at this juncture was a challenge. Something that would permit her to test her . . . mettle.

Joshua Turnbull, spiritual leader of the tiny Jewish community in King's Neck, had in recent months become a figure of modest controversy. It began when he announced plans to amplify a Friday night service the following month with a rock 'n' roll group known as "Jonah and the Wails." It was this announcement that qualified the rabbi for a guest appearance on the *Billy & Gilly Show*. And the rabbi's public relations man had said Rabbi Turnbull would be delighted to come.

So it was that William Blake—philanderer, cuckold and moderator—looked on naïvely that Monday morning as Gillian hoisted sail. Rabbi Turnbull was difficult from the outset. Not only was he oblivious to Gillian's charm, he even seemed unaware of her presence, and he directed his conversation to the radio audience. He wasn't responding properly to her sallies. He answered them obliquely and continued following a course of his own charting. Gillian added canvas, sailed recklessly after him.

Turnbull, a product of Union Theological Seminary in Cleveland, was a beefy, thick-muscled man in his mid-thirties who sported an ash-blond Vandyke, jaunty salt-and-pepper tweeds and no yarmulke. William noted a resemblance to Skitch Henderson. Rabbi Turnbull sprang from a family of Reform rabbis that had emigrated to the Midwest from Germany before the Civil War. Rabbi Turnbull was considerably more than reformed; he was reconstructed. American to a fault, he was the residual of four generations of reformed Jewry that had refined the stiff-necked, insulated, and anachronistic worship of a desert God into a white precipitate of acceptability and consensus that bordered on the Episcopalian.

Rabbi Turnbull's Sunday School, for example, happened on Sundays. The rabbi had constructed a Temple of steel and glass that was the envy of all the other faiths in King's Neck. (He sometimes took delighted malice in the Greek epigram: "The crucified martyr made light of his loss/ Till he spotted another on a higher cross.") The Temple was built with three prongs jutting skyward, symbolizing the Hebrew letter "shin," a symbol that burst with significance in Jewish lore but was also a symbol that could represent any trinity that one cared to apply. Detractors said it looked like Neptune's trident thrust through the earth, and they claimed it would not be surprising if a huge pagan fist reached up from the waters of Long Island Sound to reclaim it. Vandals from the city had once desecrated the building by painting the words, "By you, this is a shule?" across the front doors.

But the most unpleasant incident connected with the Temple occurred during the dedication ceremonies. Rabbi Turnbull had arranged to liberate a hundred balloons and, as the balloons soared aloft, the string on one of them became entangled on the forked tongue of the Temple's left prong and bobbed there insistently. In effect, the letter "shin" was dotted on the left which, unfortunately, turned it into the letter "sin." And to the rabbi's anguish the balloon remained there for half a day until one of his congregation shot it down with an air rifle.

Despite its beginnings, the Temple prospered. As did Rabbi Turnbull. Gaining some small fame as an ecumenical bridge, the Temple primarily served as the social locus of the Jewish community of King's Neck. The Jews of King's Neck, thoroughly assimilated and distributed, were members of that ultimate ghetto—the dispersed one.

Turnbull always observed that tolerance breeds selectivity. If a community bends over backward to be publicly liberal, it can give itself the bonus of private snobbery. In such a hotbed of tolerance it was perhaps inevitable that the rabbi and his Temple would flourish. Only last year, Turnbull, the father of three, had been named one of the ten most outstanding young rabbis in America. This was followed by a genuine heaven-sent gift—the King's Neck (Reform) Temple Beth Manasseh received a three-page color spread in a *Life* Magazine series entitled "The New Look in Religion." Shortly thereafter, Rabbi Turnbull received a CORE citation for his Civil Rights efforts. He had marched in Washington and St. Augustine, and his picture had been flashed across the nation when an Associated Press photographer spotted him attempting to reason with an outraged redneck in Selma. Turnbull circulated five hundred of these photographs to leading church, state and community officials at his own expense.

But Rabbi Turnbull's latest venture, hiring Jonah and the Wails for his Friday night service, had caused a stir even among his fellow reformers, most of whom objected on aesthetic rather than ethical grounds. The rabbi dismissed this as so many sour grapes. He had simply stolen a march on them again.

The controversy spread throughout Long Island, with the community about evenly divided. A *Newsday* poll revealed that the division was among those who thought the rabbi was a charlatan (5 per cent), those who thought he was sincere (5 per cent), those who thought Jonah and the Wails were sincere (20 per cent) and the rest who had not yet formed an opinion. In the face of criticism, Rabbi Turnbull stoutly maintained that Judaism was an organic faith which must adapt or die.

"I am improvising on the keyboard of faith," he told Gillian, or rather, the microphone. At that moment Gillian decided, if the rabbi planned to champion reform, she would fight the battle of tradition.

Rabbi Turnbull noted that music had been malleable and contemporary in Jewish culture from the time of King David's harp; as evidence he named such composers as Arabanels in Spain and others such as Mendelssohn and Halévy. Gillian countered by observing that no one on the list composed ritual music. Rabbi Turnbull recalled that even the pious Hasidic rabbis had composed a march of welcome when Napoleon entered Galicia.

"Yes," Gillian said, "but surely you will recall that they scrupulously refrained from using that march in their liturgy. And certainly you're not going to compare the Hasids to . . . Jonah and the Wails?"

The rabbi turned red around the neck but went on ignoring Gillian. He pointed out that, if the tradition were literally adhered to, the great commentaries on the Bible, the Mishnah and Gmorrah, would never have been written, and the Jews would still be mired in pre-Herodian ritual. What were the commentaries, he asked, but a restatement of the Bible in contemporary terms? He likened the Bible to a Rorschach ink blot and the commentaries to the thought associations of generations of rabbis.

"Careful, rabbi," Gillian said.

"And what is the Reform movement," he continued, "but a restatement of Judaism in contemporary terms? And, consequently, in the direct tradition of the great rabbis. Like your own earlier Christian Reformation, it is an attempt to breathe new life into an ancient faith. And if we are to rephrase the religious idiom, would it not be a breach of faith to stop short at the music?"

Gillian had majored in Far-Eastern Religion at Bard College- that was before she left school and lived off-campus with Charlie, a blind jazz pianist—and she was not so easily put off.

William turned away and sighed. He knew what was going to happen. Whenever a male guest showed a flourish of intellectual vigor, Gillian would first attempt to match erudition—this through an instinctive ability to marshal the right quote, cite the differential case and, at times, invent the properly unnerving statistic. And if she didn't win in this manner, she would resort to banter, ruse and twittering. Then, if the guest genuinely knew what he was talking about, Gillian would ever so deftly suggest that he was a wee bit pompous, lacked humor, took himself more seriously than was absolutely warranted. And, in extreme cases, when the guest was preparing to lash back, Gillian would simply cut him down with a fusillade of charm. Which would it be this time?

"But isn't it true," she began the assault, "that medi-

eval rabbis had interpreted the Law within the tradi-
tions of ritual—which you are clearly not doing? And
isn't that ritual which you are forsaking essential to
Judaism, not necessarily for its own sake as you imply,
but because it reaffirms the holiness of each human
act?"

"My dear lady. . . ."

"Just let me finish, rabbi," she interrupted him. "As
for the analogy between Jewish and Christian reforma-
tions, I'm more than a little surprised that you would
overlook such a basic matter as intent. The original
spirit of the Protestant Reformation was to purify, to
return to the past, whereas the Jewish Reform sought
to streamline and move toward the future. And finally,
it will seem strange to some of our listeners that a man
of God would allow what is most crude and frivolous
in our society into the sacred halls of a temple—not as
penitents, but as preachers."

"Is there a question in all that?" For the first time
Rabbi Turnbull took note of the opposition.

"Take your choice," Gillian said.

"It was Rabbi Meir," Turnbull said, "who was
once asked why he remained friends with an outcast.
His reply should serve me as well: 'I found a pome-
granate; I ate its contents and threw away its husk.' "

William was getting nervous. Not only did he question the relevance of pomegranates, he could almost
hear the radios being turned off. (That talky kike is
worse than my gabby wife, he thought.) He was aware
that he had become less than peripheral once again.
He had vanished, vanished like a rabbit through the
magic of others being unaware of his presence. The
one thing he was certain of, the conversation was becoming too damned metaphysical for a chatty morning
radio show. Who did she think was listening, Reinhold
Niebuhr? That crack about Protestants purifying the
church, that was going to go over big with the Catho-
lics.

"Gilly," he interrupted, "darling, don't you think

that what the rabbi is trying to say is that religious music can benefit from new sounds, even rock and roll?"

"Not exactly, Billy," she said—control, control—"sweetheart, I think the rabbi is saying much more than that. I think he is suggesting a religious structure that is not so much opposed to tradition as outside it. Isn't that so, Rabbi Turnbull?"

They were off once again, Gillian leading Turnbull a merry chase through the forest of tradition and reformation. The rabbi was dazzled by Gillian's fund of knowledge, dazzled but not cowed, and he took to the game with relish. But when he cited an arcane Babylonian scholar, Gillian managed to recall what the sage's equally arcane nemesis had said to refute the argument. Turnbull was fascinated. Up until that moment it had been a game. Suddenly it was a contest.

In the next fifteen minutes, Rabbi Turnbull had invoked the sum of his learning at Union Theological and beyond. Gillian had, by this time, changed her tactics, shifted to intellectual guerrilla warfare, sniping, hitting available targets, retreating, twitting and teasing. When the show finally ended, Gillian reflected the infuriating impression that she had won. The issue of Jonah and the Wails had somehow been put in camphor.

"You are an army of scholars, Mrs. Blake," the rabbi conceded. "We must continue this some other time."

"I'd love to, rabbi."

The rabbi nodded absently at William and left. He had hardly closed the studio door—

"What the hell did you think you were talking about?" William was asking. "Where did you think you were, one of your Radcliffe seminars?"

"Bard," she corrected him. "And kindly be quiet for a moment and do some thinking. It doesn't matter what I say. We could be talking Urdu—all that matters is that all those little housewives think I come out on top. In case you've missed the point, that's what this show is all about."

"Try talking Urdu a few times," he said. "And see what happens."

The following day Rabbi Turnbull phoned Gillian and asked for some program tapes. She said she would have them the next evening if the rabbi wouldn't mind stopping over at the house for them. He said no, he wouldn't mind. She said fine.

Gillian had figured right; Wednesday had become Phyllis night. When Rabbi Turnbull arrived at the Blake home, Gillian greeted him in a low-cut dress which covered her midsection and not much else. She had completed the costume with hooped earrings and matching silver bracelets.

"Rabbi, how good of you to come," she said. "I didn't hear you drive up."

"I parked up the block," he said. "I was afraid I might clutter your driveway."

Was it possible? Was it possible that even the rabbi would be so willing?

"But that's what the driveway is for, rabbi," Gillian said. She led him by the hand into the living room. The decor was Spanish—everything low and wide except the mortgage.

"From the outside," the rabbi said, "I expected to be greeted by Henry VII."

"Imitation Tudor," she said. "And I hate imitation anything. William always says that all this castle needs is Anne Boleyn—but I guess I'll just have to do."

"She ended badly," Turnbull observed.

"But she lived so well."

"May I ask," he went on, "where Mr. Blake is to-night?"

"William is working late tonight," Gillian said. "He works late on Wednesdays and on Mondays and some-times on Sundays. And on those occasions, he leaves me with his dog. Rolf. I don't like dogs, however, and I especially dislike Rolf."

"Where is Rolf?"

"I've locked him in the garage," she said. "I always lock him in the garage when William's gone."

"But isn't that cruel?"

"Not at all," she said. "He's supposed to be a watchdog. He watches over our broken lawn mower."

Gillian offered Turnbull a drink. His rapid acceptance of the offer amused her.

"What's the blessing on a martini, rabbi?"

"It depends on how well you make it, Mrs. Blake."

Gillian returned to join Turnbull on the couch. The conversation went from the tapes to the show and then, with increasing animation, to the age-old struggle between good and evil. Turnbull mentioned that evil was known everywhere, even in the rabbinate. He concluded that even the sages—no, especially the sages —were not free from temptation.

"Why the sages *especially?*"

"There is a saying, Mrs. Blake," he said. " 'The greater the man, the greater the inclination toward evil.' "

With this Turnbull snorted, as if to clear his nostrils, and reached out to grasp Gillian's wrist. She twisted her arm from his grasp, went into the dining room and returned a moment later.

"Here are the tapes, rabbi," she said. "I believe these were what you came for."

"I mistook you, Mrs. Blake." Turnbull rose and strode over to her. "I hope I didn't upset you."

"No," she said.

"I hope we can still be friends."

"I understand, Rabbi Turnbull, that you're married and that you have three children."

"Yes."

"And your marriage is considered a model for the community?"

"Models are for show windows," he said.

"Then you are unhappily married?"

"That is a redundancy, Mrs. Blake."

"Have you been unfaithful before?"

"Why all this?" he asked. "Is this another taped interview?"

"Before you buy the goods, rabbi, you want to know the quality."

"I will talk straight with you," he said. "I have a need for variety which my wife, dear woman, cannot fulfill. I am not a believer in abstinence."

"But isn't abstinence the sign of a holy man?"

"Only according to your saints, Paul and Augustine, both profligates of the worst order trying to repent for their own sins. Abstinence and profligacy are two sides of the same coin. To be obsessed by one, you must be fascinated by the other."

"This *is* beginning to sound like an interview, rabbi," she said.

"Let us return to the goods, Mrs. Blake. Have we made a sale?"

"Call me Gillian," she said.

"I take it then"—reaching for her—"that the goods are in hand."

"Not until you get your hands on them."

Gillian laughed, slipped away, behind the couch, into the master bedroom. Snorting, the rabbi gave chase. His beard was bobbing. He cornered her in the bedroom against a low Spanish bedpost and pushed her toward the bed.

"Wait," she said, "I must ask you something."

"Honey," he said, "we have talked enough."

"But do you really believe that you'll be damned in hell for this, for what you're trying to do?"

Turnbull studied her for a long moment. Was she joking, crazy? What then? " 'There is neither judgment nor judge'—Rabbi Elisha." With that he thrust Gillian back onto the bed and made a flying leap with the clear intent of pinning her down to stay. But she swerved to one side and the holy man, stiff with lust, came down standard-first on the bedpost. For a full two minutes he did not rise; he lay there, crumpled up, hissing incoherently.

"Rabbi Turnbull, are you all right?"

"Never mind me," he hissed. "Think of Rabbi Elisha."

Gillian was solicitous. The poor man was in obvious pain and she searched for ways to comfort him. "Would you like a massage?" she asked. The mere suggestion caused Turnbull to swoon into a comatose state. A half hour passed before his moribund powers were restored. And no sooner had feeling returned to the affected parts than he once again reached out for Gillian.

"Your clothes," he gasped. "Take off your clothes."

She laughed, pulled away, teased. That crazy *shiksa*, she wants me to work. In this condition, she wants me to work. He managed to rip off her dress. The sight of her long, faintly tanned legs below black net panties set off new explosions of lust in his belly. Avoiding the bedpost, he pounced again. Gillian tried to kick loose, but he had her pinned this time and was covering her mouth with wet kisses. Then, holding her fast, he began working his way down. He traced her navel with his tongue and reached for her smooth, high, arched buttocks when the phone on the night table began ringing.

"Don't answer it," he whispered.

"Why are you whispering?" she said.

The phone kept ringing, insisting, a noisy witness to an act rendered suddenly ludicrous.

"Forget about it," the rabbi said. "Forget about that fucking phone."

"*Rabbi!*" The shock in her voice caused him to loosen his hold. "I can't forget it, it's probably William. If I don't answer, he'll be suspicious."

Turnbull groaned, relaxed. She rolled away from him and picked up the phone.

"Hello. Yes, everything's fine. Why?"

"William?" the rabbi whispered.

No, she indicated. Turnbull clapped his hand over his eyes, groaned aloud. Gillian continued to chat aimlessly for fifteen minutes despite his imploring hand signals. It seemed to be the smallest talk possible. From time to time he reached out to touch her, but she brushed him away. By the end of the call, he was doubled over on the bed again, muttering incoherently. As the thought of strangling her with the phone cord came to him, Gillian calmly hung up.

"Why didn't you hang up right away?" he asked.

"Am I answering to you already, rabbi?"

"Joshua," he said, "call me Joshua."

"Well, Joshua, that happened to be Mario Vella."

"The gangster fellow?"

"The same," she said. "I don't understand why he calls me, but sometimes he says he just wants to talk. And I don't think it would be particularly wise to hang up on him."

"But Mrs. Blake, Gillian, when a man and a woman are in bed. . . ."

". . . The world doesn't end," she finished it.

Turnbull looked at her for a moment. She was kneeling opposite him on the bed. He unhooked her brassiere, and this time Gillian offered no resistance. He removed it and bit softly at her breasts. They waved at him, pennants in the wind of lust, and he bit deeply into the acid of her dugs. Then he pulled off the black net panties—there was a cellophane sound as they were peeled past her thighs. They stuck at her knees. What he had hoped (and prayed, even) would be a smooth operation was spoiled as he had to fumble about her knees and she arched to let him finish slipping them off. Turnbull rose from the bed and then, clad only in his beard, rejoined her. He watched with the patience of the sages as Gillian removed the earrings and the bracelet.

Turnbull delayed it, made it last, stared at the naked woman waiting on the sheets for him. Then, as if mak-

ing an elaborate bow, he took hold of her and pressed
hard against her slightly parted legs. He sewed her
body with a thread of bites and kisses, dwelling on the
tight high pack of her working hips and patching them
with little pink squares. Finally he rose up over her,
shadowed her with the majesty of his manhood, noticed
that her legs were still closed.

"Not yet, Joshua," she said. "Not yet. Kiss my knees
first."

"Your knees?"

"My knees."

"Would you prefer the caps or the hollows?"

"Just kiss them, Joshua."

One nut-girl in this town, he thought, one lovely
shiksa nut-girl and I had to pick her. Turnbull bent
uncomplaining to his new labors. Gillian's knees were
well fleshed and dimpled and certainly not unattractive, if one happened to be a kneeman. For ten long
minutes he improvised on the knee theme—it wasn't
his specialty, but he was always flexible in such matters—and he was rewarded by the sounds of irregular
breathing and little growls. He felt her knees starting
to part and he rose, but she stiff-armed him neatly.

"More," she cried out.

Oy, oy, oy. Trying to preserve his patience, the rabbi
returned to the knees. The growls deepened. It
sounded to Turnbull almost animal-like and, in some
uncanny way, as though the noise was coming from behind him. A moment later, in horror, he realized it was
coming from behind him. It was Rolf. The dog. The
dog who had somehow escaped from the garage, from
the lawn mower, and now he stood in the bedroom
doorway growling at what must have been an incom-
prehensible sight.

During the instant of recognition, Turnbull, buttocks exposed, knelt frozen in terror. And that one
instant was all he had. Rolf leaped. Turnbull felt a
searing pain flash through his right hip. Then a
clamped set of needles dug into his rump and held

fast. Gillian at first felt the rabbi had been transported into a state of exultation that beggared her past experience, and it was only his wild bellowing that made her realize there was an intruder. She crawled around Turnbull, pulled Rolf by an ear and smacked him.

"Naughty dog!" she said, slapping him repeatedly. The beating did no more than cause Rolf to seek an even tighter grip on Turnbull's rump. Finally, tugging at both ears, Gillian managed to pry him from his prey. It must be said to the dog's credit that he did not loosen his grip. It was simply that a portion of the rabbi came free with the dog. Turnbull collapsed on his stomach, moaning, holding his wounds.

"Naughty, naughty dog," Gillian continued. "Now drop that."

Rolf refused to discard his small prize, and Gillian led him to the garage and once again locked him in. Turnbull had not moved.

"I'll get rabies," he moaned.

"Rolf's had all the shots," she assured him. "And it's not all that terrible. William's been after me to throw out this bedspread for an awfully long time."

She found bandages in the bathroom medicine chest, returned and patched Turnbull up.

"You mustn't worry about Rolf," she said again. "He may seem a little testy, but he's certainly not insane. There, that should be better. Well, what did you have in mind next?"

Gillian was sitting cross-legged on the bed before him. The view was too much, even for a newly wounded man. He reached out for one of those magnificent legs, then the other, and he propped himself up on them. Her thighs, he noticed, were springy and firm, the haunches of a lioness. He embraced her in a clumsy bear hug, pushed her heavily down on the bed. He was through with the game playing. He grabbed at her moving thighs and kneaded her swift buttocks. He bit her neck, then her shoulders and pressed himself down on her. Her lips were open in a small smile. Her eyes were closed. The sweat of her body made him weak with desire. Her legs were parted in a wide welcoming arc. The moment had come. Turnbull mounted over the throbbing, waiting woman.

The doorbell rang.

"My God, what's that? What now?"

"Oh, drat," she said. "It must be the girls from the bridge club. I wasn't expecting them until nine."

"Bridge club?"

"I just joined last week," she said. "They meet Wednesday nights."

"Don't answer the door," he pleaded. "Tell them you weren't home."

"The lights are on," she said. "The car is in the driveway. My, wasn't it fortunate you didn't park your car in the driveway. We can be thankful for that."

The bell rang again and Turnbull rolled off.

"Mrs. Blake," he said, "if you knew you were going to have company, why this?"

"It might have worked out," she said. "You'll have to admit, Joshua, you did fumble a bit."

Another ring.

"Joshua, you really have to leave."

"How am I going to get out of here?"

Gillian quickly charted the escape route. Down the stairs, into the den, through the plate glass windows, onto the patio and out the driveway. She would entertain the ladies in the dining room while he made his escape. Even as she was explaining his retreat, Gillian straightened the bedclothes with quick precise movements. Then she climbed into a long, modest frock and, without once looking back at her aspirant lover, left the room.

Turnbull, eyes glazed, sat on the bed until the door clicked shut. Then, still in a weakened condition, he managed to pull himself together. He scrambled into his clothes and, carrying the bloodstained bedspread under his arm, managed to creep out the back way. Despite a narrow escape from a swimming pool waiting for him in the night, the rabbi managed to find the driveway, then the road, then his car. Seated painfully in the safety of his automobile, the rabbi began to consider the entire evening. Was it possible? Was it possible a woman could plan something like that? The invitation, the ferocious dog, the bridge club, even the moans—was it possible that this had been staged for his benefit? Yes, he decided, it was possible.

The following week, Gillian received two phone calls from the rabbi. She was noncommittal, evasive. The next four phone calls she was politely unavailable. The following week—and by this time he heard rumors that Gillian Blake had been seen at a drive-in hamburger stand with Mario Vella, a common gangster— Rabbi Turnbull began sending her presents. The gifts were returned, unopened, to his office beside the Temple.

The more she rejected him, the more he craved her. For just the chance to kiss her knees. He decided that even the dog, Rolf, was not too bad, quite probably a very effective watchdog.

And then he began to hate her.

Love and hate, mingled as they often are in the same current, coursed through his veins and pounded at his temples. Turnbull could not control the demons. And when Gillian began to hang up the phone at the first sound of his voice, he knew the demons would claim him.

He snapped at the members of the ladies' auxiliary. At Temple meetings he seemed distracted and morose, then engaged some of the most important donors in senseless argument. He arrived drunk at Friday night service. Saturday he was seen at a roadhouse with a notorious woman. Acquaintances sought him out to talk to him, but he would have none of it.

In a way, a strange way, Turnbull became more popular in the community than he had ever been.

Scandal is a community service and a free entertainment at that; witnesses generally feel obliged to pay admission with sympathy. Turnbull scorned their sympathy, slapped his wife, shouted at his children and, just before the scheduled appearance of Jonah and the Wails, disappeared for three days.

Cooler heads in the Temple said that this was all for the better, and no police report was issued. Rabbi Lerman, Turnbull's inarticulate assistant, was given specific instructions to get the services over with as quickly as possible.

The services that Friday night were expectably well attended. Reporters and photographers fattened the congregation considerably, and the first half of the proceedings went smoothly. Jonah and the Wails, four grave young men dressed neatly in Mod black, made a fairly conservative entrance if one could overlook the blond wigs. They wore wide leather ties with leaping sperm whales spraying toward the knots. They made their music with two electric guitars, a tambourine and a whale's jawbone that was banged against a single kettle drum. The second half of the service began with the Torah removed from the holy ark and Jonah leading the group in song—

> Open the doors
> Git out the book
> Uh—Uh—uh—uh—uh
> And take a look.
>
> We all prayin'
> (Yeah, yeah, yeah)
> We all prayin'. . . .

It was an instantaneous success, and some in the audience saw a twinge of irony in the fact that Rabbi Joshua Turnbull could not be there to savor his most hard-fought victory. The second song, "Kneelin' and Feelin' and Prayin' and Sayin'," was launched in splendid fashion, with flash bulbs providing punctuation, when the spectre appeared.

Rabbi Turnbull, mantled in a potato sack, his eyes red and wild, marched upon Jonah and the Wails, commanded them to stop. They did. Turnbull mounted the lectern and, foaming with rage, denounced Jonah as a false prophet. He turned to his horrified board of directors and accused them of the sin of the biblical Jonah, ignoring the will of God.

"We are in mortal peril!" he shouted.

Turnbull, holding onto the lectern like a forecastle, felled three Temple vice presidents and was holding his own with a fourth when the police arrived.

"Philistines," he cried, "I'll take the jawbone from this ass and lay your thousand low."

Jonah gave up his bone and fled into the crowd. Turnbull, discovering that it was rubber, threw it at the last of the retreating Wails. Finally, hemmed in by superior forces, Turnbull was overpowered and carted off. The remainder of the service was canceled. And, though the Temple did not press charges against its rabbi, he disappeared forever from King's Neck.

It was rumored in later years that he had changed his name to Brodsky and had found employment as a beadle in a deteriorating Orthodox synagogue in East New York, where he remained, penitent, recluse, who flagellated himself ritualistically. But that was only a rumor, of course.

Billy: Yes, Gilly, with Thanksgiving gone, can Christmas be far behind?

Gilly: And don't forget Chanukah. Equal time, you know. Anyway, that comes first, doesn't it?

Billy: I think so. By the way, Gilly, I think we should express our regret at what happened to Rabbi Joshua Turnbull, who was on the show with us not long ago. I'm sure everybody read about his unfortunate breakdown.

Gilly: Yes, the papers certainly had a picnic with it.

Billy: The man must have been under fantastic pressure.

Gilly: You can't imagine how sorry I felt. That good, saintly man. It just proves what a strain religious leaders are under today. It's the world we live in.

Billy: Right. I'll tell you, Rabbi Turnbull was especially interested in reaching young people, and that could have done it.

Gilly: I'm not sure I follow you, dear.

Billy: Well, these kids today, they don't care about anything. They don't identify with anything.

Gilly: Wait a minute, dear. Certainly today's young people show a great deal of alienation, but I think you're being extreme. I'm sure youth has its important values.

Billy: Yeah, marijuana and LSD. Look, how about the kids you see walking around the Village?

Gilly: Those are hippies. Or they want you to think they are. And anyway, I don't think they're representative of all young people.

Billy: Maybe not, but there are an awful lot of them. Listen, you even see them in the suburbs nowadays.

Gilly: That's true. But even then, you can't always judge a book by its cover.

Billy: Well, all I can say is that some of them, the ones with super-long hair and sandals, have some pretty unappealing covers.

Gilly: Perhaps, but I can remember what it was like when I was in college. We weren't all angels.

Billy: You were, dear. I'm sure you've always been an angel.

Gilly: Well, it's nice of you to think so.

Billy: Seriously, sweetheart, some of these kids today are frightening. Take sexual promiscuity, for instance.

Gilly: Yes, I know what you mean. But I think you're generalizing.

Billy: I'm not so sure.

Gilly: I still think most young people are terribly stimulating.

ARTHUR FRANHOP

Raina Franhop slipped the amphetamine tablet into Cat's water bowl with the sincere hope that it would compensate for his waning sex life. (Domestic animals, of course, were not permitted to run free in the unincorporated village of King's Neck and, on his last excursion into the great outdoors, Cat had attempted to mount a gray squirrel, only to be severely rebuffed.) The drug took effect immediately. Unfortunately, Cat overreacted. He sped from one end of the living room to the other, banging his head noisily against the wallboard to mark the end of each lap. Arthur Franhop could not help but notice that Cat was caught up in an orgasm of ecstasy.

"Barbaric!" he screamed.

"Hypocrite!" she screamed back.

Raina realized that Arthur's concern was over the loss of the pill, not for the well-being of her beloved Cat. And, all too true, it was becoming harder and harder to score safely. But they still had the twenty pounds of Acapulco Gold they had smuggled out of Mexico in whimsically painted Christmas balls, and Arthur had no right to blow his cool over one lousy goofball.

What really upset Raina was being called barbaric. She did not like, and she did not need, to be reminded of it. Often she felt that she was just about to slip over the edge of humanity into an abyss of pure violence. During a recent LSD session she had been transformed into a banzai-shouting, teeth-baring maniac; she still wasn't sure she had returned safely from that particular trip.

Eventually Cat slowed down and collapsed. By that time, Arthur and Raina were lying nude on the Mexican serape reading the *East Village Other* and some lesser publications.

"Here's one," Arthur said. "Pretty groovy. 'Housewife, 42, interested in chains. Formal practical nurse, has knowledge of piercing. Willing to oblige women in particular.' Interesting."

"Yes, but her address is Kenosha, Wisconsin." Raina said, reading over his shoulder. "You don't have the bread to bring her all the way out here."

Raina never neglected an opportunity to mention Arthur's relative poverty. Her father had paid twenty-eight thousand dollars for the split-level home on the outskirts of King's Neck—quite likely with the hope that a material possession, especially one in the world capital of material possessions, would give them some sense of responsibility. Possibly even push them into formal marriage. (Though they shared Arthur's last name, the marriage ceremony had never been performed by a lawfully appointed official—it was sanctified by a bearded nineteen-year-old Zen-reader during a monthly meeting of the Los Angeles chapter of the League for Sexual Freedom.) At any rate, Raina liked to keep reminding Arthur that, even if she wasn't indispensable to him, her father's money was.

Arthur ignored it. He had a great ability to hear only the things that really interested him.

"Okay, here's something even better," he said. "'Father and mother, both 32, with son, 12, and daughter 8.' It goes on to say they raise muskrats but they're very interested in leather, especially boots."

"Leather, for God's sake," she said. "Don't you think that's a little passé? And look at the address. Taos, New Mexico. How would you figure on getting there?"

"Hey, do you think they're Indians?"

Arthur brightened for a moment. His experience up to this point had been strictly with Negroes and whites. He wanted some Orientals to round out the picture, but Indians—Jesus, they'd be something else. He stared at Raina. That long, straight black hair. A little snarled, maybe, and most Indian women kept their hair in tight, neat braids. But it was passable. Hell, more than passable. It would do. And those dangling silver earrings. They had turned her ear lobes black, but even that gave it a touch of authenticity. Not too many bathtubs around those little Indian villages. Yeah, she'd do. For the moment, anyway.

"*Querida*," he said, grabbing her left ankle brutally. "Say something dirty in Uxmex."

"Fantasy-break time again?" She stared back at him balefully.

The question turned Arthur off. He liked spontaneity—in fact, when he had first met Raina a year earlier, that had been her most attractive and endearing quality. When he wanted to play Unicorn, she had obligingly curled into the shape of a horn. When he had wanted her in the chapel, she had sweetly stretched herself into the form of a crucifix and—no questions asked—accepted his love-making in Latin.

(*"Vidi, vici, veni"*—he had been inspired by the sight—
"I saw, I conquered, I came.")

But now it was a totally different story. Raina moved
away from Arthur and eased her thighs into the Lotus
position. She was let down, bruised to the depths of
her superego. Perhaps Yoga could help her. It was better than pot or LSD, especially Tim Leary's much
touted LSD trip without LSD (you sat barefoot in a
quiet setting contemplating a tin can and fruit seed).
Tim Leary, what a sellout. It was all right, of course,
for producing visions, but she didn't want visions now.
She wanted calm, higher understanding.

What upset her was not the fact of rejection. That
would pass. The thing that bothered her was that they
had played Indian before. Arthur was *repeating* a
fantasy. Jesus H., if things were going to get boring,
that was it. Boredom was Raina's major fear in life;
it was the one evil to be avoided at any cost.

She waited there, in the Lotus position, waited for
inspiration to overtake her. Arthur tried to pull the
serape from beneath her and wrap it around his neck,
possibly in imitation of a lei. ("Welcome to Hawaii,"
he said.) Unamused, thoroughly unamused now, Raina
stood up, the serape still wrapped around her, and
walked out of the room with dignity.

Arthur didn't give her a second thought. He rarely
concerned himself with thinking about other people.
His own moods were so much more fascinating. He
began thumbing through the magazine again. And
just as he hit upon another intriguing item—"Husband
and wife, 21 and 19, both like hairy men—no women
need apply"—the doorbell rang, and Arthur got up,
still nude, to answer it.

It was Dexter, a huge Negro who had been Arthur's
buddy in the army. (Arthur had allowed himself to
be drafted a year after flunking out of Brandeis. So
many of his friends had burned and urinated on their
draft cards, feigned catalepsy, encouraged hideous
rashes, learned to lisp and so forth that the only cool,

the only truly cool, thing left to do was to go into the
army, and so Arthur had allowed himself to be drafted.
His friends had congratulated him on his imaginative
stand, and Arthur was not unhappy about it himself.
Actually he had enjoyed the army. Being an MP directing traffic on a Nike base in Maryland was a whole
new bit. And even when he was discovered chewing
morning glory seed on duty—his clearance had been
lifted—he found that being a typist in personnel was
just this side of wiggy. He had spent most of the time
drawing obscene portraits of the thyroid-eyed WAC
who sat opposite him and telling her such wild stories
that, by the end of his stint, her mind was completely
but permanently blown and she was reduced to mop-
ping floors in Headquarters Battalion's psychiatric
ward.)

Fond memories aside, here was Dexter. Good old
Dexter. A tall, silent Black who communicated only
in two-word sentences. "She fly," he would frequently
say, meaning "She's good." Or he might say "She
bad"—also meaning "She's good." "Woofing" (putting
down) and "jammed up" (crazy) and "rapping" (playing up to) were some of his other judgments.

He seemed more excited than Arthur had ever seen
him. Arthur looked at him with a tender smile spread
across his pale bony face. He liked Dexter, truly liked
him. Dexter never got mad, never asked questions,
never thought about anything. He just grooved along
from one day to the next, so cool he was almost dead.
Arthur liked him so much, in fact, that if he ever got
up the nerve to have a homosexual fling, Dexter would
be his man. (Though he was loath to admit it, Arthur
had never been able to make it with a man. He felt
ashamed of the idiosyncrasy but could do nothing to
conquer it.)

"Man." Dexter was staring at him, glassy-eyed as
usual. "I have just had me one real-life experience."

"Yeah?"

"There am I, buzzin' through this supermarket you

got here, lookin' to cop a salami, somethin'. [Dexter knew that if he wanted something to eat, he'd have to bring his own provender. Brown rice and nuts filled the refrigerator, and that was not Dexter's idea of soul food.] All of a sudden what do I see but this chick who is the most fly chick I have seen in my life *ever*. This one I say, this one, baby, is a trip and a half, only she is crying there.

"So right away I ease myself up to her and say why is she cryin'. She is sayin' a friend of hers has checked out. So then I tell her I'm from SNAC. And she says, very cool, 'a breakfast cereal representative?' And I say I mean SNCC, you know, baby, civil rights, you know, integration and like that. And by this time she is laughing. Hooowee and a half, baby, she is something else."

Arthur drew his buddy into the house. Never in his three-year friendship with Dexter had he heard him communicate so long, so enthusiastically and so coherently. However, his sense of hospitality had not deserted him altogether.

"Wanna smoke some grass?" he said.

Dexter nodded almost imperceptibly and Arthur reached for the Christmas ball on the mantelpiece, cracked it open and offered his friend some marijuana. The two of them sat there for a while, smiling at the wall, until Arthur broke the silence.

"You get her name, Dexter?"

"Gilli-Anne, brother, Gilli-Anne Blake."

The rest of the story came from Dexter in barely coherent fragments. She was tall, blonde and slim. Her breasts were full without being maternal. Dexter had, of course, propositioned her. She claimed to understand the meaning but the phrasing troubled her. At any event, she had turned him down, but charmingly. Dexter took no offense. Living in New York as he did, his sexual experience had been rather severely limited to one type of girl—fleshy, Jewish, painfully liberal and painfully frustrated. It even pained

Dexter to think of the last one, a flabby-thighed, snaggle-toothed young lady named Minna who had clutched him to her pendulous bosom and offered him corned beef sandwiches and sympathy after he had done his best to devastate her. He had sensed that her basic goal in life was to feed, mother and talk him to death, and he wasn't having any of it. This Gilli-Anne was much more his type.

Arthur assembled the fragments, and came up with a reasonably accurate reflection of Dexter's meaning. He allowed that he had seen the woman in question, had spoken to her three times, once at a party and twice on the street. And that it was too bad it didn't work out so that Dexter could ball her because that would be something else.

"Yeah, but baby," Dexter said, "when I tell her I know you, she say you her *type*."

"Her type?"

"She say she want *you*, baby."

The meaning of this was unmistakable. And, while Arthur in no way trusted Dexter's recollection of the conversation, he fully trusted Dexter's instincts. If Dexter believed that Mrs. Gillian Blake wanted him, well then, in all probability, she did. And if Dexter wigged out like that over her, he probably sensed that she would be wilder in bed than a female rhinoceros. Rhinoceros, hmmmm.

"Time for a little bike ride," Arthur said. Dexter blinked, meaning yes.

Arthur stepped into a pair of white levis, snapped on the big white helmet, the jacket and the boots. The two of them strolled out to the garage where Big Momma, Arthur's Harley-Davidson 1200, rested in all its multi-geared splendor. And fifteen cursing neighbors later, the machine was idling in the Blake driveway.

It was easy. Dexter banged on the door. Gillian had opened it and smiled. The smile was her mistake.

Dexter lifted her off her feet, hoisted her over his right shoulder and carried her onto the waiting motorcycle. Within five minutes they were cruising back to Arthur's house, Gillian slung across the center of the motorcycle.

Gillian had complained, then pleaded, but her cries were drowned out by Big Momma. She decided to take it slowly and did everything in her power not to smile. In a nutty kind of way it was almost romantic. Not candlelight and champagne romantic, but nutty romantic. Nothing like this had happened since college, since the time her Medieval Philosophy professor tried to make love to her under water while a chilly April moon glittered over College Pond.

When they finally arrived at their destination, Raina opened the door to meet them. She took one look at Gillian and floated off—ethereally, she hoped—to the upstairs bedroom, where she sucked on an LSD-saturated sugar cube and pondered life's inequities. A little mind expansion was sorely needed. Arthur's total insensitivity had stretched both her heart and soul to the breaking point. She was sorry for a moment that she hadn't played Indian for him—even a second time.

No one had yet spoken to Gillian—at least not directly. She walked, of her own power, into the living room. She was struck by the frightened look on the face of the young woman who retreated up the stairs. When she turned around, Arthur was in the process of removing his levis. Dexter had wandered into the kitchen to munch his salami sandwich in peace.

"Was there something you wanted to tell me?" she finally asked.

"Nope," he said.

"Was there some reason for the ride, for being kidnapped?"

"You can split any time you want," Arthur said. "No one's making you stay."

Gillian was not frightened. She realized, in a way,

that Arthur had undressed in order to make her feel more . . . comfortable. She tried not to look at him, but the lean, young body struck a chord, a chord of memory rather than desire, and she was happy at least for that. It had been a long time, she realized, since a boy had held any interest for her.

"Are the two of you married?" she finally asked.

"No," he said. "Dexter's just a buddy from the army."

"Not Dexter," she said. "I'm talking about the little creature who just took such an obvious powder."

"That depends on what you mean by married," Arthur said. "We share the pad. And she uses my name, if that's what you mean."

"I take it, then, it's a common-law marriage."

"Who knows?" he said. "Do you smoke?"

"I've got my own"—she patted the handbag containing a package of Luckies.

"Crazy," he said. "I could tell you'd swing. Excuse me then while I light up."

From the manner in which he inhaled the smoke, the exaggerated swallowing with eyes closed, and from the bittersweet smell of the exhaled smoke, Gillian realized the boy smoked marijuana. She was neither shocked nor caught off balance. Charlie, in college, had smoked marijuana, and the small furnished room in the town of Annandale was often filled with the same smell. She often thought that those had been the best times of all. Never mind that in a very real sense they were all blind; at least they all tried to find some light.

"You remind me of someone I once knew," she said. "You remind me of someone I knew in school."

"You don't," he said.

"Don't what?"

"Don't remind me of someone I once knew in school," he said. "Don't remind me of anyone ever. You're something else. That's why you're so wiggy."

"He was blind," Gillian went on. "He was a blind

piano-playing boy and he used to sit around like you are, without clothes, and he'd talk and talk. The things we were going to do, the things we believed in, the world problems we were going to solve."

"That's cool," he said.

Dexter returned to the living room, munching at a new salami sandwich. He evinced no surprise at the sight of Arthur completely stripped except for the motorcycle helmet. He asked where Raina was and then walked upstairs.

"You let your wife . . . ?" Gillian didn't complete the question.

"She's got her life," he said. "I got mine. Where shall we go?"

"Where?" Gillian said.

"Where?"

The question *where* had, in fact, been on Arthur's mind for the past five minutes. He and Raina had made love in every available square inch of the house, everywhere from the broom closet to the refrigerator (a little cramped even with the shelves removed, but delightfully cool in August) and now, with a new chick, it seemed only right to find a new spot.

Gillian almost said no. She came perilously close to exiting from the absurd little drama, but something made her stay. The thought of destroying a union as ephemeral as this one, this semi-marriage of Arthur and Raina, seemed more than redundant. There seemed no way to rationalize coupling with this youthful madman.

Maybe it was his very youth—that frail, pale little boy, his chest bare of hair, his little-boy face twisted in effort as he thought of a suitable spot to carry his lover. The incongruity of the moment. The contrast between Arthur and Rabbi Turnbull. Arthur's naturalness compared to Turnbull's pomposity. Who'd ever have thought the rabbi would turn out to be such an ass? The episode had left a bad taste in her mouth. Perhaps the boy would help purge it.

"Wherever," she said finally.

"I can't think," he said. "I can't think of a place."

"Well, really, dear," she said, "not here. I'm sure your wife is very understanding about this, but . . . not here. Shall we adjourn to the bedroom?"

The *bedroom*—Arthur was amazed. The bedroom, of course. Floors, fields, beaches, even once in a sewer —but the bedroom? The thought had never occurred to him before. The bedroom? That was even better than a snowbank. This Gillian Blake was unbelievable, unbelievable!

Walking up to the bedroom with Gillian, Arthur suffered through a curiously deflating moment or two. It was personal recognition of the clearly superior imagination of the woman beside him. This was a woman who had some things to teach him, and he only hoped she would find him an apt pupil.

Passing by Raina's Meditation Room, they noticed that the door was open, and they paused to study a curious tableau. Dexter, completely nude, was stretched out on the Prayer Table, his manhood rising toward the ceiling. Raina had scattered talcum powder over his entire body, and the effect was one of salt and pepper. She was at that moment gently massaging him at his point of greatest altitude with a bottle of pink Johnson & Johnson baby lotion. Gillian surmised that it was a religious ceremony, possibly something directly from the *Kama-Sutra*, and she said nothing irreverent. Arthur, on the other hand, realized they were playing the Baby Game and was vaguely disappointed in Raina's lack of innovation since the last time.

Hand in hand they approached the door of the second bedroom, and Arthur hardly dared ask again. He didn't have to this time. Gillian walked straight over to the bed, removed her pink-flowered muumuu and stretched luxuriously across the bed. Arthur loped across the room after her.

The *bed!* Of course, the bed. All thoughts he had

been entertaining quickly slipped from him. The ascetic sensations of the glass-topped cocktail table, the cooling joys of the refrigerator, the exoticism of the attic trunk—these images passed immediately from his mind. The bed—comfortable, soft, capacious—called out to him. Why hadn't he thought of it himself? How could it have been anywhere else but the bed?

He looked at Gillian, at the slender winding body covered with tiny blonde hairs, at the full lips parted slightly as they awaited his throbbing mouth, at the rhythm of her rising breasts. And suddenly he knew. He knew that hanging from the chandelier with her poised happily under him—this was not for Gillian. That leaning over the bed's backboard with toes curled toward Mecca—that would never satisfy her. That somersaulting into the mainsprings—that would never do.

There was only one thing left to do. He flopped onto the bed and climbed atop Gillian, arranging himself in the position that had been handed down from generation to generation since the beginning of time.

"Normal," he thought, "normal for the first time."

The word was no longer anathema to him. As he climbed aboard, a vision came to Arthur Franhop. It was a vision of life—a life of calm, steady sex, of marriage even, of charming little children whom he could teach all he knew about sex and drugs, or perpetuating the race in this natural and noble manner.

As they rocked back and forth—Gillian with dazzling expertise, Arthur with mounting ecstasy—back and forth, back and forth to the heights of burning, genuine joy, they failed to notice Raina as she came into the room, carrying a water balloon, standing then at the foot of the bed. Back and forth, back and forth, the sensations were all-encompassing, sweet and natural, and it was not until the moment of explosion that Gillian looked up and saw the audience. Raina's face was twisted in anger, contorted in indignation and her voice rasped when she finally managed to mouth her hatred.

"Arthur, you are *square!*" she screamed. "You are an incredible, incurable square!"

EXCERPT FROM "THE BILLY & GILLY SHOW," DECEMBER 7TH

Billy: It's hard to believe that Pearl Harbor was that long ago, Gilly.

Gilly: I was a child then, but I'll never forget it.

Billy: Neither will I.

Gilly: And what you wonder about is whether we learned anything from it. When I say "we," of course, I mean mankind in general.

Billy: You certainly do wonder. The world seems to be in as much of a mess as ever.

Gilly: Yes, and not just nations, but people. We just don't seem to care about one another.

Billy: The whole bit is going on, all right. War, killing, violence, man's inhumanity to man.

Gilly: Yes.

Billy: Take organized crime. It's become an accepted part of everyday life.

Gilly: That's so true. The crime seems to be in getting caught, rather than in doing wrong.

Billy: Take the Cosa Nostra. It's everywhere.

Gilly: I wonder about that, though. You know, whether it's all true. All that melodramatic stuff about families.

Billy: I believe it. Today's gangsters are organization men hiding behind business façades.

Gilly: Team men.

Billy: Definitely.

Gilly: It's too bad we don't know one we could have on the show. Wouldn't that be fun?

Billy: If you'll pardon the pun, it might be a blast.

Gilly: Oh, Billy.

Billy: No, you might get a real bang out of it.

Gilly: You're just too much today. Actually, Billy, a genuine gangster would probably be a very exciting person.

Billy: No doubt, but I think we should leave the gangsters to the crime committees. Let the government interview them.

Gilly: I suppose so. Anyway, we don't know any gangsters.

Billy: Don't be too sure. Like I said, they all have respectable fronts nowadays. For all we know, there might be one living in our own neighborhood.

Gilly: Mmmmm. Isn't that a marvelous thought?

Billy: I thought it would get you.

Gilly: Mmmmm.

MARIO VELLA

Mario Vella eased the black Bonneville down the feeder road, mashed down on the accelerator, and spurted onto the Long Island Expressway. He liked the quick surge of power under his foot. That's where power should always be, he mused, under your foot, ready to be squeezed on or off with the slightest pressure.

He lifted his foot and the car slowed down to the legal limit. He would keep it that way for the next fifty-eight minutes, to the King's Neck turnoff. From there it was just twenty minutes on 25-A to the Dunes Motel and Gilly. He hoped she'd be on time. She always had some kind of excuse. Since the first time two weeks ago, she'd been arriving progressively later each time. He'd have to clamp down.

It was only 3:30 p.m. and he was out in front of the rush-hour traffic. His eyes flicked from the speedometer to the speed-limit sign at the Queens Boulevard exit. He had been commuting to King's Neck for two years now and he knew the speed limits as well as he knew the names of his children. But he was a careful man. That was his value to the Organization; he not only knew the system, he lived it. And one of the cardinal rules was: Don't break the little laws. That was for kids, not for professionals.

Mario Vella had succeeded where some of the best men in the Organization had failed. He had blended into his environment. To most of his neighbors he was Mario Vella, thirty-six, the darkly handsome owner of the highly successful Bella Mia Olive Oil Company and the equally affluent Fort Sorrento Construction Corporation in nearby Port Jefferson. He was also known to dabble in the entertainment field, most recently in the career of a fast-rising ballad singer, Johnny Alonga.

The young singer had waxed only one solid hit, "A Dying Love," but it had remained either on or reasonably near the top ten for eighteen months. Careers had been made on less. And Vella had produced the boy as a free entertainer at several local charity affairs and political dinners; he had even appeared twice for Vella at the King's Neck Country Club. Vella now was being flooded with invitations to become a board member of every worthwhile organization in sight. He could never be sure whether his popularity was attributable to Alonga or to his own ready checkbook. The Organization had helped. Whenever Vella lent his name to a fund-raising concern, journal ads poured in from construction and garment firms throughout the state.

There had been, of course, rumors of gangster associations, but they were hardly ever more than rumors. The newspaper that made the mistake of referring to him as a "friend of the underworld"—and that was eight years ago in another town—paid $45,000 for its error.

Next spring he was slated to be honored as Man of the Year by the Society for the Prevention of Rickets in Children. And in January he would assume office as president of the League to Preserve Italian-American Dignity (LPIAD). He had helped to found that one, and the Organization credited him with a master stroke. Two city newspapers had attempted to build circulation with investigations of the Organization, but a few LPIAD picket lines had discouraged the publishers. Television, always gutless, canceled a scheduled documentary. And now politicians came to Vella seeking advice.

Mario Vella jabbed at the button with his manicured finger and opened the driver's window. It was a warm day for November and his eyes had been smarting from the cigarette smoke in the sealed car. He pushed the buttons on the car radio, pushed them until the car was filled with the syrupy sounds of Johnny Alonga singing "A Dying Love." He listened for a few seconds, then changed stations again. The song still made him want to puke. It reminded him of Donna Marie. They had been married for ten years. Ten years of rotting waste, studding Man O' War to a milk cow.

He'd had that same thought earlier in the day. He had awakened at six thinking about Gilly. He reached over to the night table, lit the cigarette, lay on his back, motionless, staring up at the absurd sky-blue canopy that Donna Marie had insisted on having custom made. He tried to keep his thoughts on Gilly, but Donna Marie was stirring at his side. He imagined Gilly kneeling in front of him, her honey blonde hair bobbing at her shoulders. He could visualize the severely tailored white blouse unbuttoned to the bottom button and half-draped over her firm upper arms. He could see her cupping her erect, compact breasts in her hands, gently massaging the pink nipples with her index fingers. Her breasts seemed a creamy contrast to the fading tan. Her brief pale green skirt was pulled upward against the strain of her body, exposing an eyeful of nylon-sheathed thigh.

He saw himself standing, his clothes thrown to the side. He saw her wriggling closer and playfully massaging the inner part of his legs with her breasts, up and down and up then down again. Gently. She never came all the way up, always stopping just a little short. The suspense surging within him always turned to agonized impatience. She would look up at him with that smile. "Are you still afraid of me, Mario? Do you still want me to go away?" He leaned over and pinched her ear lobes, delicately, lovingly, and then carefully guided her unresisting head up, up—

"Mario!"

Donna Marie's voice had slashed through his dream. He jacknifed into a sitting position and turned to face his wife.

"Your cigarette," she said. "You dropped your cigarette on the bed. Do you want us to burn to death in our own house? Look, you've burned a hole in the comforter. My father gave that to us. A hundred and fifty dollars it cost, all the way from Italy. It's ruined. What will we tell him?"

He shrugged his shoulders, a half-hearted gesture of apology. He poured a glass of water from the night table onto the smoldering satin comforter. Secretly he was pleased. He had always hated the comforter, an unreasonably faithful embroidery reproduction of sunset over the Bay of Naples. It was just like his father-in-law Septimo. Vintage wop.

He reached over and pulled Donna Marie to him, the hunger for Gilly still racing in his blood, hoping that this time it might be different. As always, Donna Marie was submissive. She had been raised to submit to her husband, whoever he might be, unquestioningly, sick or well, night or day. Men are that way, her mother had explained. It was a wife's duty to give, not to expect, at least in the bedroom. Her long black hair, lustrous from a lifetime routine of one hundred brush strokes a night, streamed across the pillow behind her head.

Mario snaked his hand under the hem of her short flannel nightie and flattened it palm down on the broad expanse of her belly. There was not the slightest quiver of movement in return. He moved his hand upward, over a soft bulge of fat, to her great flaccid breasts. God, he wondered, do all Italian girls get this swollen after three children? He pulled his hand away and Donna Marie automatically rolled over on her back, hiked her nightie up and spread her legs. She waited patiently. He did it, hating both her and himself.

As he rolled away, she sat up and asked: "Are you going to be home for dinner tonight? I'm making lasagna and broccoli with garlic. You know you like that, Mario. But you have to tell me now—the broccoli is no good heated over."

Just like Donna. All the while he was doing it, she was planning out her goddam lasagna and broccoli with garlic.

"Maybe you could bring Louie and Danny home with you," she went on. "It's been a long time since you brought anyone home with you and you know how they like lasagna. And the kids love to see them. You know that."

Fat chance, he had thought, as he glanced at his wafer-thin platinum watch. It was 7:00 a.m. That meant it was 6:00 a.m. in Chicago and if Louie and Danny were doing their job they were in Chicago right then. If they were on schedule, in a half hour Louie would be slowly strangling the life from some fink stoolie with a piece of piano wire and Danny would be flicking him with a knife for kicks. It was a funny thing about Danny and that knife.

"Are Danny and Louie still in the undertaking business?" Donna Marie asked.

"Yes," he said. "But they can't come tonight. A very very rich man died in Chicago and they had to fly there to make arrangements for the body. I won't be home myself, not until late. I have to take Johnny over to the studio to make a record." Then, an after-thought. "I may even stay over in town if it gets too late."

Donna shrugged, moved to her bottle-littered vanity table and began to pin her hair into a bun. She looked over her shoulder, her face impassive.

"By the way, Gillian Blake called last night. She said she wanted to speak to you, that it was very personal. What in the world could she want to talk to you personal about?"

Mario didn't like that. Gilly should have the brains not to call him at home. She had never done it before. Why now?

"She probably wants to get Johnny on that show of hers," he said. "They all do."

"And something else," Donna Marie said. "My father called you last night. Twice. The second time he sounded mad. You haven't been doing anything to upset him?"

"No." Mario answered carefully. "He's impatient because the new oil shipments haven't come through. I'll call him today if I get the time."

Now, heading east on the Expressway, Mario Vella wondered about Septimo. He had called all over for him that morning and hadn't been able to reach him. But that wasn't what worried him. It was something he sensed, a difference in the voices. Mario had used all the proper codes, but everyone had answered in a strangely short way. He'd called all the New York operations—Galaxy Liquors, Deuce Lathing, Tornedo Linen Supply, Septimo Construction over in White-stone, even the four restaurants. At every outlet, the same answer. No one knew where he was. Even Seraphina, his mother-in-law, she didn't know. And all of them seemed distant on the phone. Yes and no, that was all.

Septimo Caggiano was very important in Mario Vella's life. It might have been different if Mario's own father had lived. His father, Onofrio Vellaturce, wanted for two murders in Naples, had jumped ship in Hoboken and settled down to life in America. The Organization welcomed him like a long-lost brother, and inside of twenty years he'd headed the largest Organization family in the New York area. From a castlelike home on the Palisades, Onofrio ruled everything in sight—docks, produce, trucking, terminals, narcotics, gambling, labor unions and politicians. And in Brooklyn, Sicilian-born Septimo Caggiano began to worry that Onofrio might begin to lust after his organization. They set up a union, a union sealed by the marriage of Donna Marie and Mario.

Mario, the son of an Organization leader, understood what was expected of him. Two kingdoms were to be joined. Donna Marie—doe-eyed, dark-haired, plump— had a peasant's taste in clothing, running to sequins and ornate embroidery. She would cook, bear children and keep a house as well as its secrets. Onofrio had told him to overlook the girl's bad points. There were always girl friends, he had said with a wink; and, as long as they were kept at a distance, they would bring no shame to the family name. One must never overlook, his father had said, the peculiar Sicilian ideas about honor.

The two young people had had a total of three dates, all of them well chaperoned. They were married at Salve Regina Church in Brooklyn. The reception in the grand ballroom at the Hotel Commodore was a convention of politicians, monsignors and Organization luminaries from both coasts and most of the states in between. And that night Mario dimmed the light in the bridal suite and learned that he had married a sexual zombie.

One week after this depressing discovery, while honeymooning in the Laurentian Mountains north of Montreal, Mario received a phone call telling of his father's sudden death. His father had apparently dozed off behind tre wheel of his Fleetwood in Jersey City. And for some reason he had selected that night to give Louie, his bodyguard-chauffeur, some time off. The car had plunged through the guard rail just south of the Park Street viaduct and spilled down the cliff onto Hoboken, exploding in a ball of flames.

A meeting of the board was held. Septimo took over the joint Organization with his father's old friend, Gino Viccardi, as underboss. It was agreed that Mario should start at the bottom. He would have to be blooded. If all went well, Gino would retire in eight years and Mario would take his place as underboss. And some day, when old Septimo decided to step aside, Mario would be expected to fill his shoes. He had done as he was told. He had been blooded in Cicero, Illinois, and he would never forget that first kill. He had met the rebellious union reformer behind the Giaconda and blown off the back of his skull with two .45-caliber slugs.

Though Mario had always used a gun, he got no pleasure out of killing. It was a job that had to be done. And a gun was the quickest way to do the job. Men like Louie and Danny liked to make death last. They used piano wire and knives. Louie was an expert at loosening the wire just before his victim passed out, then tightening it again, then repeating the cycle. Danny could probe his knife in just short of a vital spot and then twist it out for still another jab. They liked what they did; maybe that's why they were still doing it. But ten years had passed and Mario no longer had to do the dirty work. He had no criminal record, and now he was the underboss of the combined Organization.

Gillian Blake. He savored the name as he repeated it. Class, just like Gilly herself. She was a thoroughbred. Class. The way she floated into a room. The way she dressed. The way she talked. The way she ate.

Why hadn't he plowed her when they first met for lunch? He could have, he was sure. There had been women in Cicero, in Jacksonville, in a dozen other towns where he had paused to kill on contract. He knew he appealed to women. His black hair was frosted at the temples but he kept himself in shape. His taste in clothing was expensive but not flashy— Sulka shirts, Brooks Brothers suits, rep ties. They had met at the studio to discuss the possibility of having Johnny on the Billy & Gilly Show. Her husband, Bill was his name, had left them—had said there was a squash match at the Racquet Club. It wasn't until that moment that he had figured Gilly for a score.

"Why don't we have lunch, Mr. Vella?" she had said. She had been wearing a sack dress, and only two parts of her touched the material. Sure, he had answered.

She had suggested Michael's Pub. She had ordered a martini, specifying the gin, telling the waiter "just a breath of vermouth." Class. He stuck with a tall Scotch and water and she stuck with martinis, three of them. She knew exactly what she wanted and she made certain that she got it. After lunch he suggested that he drive her home. She had said that would certainly be preferable to the Long Island Rail Road.

It had been Gilly who suggested the tour on the way home—she had asked him to drive north to Oldfield so she could see the winter sun set on the Sound. "If we watched from our own cliffs," she had said, "people would think we were lovers." They parked at the road's end. She sat staring down at the water and his body ached to possess her, to tear off her clothes and crush her to him, to explore the smoothness of her body with his hands and mouth, to hear her. . . .

But it was she who made the first move. Her arms were about his neck and her face was against his. "Poor Mario," she had said, "you want me so much." Her lips brushed his and her warm tongue darted into his mouth.

He stared at her, fighting it. And then he had said, "It's late. We better get home."

She had laughed at that. "I like you, Mario. There's something about you, something menacing, and that's intriguing. And you're afraid of me and I think I like that too. But chase away your ghosts, Mario, I may not like you forever."

Why hadn't he accepted her invitation then? God knows he wanted her. And she was right about that other thing, about being afraid. But not of her. Afraid of old Septimo and his Sicilian family honor. How could he tell her about a $500,000 Organization investment predicated upon his keeping his nose clean?

Twice that week he had called her. Twice they had met for drinks at the Dunes Motel. Each time it was the same. She fascinated him, stirred him. Each time he had driven her home untouched, unable to quell the instinct that had kept him alive when better men had died. Then she had worn that sack dress to a lunch at Peacock Alley. And it was then, over coffee, with her small, firm chin resting above her folded hands, that she said—

"I'm not going to see you any more, Mario. You're beginning to bore me."

His first reaction was boiling anger. He had thrown the money on the table. He had said "So long, bitch," and walked out. He had walked and walked and he could not erase that final smile on her face. It was a Mona Lisa smile and Mario suddenly understood why the Mona Lisa smiled. It was because she was unattainable. It was because men were crazy to hold her breasts and suck the sweetness from her mouth, and it was an impossibility. It was impossible because then she would be just another woman with a silly smile.

But Gilly could be attained. He called the studio that afternoon. He called the studio four times before noon the next day. Each time a fag bastard had answered that Mrs. Blake was too busy to come to the phone. He waited for her later at the studio entrance, but she was with her husband and he had ducked into an alleyway.

That same afternoon he had ignored a legitimate tip and the feds had raided one of the Organization's best cutting plants in the Bronx, nailing three men and six kilos of pure heroin. He had broken two appointments with Septimo the following day. And then, when he had given up, she was on the phone. Had he been calling her? she asked. Would she meet him for a drink on Tuesday night at the Dunes? he asked. A drink? she had asked. No, he had said, for more than a drink. She promised to be there and then the line went dead. Later he thought about it—had he said anything on the phone that could harm him?

Mario nosed the Bonneville down the steep cliff road leading to the Dunes. Even Septimo didn't know about this one. Charlie Friars, a Smithtown politician who got rich approving zoning changes for builders doing business with his insurance agency, had gotten a severe case of the shorts while building the Dunes, a modern motel-cocktail lounge complex. At Charlie's request, Mario had paid the unpaid bills and now had a hidden half ownership. It wasn't likely he would run into any of Septimo's bird dogs, not here. Organization men didn't get the red carpet treatment at the Dunes, and they naturally favored the mob-owned places.

Gillian was already at the bar. Mario sucked in his breath and stood for a moment at the door, licking her with his eyes. She was talking to the bartender. Her slim legs were crossed at the knees and a lit cigarette was in her hand. The martini in front of her was untouched and moisture still frosted the outside of the glass. Good, she had just arrived. He was momentarily irked that he had not spotted her car outside. It was second nature to check a building before entering, even your own home, and he had forgotten.

"Hello, miss," he said. "Are you lonely?"

"I thought you might keep me waiting forever," she said.

He cupped her hand in his and she squeezed. Later

they sat opposite each other at a small candlelit table, staring into each other's eyes, holding long wordless conversations. They didn't touch the filets. Mario felt the electricity when their fingers touched.

"How much longer are you going to make me wait, Mario?"

He took her hand and they moved out the door and down the carpeted corridor. The room door was ajar. Giant orange crysanthemums glowed like a sunset from a vase on the coffee table. Next to the bed two bottles of Pinay '61 were chilling in a glistening wine cooler heaped with crushed ice. Charlie had thought of everything.

He turned then to face Gilly. She kicked her shoes off and stood in front of him, her arms outstretched. He reached for her and folded her into his arms. Their lips met, hard and fierce at first, gradually relaxing into a soft, sucking pucker. Her head came barely to his shoulders. Without breaking the kiss, he reached down and pulled her up, his arms circling her legs just below the round of her hips. They stayed this way for moments, and then, scooping her into his arms, he gently carried her to the bed.

They lay side by side, still clothed. His hands played up over her breasts and she shuddered. Then he felt a shock as her knee, gently but insistently, pressed up into his groin. Her hands stayed behind his neck, her fingernails softly tracing up and down the nape. He turned her yielding head and, taking the lobe of her ear in his mouth, he sucked it between his lips, licked it with his tongue. Then he moved his head higher, pressing his tongue into her ear. She gripped him tightly, her knee working against his crotch, her body moving now in an undulating rhythm.

"Wait with me a second," he murmured, kissing her softly on the lips again.

He rose from the bed and crossed the room. He undressed quickly and turned to face her. She came to him and, as he reached out, she pirouetted on her toes and came into his arms backwards. His hands clasped her breasts. She looked up at him over her shoulder.

"Unzip me," she said. "Please."

He slowly pulled the zipper down to its nesting place in the round of her back and, with a quick movement, she stepped out of the dress. She stooped, snatched up the dress, dropped it on a chair. Then, her hands clasped childlike behind her back, she turned to face him.

She was wearing no bra and her firm small breasts stood erect, her little pink nipples already hard from desire, pink-white peaks rising from the residue of her tan. So much like the dream, so close to the dream. She had the supple body of a long-distance swimmer, so slim, so frail compared to what Mario had known.

"Come, Mario," she said, "come with me."

She took his hand and almost shyly led him to the bed. She snuggled to him as he moved his lips and tongue along the hollow of her shoulder and neck. He circled her nipples with his tongue, never touching until impatiently she thrust them into his mouth. Their fever mounted and their bodies moved together as he unsheathed her from her panties.

"Now," she gasped, "now."

It was a plea and a command, and he obeyed. It was almost over before it started. Her willingness, her desire, had caused him to explode almost as soon as they joined. He leaned heavily on his hands, praying for strength. Her hips kept moving and she stared up at him, her eyes clouding. Was it disappointment? And then, almost as it disappeared, he felt his manhood growing again inside her and he smiled down at her.

"What's the matter, Gilly?" he said. "Didn't you know about Italian lovers?"

"Shhh," she said.

A few moments later he felt her climax, and again,

and a third time before he exploded again and collapsed into her arms, kissing her hands, her breasts, her neck, her ears, her mouth. He felt her going to sleep and he let her go and the last thing she said was—

"You're not afraid of me any more, are you, Mario?"

He woke to a cold feeling on his feet. Gilly, her hair bobbing freely, was splashing champagne against his feet. Her breasts were suspended seductively as she bent toward his toes.

"That's good champagne," he said. "It's made for drinking."

"Is it?"

Her pink tongue darted over his feet. One by one she caught his toes in her mouth and gently sucked on them.

"Champagne lollypops," she said.

She splashed the champagne on his legs and followed it with her tongue. As she moved up, her breasts rubbed against his feet and then his legs, and finally his thighs. He groaned, let her continue and, when he could stand it no more, reached for her. This time it was slow, measured and sure and they climaxed together, ending with their arms entwined and their lips pressed together. And again sleep came. Mario slept for fifteen minutes. When he awoke, Gilly was dressed and standing by the bed.

"Goodbye, Mario," she said.

"What are you talking?" he said.

"Just goodbye, that's all," she said. "And you might think of me every time you screw that cow."

Before he could get to his feet, she was gone. On her face, that smile again. Bitch! Mario rubbed the sleep from his eyes, stepped into his trousers, cursed her again. Why? He had been better than any three men, better than that whore had ever seen. He walked out to his car. Tomorrow he would have her again. Tomorrow, he knew, he *had* to have her again. Tomor-

row the phone would ring and she would come crawling, begging for the chance to lick the champagne
from his toes. They were all alike finally. Cows or
whores, whores or cows. And whatever he thought at
that moment, he knew Gilly was no cow.

Sliding the key into the starter, he glanced up at the
rear-view mirror. He found himself staring directly
into Louie's eyes. He swung around swiftly and looked
into the back seat. Louie and Danny were both there.
Both were wearing overcoats with the collars turned
up around the neck. Danny's hand was wrapped
around the Beretta, its silencer gleaming wickedly in
the courtesy light.

"What the hell you guys doing here?" Mario said.
"You're supposed to be in Chicago."

"Septimo canceled the trip," Louie said. "He's waiting for us at the top of the cliff."

Mario tumbled the odds. Septimo hadn't come out
here to scold him. Mario's two best contract men would
never hold a gun on him, not unless the old man had
given direct orders. And having done this, they could
not hope to live unless Mario himself were dead.
Mario couldn't believe it. But there it was. Septimo
wanted to kill him, his own son-in-law. As he reached
for the emergency brake, he remembered the built-in
panel. Three upward taps on the brake and the panel
would slide and a loaded .38 would drop into his hand.

"It ain't there," Louie said. "Remember, I'm the
one had it put in for you."

The road widened on the cliff side into a small parking area at the top. A frail wooden fence bordered the
two-hundred-foot drop. It was quite a spot, Charlie
had told him, great for cheap lovers. He nosed the car
against the fence and stopped. Septimo stood beside a
rented car.

"I've been waiting for you, Mario," he said. "You're
scum, like your father. Only you done worse. You dishonor my daughter. You dishonor the name Caggiano."

Septimo pressed his lips to his hand and then

pressed the hand to Mario's face. *"Bacce del morte,"* he said and turned away. Louie stood outside the car, covering him with the gun. Danny reached over, turned on the radio full blast and got out. Danny returned and dumped three bulging plastic bags in the front seat. Mario could smell the gasoline.

The two killers pushed the car slowly toward the fence, and Mario was frozen with fear. Septimo applied his butane cigarette lighter to a sheet of newspaper and, as the car rolled by, he tossed the flaming paper through the window. The explosion came as the car went over the edge and tumbled twice. Then it struck the rocks below.

EXCERPT FROM "THE BILLY & GILLY SHOW," DECEMBER 16TH

Gilly: Well, it's time to deck the halls and do the Christmas shopping, dear.

Billy: Deck the halls with boughs of holly, fa-la-la-la-la, la-la, la-la.

Gilly: You've got a lovely voice, dear, but let's keep this a conversation show.

Billy: Okay, so I'm no Johnny Alonga, but I think I carry a tune rather well.

Gilly: Speaking of Johnny Alonga, I'm just heartsick over what happened to his manager, that nice Mario Vella.

Billy: I know. And the police said it wasn't a suicide or an accident. So it had to be. . . .

Gilly: Never mind, I think that's just too morbid for words. Anyway, let's get back to Christmas shopping.

Billy: That's something else I'd rather not contemplate.

Gilly: I know. We seem to be doing our best to keep the commerciality in Christmas.

Billy: Yes, all you need for a merry Christmas is money.

Gilly: Ummm. Money. Why is it that you never have it when you need it most?

Billy: Probably because you always need it. I mean, if it's not Christmas presents, it's the old faithfuls—the telephone bill, the mortgage, the fuel bill, and all the rest.

Gilly: That's part of the joy of being a home owner. It's the emergencies that hurt.

Billy: You sound worried, dear. Don't tell me you've

gone and run up a gambling debt, or spent the milk money on demon rum?

Gilly: Oh, you're so silly. No, I'm just speaking figuratively. It's simply that money can be a problem.

Billy: Yes, but you know what they say. It can't buy happiness.

Gilly: Perhaps not, but there are times when it can quell anxiety.

MARVIN GOODMAN

It was the week before Christmas, traditionally a time of heightened emotion, and two residents of King's Neck shared the feeling that the world, or at least their private worlds, would soon end. Neither of the two anticipated a particularly pleasant finale. Marvin Goodman was once again on the verge of bankruptcy. And Gillian Blake was pregnant.

Marvin Goodman groped anxiously toward the Danish modern mailbox that hung from the rough-hewn shingles of his Custom Split, and extracted a dozen envelopes of various sizes, shapes and colors. The sight of the cellophane windows was sufficient to justify his next-to-worst fears, to induce his recurrent daylight nightmare.

He walked noiselessly through the foyer into the living room, barely conscious of the thick velvet pile ($22.50 a yard) that cushioned his steps. He totally ignored the climate control system that nurtured his well-being, the Tanganyikan carvings, the pre-Columbian figures, the abstract expressionist oils, the limited-edition art books that fed or stimulated his aesthetic needs.

Marvin tore open the wide manila envelope first and watched as the garish illustration of a one-time comic book hero and erstwhile companion of his youth fluttered to the floor. "Bat-shit," Marvin said, resisting the temptation to grind his heel into his fallen idol's groin. The sadistic smile that had accompanied the impulse faded as speedily as the gray winter sun over the Lombardy poplars marking the Goodmans' rear property line.

"Bat . . . shit," he reiterated slowly, while a dozen mauve, perfumed sheets fell from a squarish envelope tastefully imprinted *Saks Fifth Avenue*. A remaining sheet, imprisoned between Marvin's thumb and forefinger, indicated that $249.89 worth of unpaid merchandise had been transferred from the Saks showroom to the Goodman residence during the past thirty-day period. Added to previous shipments, still unpaid, the total due now exceeded the Goodmans' joint checking account balance by an amount approximating seven hundred dollars. Marvin did not have the strength to figure it to the penny.

Combining X-ray vision with computerlike speed, Marvin's troubled mind assessed the contents of the other envelopes. Each envelope's return address triggered a response that fed a familiar figure to the accurate accounting department in Marvin's brain. Long Island Lighting Company ($44) . . . Suburban Meats ($52) . . . Green Pasture Farms ($35) . . . New York Telephone Company ($32) . . . Dr. Hetterton ($145 outstanding) . . . and so on.

"Helene!" Marvin screamed. "Helene!"

"What do you want, honey?"

"Get your ass down here."

Through more than a decade of marriage to Marvin, Helene Goodman's cells had developed responses of their own. On the rare occasions when she sensed unqualified hatred, she sought refuge. Anger, Marvin's most familiar attitude, was met with yielding softness, unswerving agreement and the promise to improve, to really try like hell next month. Manifestations of softness on Marvin's part, on the other hand, were invariably tested for small advantages. It was the sort of thing Helene had excelled at since high school—and even then there was evidence of great and practical flexibility. She would not stir, for example, should a popular boy's hand move toward her indifferent breasts if a prom was in the offing; however, should the same young man seek to continue his explorations on the way home from the prom, he would win only rebuke.

Now in her early thirties, Helene had not appreciably changed. Her breasts, though fuller, were still indifferent. Her use of them, though refined through time, was still primarily geared toward inducing Marvin to do her bidding. Figuratively as well as literally they served as pacifiers. At this moment Helene instinctively opened the third button of her blouse to expose her cleavage more fully. She put on her fun-loving face, and as she worked her way down the abbreviated staircase she added the final touch, the hip swing.

"What's the matter, honey?" she said, at the same time catching sight of the Saks' bill crumpled on the thick carpeting. "Did Saks make another little mistake?"

Marvin flicked his head slightly, a boxer evading a left jab. He had, within his solid accountant's mind, constructed a flawless case. His profligate wife had obviously, perhaps even deliberately, overspent their available funds on personal luxuries. She had done this despite a November promise to try like hell to do better. She was wrong and she would be punished. He was the aggrieved party and would determine her fate.

But the possibility of a bookkeeping error had not been considered. Big department stores are not supposed to make mistakes and yet, as an accountant, Marvin knew how often they could and did. The possibility, however remote, destroyed the perfection of his attack. It would have to be erased before he could feel completely victimized and thus self-righteous once again.

"What the hell do you mean *another* mistake?"

"Oh, honey"—teasingly now—"you remember that time you were so angry that you got all mixed up. You called me a 'gold damndigger.' And how cute you looked when you had to apologize. They'd sent us your mother's bill by mistake. You remember that, don't you?"

It had happened, of course. Six years ago, as he recalled. He also recalled that Helene's explanations had seemed so absurd at the time that he had stopped just short of hitting her. And then Saks had admitted the error. And his widowed mother, whom he constantly held up as a model of economy, had actually run up the staggering bill. It was a multiple embarrassment and, in order to let his wife recover her self-respect, he had stood idly by while she embarked on her greatest buying spree. Wincing at the memory, he revised his strategy—after all, was not discretion the better part of malice?

"Are you telling me they screwed up again?"

Helene brushed her freshly dyed black hair away from her forehead with a calculatedly casual motion and bent over in front of Marvin to retrieve the Saks bill. She simultaneously inhaled, allowing Marvin a long look down the front of her blouse. She briefly studied one sales slip after another, and at the fifth she stopped.

"Here it is," she said. "I just knew there had to be a screwup."

Marvin studied the sales slip. It appeared entirely normal. It was for a dress that had been ordered by telephone. It had been ordered on the 27th day of November. It came to a figure of $125.

"And where's the screwup?" he asked.

"No dress, honey," Helene said. "No dressee, no tickee. Anyhow, there shouldn't be any tickee. I never ordered that dress and they never sent it."

"You sure?" Marvin remained skeptical. "I mean, that's kind of a weird mistake. They've got your name and address down there."

"What does that mean?" Helene moved closer to Marvin, close enough so that the biceps of his left arm rested against her right breast. Then she applied the pressure. "Some dumb broad writes the wrong address and the bill goes out. You think Mr. Saks checks these things personally?"

"But that's not the point," Marvin said. "It's not just a mistake. It's money. You think they're just going to take my word for it?"

"Well, what can we do—take them back the dress I didn't get? Come on, Marvin. You were ready to tell me off—how about taking some of that anger down to Saks and show them what a big man you are? Your mother would have been down there ten minutes ago."

In the garage Marvin stepped through a transparent plastic kite and climbed into his white Cadillac convertible. Batshit, he thought. As he gunned the car down the graveled street, Helene was upstairs looking at the $125 dress with the Saks label. She had once heard it said that, if he knows his client is guilty, a good lawyer tries to postpone the trial as long as possible. Witnesses can die; victims can change their minds; clients can take ill suddenly. Yes, given time, all kinds of things can happen. She shrugged, closed the closet door, went back to the copy of *Vogue* she had been reading before the interruption.

The Saks shipping department manager managed to produce a receipt bearing Helene's unmistakable signature within a half minute of hearing the complaint. Marvin's shock at the enormity of his wife's falsehood was exceeded only by his humiliation which, in turn, was exceeded only by his gratitude that the encounter had taken place in the manager's small and sparsely populated office. Publicly, at least, his image was still intact. But even that was only a matter of time. Twelve days, a month, maybe six months—the time would surely come when the men would arrive to reclaim the Cadillac, the furniture, the appliances, the home . . . the reputation.

He thought briefly, standing outside the shipping manager's office, of the offer he had received last year to handle Mario Vella's books—a most generous offer he had seriously considered until thumbing through the books one night. Now Vella was dead, murdered they said, and it was just as well he hadn't got involved. Another offer from the government tax man who tried to interest him in a bogus refund scheme. The endless opportunities to collect exorbitant fees from clients anxious to falsify their returns.

His integrity was perhaps exceeded by his fear, but there was a third factor that held Marvin back. And that was the instinctive understanding that it would be Helene—not little Barry or little Jacquie (or little Marvin, for that matter)—who would gain from any additional income. The coin was a bad one—heads, Helene wins; tails, Marvin loses. Nobody had ever called Marvin a born loser. But then, nobody ever had to.

"Marv," the voice said. "Marv Goodman."

He turned to look into the most exquisite green eyes he had ever seen.

"Come on now," the voice continued, "I know you're Marv Goodman."

He stared at the eyes, at the wide, slightly thin lips, at the small white teeth and the swift tongue that curled over them.

"Gillian," the voice said. "Gillian Blake."

Marvin was entranced at the way the tongue seemed to slip in and out with each syllable. It was moist and agile.

"I'm hurt," she was saying. "I really am. It was just last week at the King's Neck Property Owners Association meeting. Remember? I sat right next to you. You kept telling me if they increased the dues any more they'd have to form a credit association."

"Of course," Marvin said, recovering. "How've you been, Mrs. Blake? And how's . . . um . . . your husband?"

"His name is Bill and he's the same as ever," she said. "But I had to ask you why you're standing here looking so serious. I saw you in there a few minutes ago and I was certainly impressed. I had no idea you were so . . . forceful. You were certainly giving them all kinds of trouble."

"Oh, that." A forced laugh. "You can't watch these bookkeepers closely enough."

He hadn't thought of himself as forceful in at least ten years, and it pleased him enormously that someone did. But why not? He was a young thirty-six. Tennis and skiing kept him in good shape. Tennis and skiing, he thought, also make an excellent substitute for sex, if one needed substitutes. He only weighed five pounds more than when he had won the Intrafraternity Tennis Championship at Cornell fifteen years earlier. He had always thought of himself as being ruggedly handsome, and his marriage had, if anything, increased the hardness of his looks without appearing to age him. And now, in the presence of Gillian, he felt strong and young. More than that, he sensed the woman's interest in him.

Gillian's interest had, in fact, been aroused—but for not quite the same reasons. What Marvin would describe as rugged good looks, Gillian would dismiss as malevolence, even sadism. Gillian had first noticed Marvin Goodman the very day they had moved to King's Neck. He was in the Security National bank as she and Bill were establishing their accounts. He could not be missed. He was arguing heatedly with a junior executive about what seemed to be an overdrawn checking account. Then, too, he could not be missed the night of the party. On that occasion he was involved in a dispute with his wife over the fact that not one of the other wives polled required $75 a week for food shopping. (His wife, Gillian recalled, handled the incident with perfect calm, a woman who well knew the use of sex as a weapon.) The next encounter was at the Property Owners meeting. And this was the fourth time fate had joined them together. In each instance, Marvin Goodman had been wrapped up in a subject of increasing importance to Gillian.

Money. Fifteen hundred dollars was the price quoted. She knew it was high and she knew she had to raise it—and quickly. The demands of her job precluded a visit to Japan or Puerto Rico; her status as a celebrity made any unknown doctor too much of a risk. The one doctor she could trust, a highly recommended Lexington Avenue neurosurgeon with a profitable sideline aborting the unwanted offspring of the rich and the famous, charged a flat fee of $1,500.

Gillian looked at the plate glass window behind Marvin and saw that it was freckled by raindrops.

"Damn!" she said. "That spoils everything."

"What's that?" Marvin said.

"That rain," she said. "Here I thought I'd have a chance to walk a few blocks with you and maybe even talk you into buying me a little drink. Damn rain!"

"It doesn't have to spoil anything," Marvin said.

From somewhere in the past, from distant days of young manhood, Marvin felt stirrings that had been quietly laid to rest shortly after wedlock. It was not simply that this woman was desirable. Nor merely that she seemed available. What truly excited Marvin was the undeniable fact that he excited *her*, that *she* wanted *him*. Guilt? Perish the thought. There could be no sense of guilt if one considered Helene's flagrant falsehood. Yes, Helene needed to be punished. And it was up to him.

"It's 12:45 now," Marvin said. "Why don't we hop into my wagon—it's just downstairs—and take us a little drive? We'll find a spot for lunch. I mean I'm free for the rest of the day and right now I think I could use a little change."

"I know what you mean."

She put her hand around his arm and squeezed it. Marvin glanced quickly around the store. Saks' Long Island store was located in Garden City, an upper-middle-class residential and shopping community a forty-five-minute drive from King's Neck, and Marvin knew the odds were well against encountering any other neighbors. And so what? So what if he did? He walked calmly with Gillian to the parking lot, into the distinctive white convertible with the MG-1 license plates. Marvin headed directly for the Meadowbrook Parkway, and he felt the slight pressure of Gillian's left thigh against him. At that moment Marvin Goodman knew his luck was about to improve.

As the big car turned onto Northern State Parkway, Marvin glanced at the gas gauge. E—that's where the needle was flickering. He bit his lip and eased off the gas pedal slightly, allowing the speedometer needle to settle back toward fifty-five. By the time Marvin found a gas station, the meter registered below empty and he ordered the attendant to fill the tank. It required just short of twenty gallons.

"You nearly didn't make it," the man said.

"You're so right," Marvin said. "But I have a feeling this is going to be my day."

The station was one of the few in the northeastern United States for which Marvin Goodman did not have a credit card. Still, even after paying for the gas, he noted that there were almost fifty dollars remaining in his wallet. Fifty in his wallet and not much more in the world. Gillian sat beside him quietly as Marvin drove past the boat basin, now devoid of its white sails, and on toward the Throg's Neck Bridge.

"How do you feel, Gillian?"

"A little nervous, Marvin," she said—and honestly. "I wouldn't want you to think I do this kind of thing with anyone."

"I don't," he said—and, indeed, he had no reason to. It was doubtless that . . . rugged quality. "But what do you feel like doing? What are your needs?"

"I feel," she said, "thirsty, hungry and . . . sexy. And not necessarily in that order."

"We can handle that list item by item," he growled. "And not necessarily in any order."

At the Throg's Neck Bridge, Marvin dug into his pockets but couldn't locate the quarter.

"Sorry," Gillian said. "I can't help. All I've got is my Saks charge plate and my good name. Let me say, if you're ever offered a choice, take the charge plate."

He broke a ten to pay the toll and headed north. In Westchester he paid another toll on the Hutchinson River Parkway, then took the next turnoff and parked outside of Country Inn. The restaurant was decorated in a manner supposedly similar to what you might find in the French provinces, a fact that escaped most of its expense-account clientele. Marvin steered Gillian to the heavy oak bar.

"First," he said, "let's take care of the thirst."

"Martini," said Gillian.

"Two of them," he told the bartender. "Bone-dry."

"On the rocks or up?" the bartender said.

Marvin looked at Gillian, who signaled up with her thumb. Marvin did the same, and Gillian closed her hand gently over Marvin's upturned thumb.

"Got you, lover," she said in a low voice. Marvin, by way of answer, began moving his thumb slowly up and down inside her closed fist. "Mmmmmm. I'll bet they call you Marvelous Marv."

"No," he said. "No, they never have."

"Maybe they don't see what I see," Gillian said.

"Maybe they don't," he said. "Maybe that's what's bothering me. Things like this don't happen to me. They *never* happen to me. Why me? Why should this be happening to me all of a sudden?"

"Drink up, Marvelous Marv," she said. "Maybe you have something that I want. Maybe this kind of thing as never happened to me either."

They stayed long enough for a second martini. Marvin, euphoric from a combination of the alcohol and the prospect that lay ahead, left the grinning bartender a dollar tip. They climbed back into the Cadillac and continued north on the Hutchinson River Parkway. The next time Marvin glanced at his gold-banded watch it was nearly three o'clock and he realized they had not yet eaten lunch. They were almost in Connecticut when he pulled off the Parkway a second time. This time he followed a network of local roads into Bedford Village and eventually to La Cremaillere, a restaurant that *Holiday* Magazine had described as "distinguished," a restaurant that Helene had begged to visit. Well, the hell with Helene.

Lunch, if a trifle rich, was distinguished. And with a half bottle of vintage Chablis lulling his senses, Marvin for once forgot to tally up the bill, which he drowsily noted approached $25. And $5 for the young lady who offered such impeccable service. And another loose bill for the excellent young man who went to fetch the car.

"How do you feel now?" he asked Gillian.

"I'm not thirsty," she said. "And I'm not hungry. Let me see, was there something else?"

"It'll come to you." Marvin ran his free hand down her side and let it come to rest on her hip. "What you need is a conducive atmosphere. I think we passed one a few miles back."

"The one with the *Vacancy* sign?"

"That was the one."

It was all going incredibly well, Marvin thought. Too well, really. The idea that it was going perfectly sent him into a momentary panic. Something had to go wrong. Something would go wrong. Stop that! Stop thinking like a loser. That's all over now. Everything's perfect and everything will be perfect.

The panic soon dissolved as Gillian rested her head against Marvin's shoulder and traced the creases in his slacks. She started at the knees and worked her way up. Her touch excited Marvin immediately and Gillian traced the swelling outline, gently, gently, until Marvin felt the blood pounding against his temples.

"Marvelous Marv," she said, "so full of surprises."

When they reached the motel, Marvin noted with gratitude that there was a drive-in window for registering guests. He couldn't have left the car at that moment in any circumstances. His slacks still bulged from Gillian's gentle, skillful and persistent manipulations. The motel owner, a soft-spoken country man with leather elbow patches on his tweed jacket, accepted without comment the registration blank that carried the name "Milton Silver" and the "MG-1" license plate.

"That'll be $20 for the double," he said.

Marvin reached into his wallet, extracted the single remaining bill, handed it over.

"And ten more, young fellow," the owner said.

Marvin looked at the bill and went white. It was a ten. He had tipped the young man at the parking lot ten dollars instead of one! God, God, God—it had to happen!

"I seem to be momentarily short of funds," he said. "You don't happen to have anything for ten dollars?"

"Might have if you were alone," the man said. "But the best I can do for you and your lady friend is $16."

Marvin took the bill without a word, jammed the car into reverse, screeched out of the graveled parking area.

"Damn it," he said. "Damn it—I *knew* it!"

"Don't be like that, Marvin," Gillian said. Her finger resumed its tracing efforts, but the swelling had vanished in the frustration of the moment. "We can go somewhere else. We can use your name. You can cash a check."

"Any check I would cash," Marvin said, "would bounce from here to King's Neck and right back again."

"But you could cover it," Gillian said. "You could

go to the bank on Monday and cover the check."

"You don't understand, Gillian," he said. "All I could cover that check with is unpaid bills. I'm broke. I'm flat broke."

Now that it had happened, Marvin couldn't accept it. His conquest, so fortuitously begun and so intricately constructed, was collapsing like a deflated balloon. He was again, again and forever, a loser. No, not a loser. No, not a loser, *the* loser, the all-time number-one world-champ loser. And what he had even greater difficulty in accepting was the fact that Gillian Blake was convulsed in an uncontrollable attack of giggles.

"You're broke?" she said, finally.

"I am driving from here," he said, "directly to the nearest poorhouse."

"But this car?"

"I own precisely $1,350 worth of this car. And the way they charge for this car, that means I own four tires and the rear window."

"The house?"

"Will be mine in precisely twenty-eight years if I continue paying $325 a month until that date."

"Poor Marvin," Gillian said. "Poor Marv."

They rode silently then, each contemplating a private disaster. Finally, more to clear the air than anything else, Gillian told Marvin that she had been going to ask him for a loan. A loan of $1,500. A loan to pay for an abortion because she was carrying, deep in her womb, the beginnings of a beatnik, the embryo given her by a hasty hipster.

"You wanted my money?" Marvin said.

"Don't get me wrong," Gillian said. "I wanted you, Marvin. But wanting you didn't prevent me from also wanting your money. But not permanently. Just a loan. And, honestly, I wouldn't have even mentioned it except, you have to agree, it is an emergency."

"We each have our emergencies," Marvin said.

"Poor Marvin," Gillian said.

They were approaching the toll booth in Pelham. Marvin fished for a coin, found two dimes and a nickel. He searched his pockets, desperately for a moment, found another quarter. "For the bridge," he said. His words were lost because Gillian was kissing his right ear.

"Poor, poor Marvin," Gillian said.

Marvin's body jerked involuntarily as Gillian slipped her hand inside his shirt and ran her fingers along his ribs. Slowly and methodically she unbuckled his belt and unzipped his trousers. Traffic was beginning to thicken, Marvin noticed, even as he responded to Gillian's dexterous fingers.

"Maybe not so poor after all," Gillian continued, stroking him into a full erection.

"Christ, Gillian," Marvin said. "The other cars, they'll see."

"Oh Marvin, let them see. You've nothing to be ashamed of. Let them see. Let the whole world see."

"Oh, God," Marvin said. "Oh, God, that feels good."

Ahead, but dimly, Marvin saw the approach to the Throg's Neck Bridge. Rush-hour traffic, he perceived, was jamming the lines to the toll booths. As he reached for his last quarter, Gillian burrowed her head in his lap. "My God. my God, my God!" he was saying as he rocked up and down on the seat cushion. He had never known this, never known anything like this before. Never. Not anything. And he gasped as Gillian suddenly stopped, pulled back, brushed back her hair.

"No, please," he said. "Don't stop now."

"Marvin," she said, "you could still lend me the money."

"How?" he said. "I don't have it."

"You could raise it," she said. "You could raise anything, Marvin."

"Just don't stop," he pleaded.

Gillian bent down once again. The truck driver in the adjoining lane looked down in mute fascination. In the other lane a three-year-old boy was jumping up and down in his car seat, pointing, but his parents didn't notice anything amiss—just a man sitting silently behind his wheel with a silly grin on his face. Again Gillian pulled up and away.

"Please," he said *"Please?"*

"A thousand," she bargained. "You could raise a thousand."

"Five hundred," he said.

Oh, oh, oh, oh, oh, oh, *oh!* The car behind the white Cadillac sounded its horn as the space widened in front of Marvin Goodman's car. Marvin stepped down on the accelerator. In the next lane the truck driver, attempting to keep abreast of the car, crunched into a Chevrolet carrying a troop of Cub Scouts and a Den Mother.

"A thousand"—this time Gillian didn't even lift her head.

"Seven fifty," he said.

Marvin felt a kind of paralysis engulfing him—every muscle was tense and he stretched himself back against the seat. He noticed, thank God, that he was in the Exact Change Lane. No toll taker. And then he was powerless, his hands gripping the steering wheel like twin vises. There was a rapping on the window beside his head but he ignored it—it was the Den Mother from the rammed Chevrolet and she was asking whether he saw what happened and then she turned away quickly, in horror at the sight of Marvin Goodman in his finest moment.

Then they were abreast of the toll basket and the car behind him was honking furiously. Marvin pressed the button that rolled down the window. "Oh, Gillian-Gillian-Gill. . . ." Marvin found the quarter and tossed it to the basket. "Ohhhhhhhhhhhhhhh. . . ." The quarter rimmed the basket, bounced on the asphalt, wheeled on edge in a wide semicircle and finally came to rest under the left front tire of the stationary Cadillac.

The toll booth attendant saw the vast tie-up and signaled the patrolman, who gunned his motorcycle over to the parked Cadillac. He noted that the door on the passenger's side was open. He noted that the sole occupant of the car seemed in a daze, a small grin pasted on his face in a lopsided fashion. "Hey Mac . . . ," he began and "Sweet Jesus," he wound it up.

The man in the driver's seat was alight with transcendental joy. The aura of Gillian still filled the car. For the moment, at least, Marvin Goodman was a winner.

Billy: Well, Gilly, there are a lot of pros and cons involved. Abortion is a touchy subject.

Gilly: Obviously. I realize there is a definite question of morality involved. But there are also human considerations.

Billy: No matter what the circumstances, Gilly, you are taking a life when you perform an abortion.

Gilly: I know, Billy, but suppose the pregnancy endangers the mother's life. Or suppose the mother is a teenage rape victim. Look, those are only two examples. There are lots of others.

Billy: It's not an easy thing to decide.

Gilly: I mean, I can feel for these poor women you read about who have to go to some sleazy practitioner —someone who's doing that sort of thing on the side, and has all these dirty instruments and everything.

Billy: I don't think there's much question that the law needs to be liberalized. The problem is how. And how much?

Gilly: You have a real talent for summing up, Billy.

Billy: Thank you, dear. I think one of your most sterling qualities is your ability to make a man feel important.

Gilly: Oh, but you are. I think all you men are just terribly important.

Billy: We're all grateful.

Gilly: Actually, Billy, a panel discussion on abortion would make a very interesting show.

Billy: I think that's a first-rate idea, hon. We could have someone from the church and, perhaps, a representative from the medical society.

Gilly: There's only one problem.
Billy: What's that?
Gilly: I'm afraid we might have a little trouble find-ing an abortionist.

ALAN HETTERTON

Alan Hetterton is a beautiful name—the words were a small song in Gillian's mind as she stepped from the shower. Oh yes, a beautiful name is Alan Hetterton—she sang the song as she toweled herself dry in the bedroom, sang the song as she stood at the bedroom window, the towel over her shoulders, and stared out at a faraway jet wheeling in the night sky toward La Guardia. Alan Hetterton, in point of fact, was the name mentioned by Maxine of Maxine's Beauty Parlor during a casual conversation on the subject of abortionists she had known. Dr. Alan Hetterton is a beautiful name—tra-la!—and the bedroom phone rang twice before Gillian responded.

"Hello," she said.

"You got a pair of big ones," the voice said.

"Who is this?" she asked.

"I said you got a pair of big ones." Whoever he was, he was making no effort to disguise his voice. "Big round ones and never mind who this is."

The first time he had called, Gillian calmly placed the receiver in the cradle, waited a second, then called the police. The police had informed her there was nothing to be done, but should the calls continue she might want to use the new automatic tracking device. It had all seemed so much trouble.

"Are you coming to the point?" she asked.

"I come to a point," he said. "Don't worry about that. I come to a point, same as anyone else."

Gillian remembered the full-page ads—so sober, so shocking—telling women exactly what they must do if they get a harassing phone call. Screw it, she thought. It was the first time in a week she had not been concentrating on the baby beatnik in her abdomen. She didn't hang up, not this time. Perversely, she lighted a cigarette and kept talking.

"Why don't you tell me your name?" she said.

"When are you going to meet me in the hay?" the voice said. "When are you going to step out of your step-ins and hop in the old hay?"

"Please, why won't you tell me your name?" she said. "I may be able to help you."

"You've heard of Jack the Ripper," he said. "Well, I'm his cousin, Jack the Fucker."

"Why don't you tell me all about it?" Gillian said. "That's a very interesting name. If you tell me all about it, maybe I can help you."

"You *hoooer!*" he screamed. "You wanna trap me. You wanna keep me talking just so you can trap me."

"Maybe I just want to talk to you."

Click. It took Gillian a moment to realize that *he* had hung up on *her.* He had taken the action she should have taken. Gillian giggled—she had a feeling that perhaps she had just learned a lesson of importance. Maybe that was the one sure way to get rid of all the nuts in the world—try to understand them. She rested back on the bed and discovered, almost to her surprise, that the call had had a strange effect: It had excited her. She found herself sensually aroused, strangely warm, and perhaps there was a lesson there as well. Gillian didn't dwell on this.

She reached instead for the Three Towns Directory. Hetley, Hetterich . . . there, Hetterton, Alan, M.D.—office 131 Thompson Lane—KI 1-1377. This time it was the voice at the other end of the line who asked the questions. An operation? Would she care to specify what kind of an operation? No? Would she care to say who had referred her to him? No? Maxine

Schwartz? Oh, yes, would Friday evening be satisfactory?

It had not been an easy road that Alan Hetterton had traveled. The road from Kings County to King's Neck was uphill and bumpy. He had known even in medical school that he was not destined to be much of a doctor. The sight of blood saddened him, sometimes reduced him to tears. To this day he was not certain which was the tibia and which was the fibia. But somehow he had stumbled through medical school, finally acquiring the M.D. after his name— the M.D. that his parents had treated with a reverence he could never understand. Most of Alan's classmates went on to postgraduate work, but Alan was not one to press his luck. (At times, even then, he thought he might still go into his father's brassiere business, learning it, as the old man might say, from the inside out.) He settled, instead, for the life of a general practitioner. One of the few on Long Island that found it economically necessary to make house calls. And perform abortions.

In time Alan met Gerda, the sister of a nurse who had helped pulled him through his period of interning. Gerda, tiny and small-boned with fair skin and a large mouth, was everything Alan was not: extroverted, adventurous, bubbling with idle conversation. It was she who had been the aggressor, she who had provided the rubber contraceptive during their first fumbling encounter one night in June on the fourth tee of the Plandome Country Club. But even there he had failed. Four weeks later Gerda tearfully announced that she was "preggy," to use her imperishable term. Six weeks later they were married. Married for eighteen years, eighteen years of relative poverty (whenever Alan encountered a statistical study of average incomes for doctors in the United States he shook his head sadly, wonderingly), and the fruit of their union was an eighteen-year-old boy, who was seriously considering a life as a Country-and-Western vocalist, and a house a mile from the water in one of the less prestigious sectors of King's Neck.

Alan had never actually regretted marrying Gerda —but there were moments. Moments when he was lancing an ugly boil or giving an enema, and then he would reflect on his marriage. What had they in common? Other than a slow-witted long-haired son who fancied cowboy boots with silver spurs—a boy who had perhaps been the foremost reason for Alan's first having risked performing an abortion. Well, what had they in common? Gerda's never-ending quest for Louis XV mirrors bored and impoverished him; her genteel habit of eating prune Danish with knife and fork (which at first had seemed so charming) now irritated him. For her part, Gerda stolidly accepted his refusal to trade in their Rambler station wagon for a Jaguar XKE or to grow what she called an "unobtrusive little Vandyke." Gerda would, of course, accept almost anything because Alan had fathered a son she found entirely beautiful.

On Friday Bill announced a weekend trip to Chicago, a conference with a prospective sponsor, and Gillian was appropriately grateful. She decided against hazarding the drive herself and called Station Taxi. The cab driver dropped her at a drugstore at the end of town and she walked back the few short blocks to the corner of Thompson. A small unobtrusive sign beside a lamp post identified the doctor's office. The low brick building was set back from the road and was modestly landscaped—it seemed to serve as a buffer between the business buildings to the south and the split levels and spaced ranch homes to the north. A Rambler station wagon, its chrome running to rust, was parked beside the building. It had M.D. plates.

The foyer was dimly lit. To her right was the waiting room. She sat opposite the door to the doctor's office. She studied with amused interest a grouping of pictures over the deep green leather couch. Marin's Lower Manhattan fought mood, color and style with Renoir's Le Pont Noeuf. Beside the paintings was a Louis XV mirror that Gillian would have sworn was authentic. A copy of a G. H. Davis World War II sketch of German and American fighter planes in aerial battle hung tastelessly with the others. The room furnishings were less expensive than one might expect in a King's Neck office, and the imbalance of color and style was unsettling.

"Hello, I'm Dr. Hetterton. And you are Mrs. Brown, I believe."

"That's right."

Gillian looked into the full face of a man who was medium tall, maybe five feet ten, and of stocky build. He wore his graying hair in a modified crew cut, and Gillian guessed he was on the far side of forty-five. He returned the glance and gave no indication of his thoughts.

"Mrs. Brown, isn't it?" he said.

"Yes, doctor," she said.

"I have a remarkable number of Mrs. Browns on file," he said.

"That is remarkable," Gillian said. "I have no relatives here."

"Just so," he said.

"Aren't you going to ask me in?"

The doctor cleared his throat and stepped inside the small office, then led her into an examination room off to the left. He handed her a surgical gown and gestured toward a curtained-off sector of the chamber. Gillian was thankful that he had dismissed his nurse. She disrobed quickly and poked her head through the curtain.

"Come on out," the doctor said. "I don't bite."

Following his directions, Gillian climbed onto the examining table. The doctor rolled a large machine over to the table. He draped a cloth over Gillian's legs and gently placed her feet in the stirrups at either side of the table. Then, less gently, he plunged the speculum into her. He completed the check in silence, then leaned against the wall and ignited a cigarette.

"Two months," he said. "Two months into a first pregnancy."

"That's right—almost to the day. Didn't I tell you that on the phone?"

"You know"—he seemed not to be listening to her—"the women in France have babies right out in the field and then go on with their day's work."

"Bully for them." If it weren't for that damn gadget tearing at her insides, Gillian would have walked out of the room.

"I just want to be sure," the doctor said. "I don't want you to do anything you're going to regret."

"How long is this going to take?" Gillian said. "Let's just get it over with. Are you going to give me anything?"

Dr. Hetterton pressed down on the foot pedal that opened the sterilizer. Steam billowed up the wall. He reached over to a plastic container in which forceps rested in an alcohol bath. Then he seemed to have second thoughts.

"Stretch your arms straight down and clasp the edge of the table. This will be over in a few seconds."

He switched on the diathermy machine and firmly clasped the cautery gun. The intense heat spread through Gillian and she bit her lip to stifle a cry. She fought the nausea welling up in her throat.

"Easy," he said. "There, that should do it."

"You mean it's all over?"

"All over now." Dr. Hetterton handed her a prescription pad and pencil. "Here, write your name, address and phone number. Your real name. You may need me and I'll have to have the correct facts. It should happen within twenty-four hours. Call me as soon as it does."

Gillian did as she was told, precisely as she was told. Not glancing at the paper, the doctor thrust it into his trouser pocket and called the taxi. The two of them sat there in the office waiting, not speaking, and Gillian wished for something appropriate to say.

For once she was wordless. At parties she employed a selection of icebreakers that seldom failed to work— a small smorgasbord of existentialism, Zen and little known facts about obscure students of Bellini. Don't you think Sartre is very much the twentieth-century man? she would ask. Kirkegaard has a marvelously fey quality about him, don't you think? she would say. Wouldn't you say that sex is simply the last resort of two people who can't communicate? she would offer.

But none of them—nothing seemed appropriate. The doctor looked like the kind of man who would forget to zip up his trousers, a man on the edge of going to seed.

"Why do you do this?" she asked.

"I'm a doctor," he said. "I help people."

"Seriously," she said.

"Seriously, I need the money," he said. "Why do *you* do it?"

"Seriously, I don't need the baby," she said.

"You don't look to be suffering," he said. "You are married, aren't you? Is the baby your husband's?"

"No," she said. "And as long as we're being honest, I have no idea who the father is."

"*No* idea?" he said.

"Some idea," she said. "But I might be wrong on that."

"It doesn't matter now," he said.

They both heard the cab pull up in front of the office. Gillian nodded at the doctor and opened the door.

"By the way," he said, "by the way, Mrs. Brown, you are a very beautiful woman."

It was a strange way to end it, Gillian thought, closing the door behind her. The door closed away the sight of Dr. Alan Hetterton holding both hands straight out in front of him. The tremor was barely noticeable. He stopped then and answered the ringing telephone.

"I told you I had some calls to make," he said. "Yes, yes, I know what time it is. Why am I still at the office? Christ, I was in the neighborhood and had to take a leak. I think, Gerda, I'm capable of coming to these decisions by myself."

He replaced the receiver and sat staring at the phone for ten minutes or more. When he could stand it no longer he went to the locked cabinet, opened it, took down the bottle of morphine. He placed two of the tiny white pills, half-gram pills, in the belly of a tablespoon. He drew a single cc of sterile water into the syringe, squirted it onto the spoon, watched the pills effervesce. Rolling up his left sleeve, he searched out the vein and daubed it gently with alcohol. Soon, soon. Drawing the precious liquid into the hypodermic, he squirted out a drop, then jabbed the needle home. An hour. One hour to get home and shower before the euphoria would grip him.

The cramps began the following morning and by noon the abortion was complete. Gillian flushed the shapeless mass away. Bye bye, baby, she thought. She dragged herself back to bed and the bleeding did not let up. She dozed off and awakened to feel the dampness spreading beneath her legs. She barely had time to call Dr. Hetterton before passing out again.

Within an hour, the doctor arrived. He gave Gillian an injection of ergot to stop the bleeding. And some follow-up tablets for the next day.

"Gillian *Blake*," he said. "You know, I honestly had no idea who you were until I looked at the paper you filled out. I catch your program frequently."

"Do you, doctor?"

"I especially liked the one the other day, the one about the God-is-dead theory. I mean, calling it the biggest publicity stunt of the decade. Imagine! God as PR man, planting God-is-dead theologians around to start controversy, to bring His name into the limelight—that was a master stroke!"

"I'm so tired, doctor."

"But seriously," he said, "something like that can start people back on the road to doing some serious reevaluating."

"Even you, doctor?"

"Maybe not me," he said. "But some people."

"One last question, doctor—does my husband, does Billy have to know about this?"

"Not if he stays away from you, if you know what I mean."

"I know what you mean," Gillian said. "And I don't think that will be a problem."

"I'm sorry to hear that," he said. "You know there's a lot of people who feel you must have the ideal marriage. What is it your announcer says? You know, about the reality of marriage in the crucible of modern living. Well, people listen to you and you seem to have all the answers."

"I'm so very sleepy now," she said.

"Of course, of course," he said. "I'll want to see you when you're up and around."

"Good night, doctor," she said. "Good night and thank you."

"You're a beautiful woman, Mrs. Blake."

A few days passed before Gillian felt her old self again. Still, she didn't go back for the checkup. A few weeks. A month. And then on a Thursday in February, Gillian examined herself in the full-length mirror. The reflection was smooth. She thought of that old joke—the patient died but the operation was a success; she decided the time had come.

Thursday afternoon she went to the doctor's office. This time, with the pale gray end-of-day light streaming through the windows, she was unaware of the colors clashing. And this time there was a third party, a nurse—a tiny sparrow of a woman. Gillian decided, yes, a large-mouthed small-breasted sparrow.

"Do you have an appointment with Dr. Hetterton?"

"Well, not exactly," Gillian said. "But the doctor asked me to stop in for a checkup."

"I'll have to see if the doctor can take you," the nurse said. "The name, please."

"Mrs. Brown," Gillian said.

"I'll see if he can take you," she said.

Gillian had to smile at that. *If he can take you—* the waiting room was conspicuously empty, and dust had gathered on the magazine rack. That nurse, she was as dreary as everything else connected with the office.

"Mrs. Brown," the doctor was saying, "yes, of *course.* Won't you please come right in? Is there anything wrong, anything. . . ."

"I have this terrible aching feeling," Gillian was saying as the door closed behind them, shutting the sterile little nurse out in the sterile little antechamber.

"Where?" the doctor said.

"That's nonsense," Gillian said. "I feel fit as a fiddle. But you did say to stop by for a checkup."

"So I did, so I did," he said. "And I must say I'm glad you came. Any trouble at home? Any . . . complications?"

"Not a one," Gillian said. "Of course, I haven't . . . done anything that might be considered risky. I didn't dare."

"I'll write out a prescription for feosol," he said. "That will keep your pep up. I don't suppose there's anything else I can do?"

"Don't you even want to examine me?" Gillian said. "After all, you're the doctor."

"I suppose I may as well," he said, "just to be on the safe side. Why don't you go into the room while I get the nurse . . . ?"

"That won't be necessary," Gillian said. "I think I can trust you now."

When Dr. Hetterton joined Gillian in the small chamber she was standing in front of the disrobing screen. She had placed the white robe over her clothes on the small chair. Her long hair tumbled freely over her pale shoulders. Her breasts, unfettered now, seemed to defy the laws of gravity and probability. She swiveled calmly to face him; it was then she noticed the trembling in his hands.

"Are you all right?" she asked.

"Yes," he said, "in a minute. . . ."

"Don't go," she said. "I think every artist should enjoy his handiwork. . . . I haven't thanked you properly, doctor. The only reason I haven't thanked you properly is that I haven't been able to thank you properly. Am I able to now?"

"Mrs. Blake, you're able to do anything now. Anything at all. You don't need me any more."

"That's where you're mistaken—can I call you Alan? That's where you're mistaken, Alan. If I can do anything at all, then I need you right now."

"But the nurse. . . ."

"The nurse is out there," Gillian said. "She is out there two doors away and we're here."

"That nurse is my wife; she's Gerda."

"Come here, Alan."

He didn't move, and Gillian walked the three short steps to him. His arms moved slowly to hold her and she reached her hands to his neck and stroked his hair gently. Then she urged him with her hands to follow her backward to the examination table. She fell back onto the table, her feet still touching the floor, and he bent over her. Gillian nibbled at his ear lobes, and her lips ran feverishly over his throat. His mouth groped for her mouth before he moved down toward her breasts.

As he continued to kiss her breasts and then advanced upon her stomach, Gillian remained calm. So strange. She felt no physical attraction to this strange round-faced man who was coming at her with increasing urgency. She did not particularly like his looks. She felt nothing but embarrassment for his fumbling ways. And yet even he—even this flawed and damaged specimen of a man—could arouse her, could lick at her center of passion, perhaps could even satisfy her.

She pushed the doctor back then and reached for his belt. She efficiently undid the belt, then the zipper, smiled as the trousers fell down around his ankles. He mounted her, entered her, probed with his rigid flesh where he had once poked with a speculum. Gillian realized idly that she had never before made love in this position. His frenzy controlled her then, and the climax of the one sparked the climax of the other, his ejection riding the waves of her spasmodic contractions.

"Alan!"

It was a scream and the two of them looked at the door, at the small woman in the starched uniform. Her mouth seemed suddenly smaller, perhaps because of the size of her eyes. Gerda had entered at the wrong moment; there was no way for her husband to stop, to apply brakes, to turn back, to explain. He drove home his final thrusting motions under the gaze of his outraged wife. Even later he made no effort to undo the damage.

Trousers around his ankles hobbled him, and Gillian's legs encircled him. He looked at his wife—hopelessly, helplessly—and the three of them seemed frozen in positions that were individually ludicrous. Then Alan felt the warmth returning, felt the motions of the woman beginning anew. He made no effort to stop himself and he responded slowly to Gillian's encouraging undulations.

"Alan, get off her right now!"

"Go away, little bird," Gillian said. "Go away unless you want to see your husband in a new light."

"Go away, Gerda," the doctor said. "This really doesn't concern you at all."

"It's better the second time"—Gillian raised her voice so that Gerda could hear each syllable—"it's always better the second time, lover."

"Alan," Gerda said, "I'm not going to ask you again."

Looking back at Gerda one last time, Alan turned then and settled his mouth into Gillian's throat. Neither of them took any visible notice as the door slammed behind Gerda. Gillian, at that moment, felt a surprising sense of disappointment. The disappearance of the audience, particularly a disapproving audience, took some of the edge off it. Live and learn, live and learn. Still, she did not convey her disappointment to the good doctor—she relaxed, rising and falling with his ebb and flow. Then methodically she drained him a second time, emptied him, calmed him and gentled him.

"I'm sorry about your wife," she said finally. "I didn't intend to ruin your marriage—seriously I didn't come here to do that."

"It was ruined a long time ago," the doctor said. "Just one thing—did you take any precautions this time?"

"Yes," she said. "But it was nice of you to ask, Alan."

"I was just curious," he said.

Before facing Gerda, Hetterton went again to his locked cabinet. This time he dropped four of the tiny pills onto the spoon. And then he sat down in his empty office and waited for the drug to take effect. When the shaking in his hands was under control, he walked over to the house and faced a strangely composed Gerda. To his surprise, she said she did not want a divorce. She said that she still loved him and would remain with him on two conditions. Alan agreed that never again would he see Mrs. Brown. He also agreed to the purchase of a $545 electronically amplified guitar for his son.

Gillian never saw Alan Hetterton again—and she was not surprised or disappointed by this. However, from time to time, she heard rumors. Rumors linking Alan Hetterton and Maxine, Alan Hetterton and a fifteen-year-old candy striper at Huntington Hospital, Alan Hetterton and a sixty-four-year-old spinster school teacher. And then in June she read the final chapter in a newspaper gossip column—

"North Shore set is still talking about the messy situation involving a local general practitioner who sidelined on the abortion circuit. Seems his frau caught him in the arms of a female impersonator and decided to do a little cranial surgery on the two of them—with a double-bitted axe. Police intervened just in time. Whole thing was hushed up by the local constabulary but both Md. and his Mrs. have left town, last seen heading in the general direction of the divorce courts."

Billy: You seem especially bright and chipper today, dear.

Gilly: Why not? It's a nice day, we're having lovely weather for this time of year, and I had a splendid time at the doctor's yesterday.

Billy: Oh . . . you didn't tell me.

Gilly: It wasn't anything important, sweetheart. Just a yearly checkup.

Billy: Well, what'd it show?

Gilly: That's just it. According to the doctor, I'm in splendid shape. Marvelously healthy.

Billy: I don't know what he gave you, but you look radiant.

Gilly: It's probably psychological, but I do feel at the top of my form.

Billy: If you'll allow me to say so, dear, your form has always been tops.

Gilly: Why, thank you, kind sir. You are a sweetie, today.

Billy: It's just my natural charm, hon. But seriously, I've always admired your ability to keep in shape.

Gilly: Well, I think it's very important for people to stay in condition. I mean, I can't see physical conditioning as an end in itself, but certainly the body does house the brain, and it pays to be healthy.

Billy: Of course, there are some people who have natural physiques.

Gilly: Yes, some athletes are like that.

Billy: That's true. But there are others who go to pot the minute they stop training. For instance, there's nothing sadder than an ex-prizefighter who lets himself get fat. Some of them turn into balloons.

Gilly: That's a shame when it happens, because I think some fighters have the best builds of all. You know, the ones with the broad shoulders and the muscular arms who taper down into narrow waists.

Billy: I remember when I had a narrow waist.

Gilly: Well, it's still quite slim, dear, thanks to all that squash and tennis you play.

Billy: Now, it's my turn to thank you.

Gilly: Also, there's something so reassuring about a strongly built man.

Billy: Really?

Gilly: Yes, I think there's a wonderfully masculine quality in thick biceps.

Billy: But seriously, don't you think women are more interested in a man's mind than in his muscles? Don't you think they're more concerned about his . . . uhm, personality, his intelligence?

Gilly: Certainly, over the long haul. But it doesn't hurt if he looks good, too. There's nothing worse than spindly shoulders and a potbelly. I'm half-kidding, of course, but muscle men are quite stimulating. After all, it's the same the other way around. What about pin-ups? And you can't tell me that a man who meets a girl with a figure like Sophia Loren's for the first time is thinking about her brain.

Billy: I'll have to admit you have a point, there.

Gilly: So it's the same with a woman. I mean you might not want to spend your life with Hercules, but you wouldn't mind watching him lift weights. Or something.

Billy: Let's watch that something.

Gilly: Oh Billy, you're awful.

Billy: Actually, I'll settle for watching Sophia Loren model bikinis.

Gilly: Right. The body beautiful in action. I think every woman enjoys watching a Pancho Gonzales playing tennis. Or a Cassius Clay boxing. I think prize fighters are especially exciting. All that con-

centrated violence. They're so direct. So beautifully brutal.

Billy: I know what you mean. It's like watching Billy Blake play squash.

Gilly: That's pure poetry, dear.

Billy: You do know the way to a man's ego, hon.

Gilly: And don't forget his biceps.

PADDY MADIGAN

The wind, which bore only a twinge of its Canadian origin, had long since blown the last of the leaves from the twin oaks in the backyard. Now it stacked them like a fragile brown dam against the bottom of the privet hedge that lined the southwest side of the half-acre that Agnes Madigan called "our estate."

That is, Agnes said "our estate" to neighbors and strangers. When her only company was her husband, Paddy, she called it "my estate." And she said it because it was so.

The deed was in Agnes's name. And so was Paddy for that matter. The money had originated with Paddy, but he had realized years earlier that without her guidance the money would have disappeared. Everything disappeared without Agnes. All that he had was because of Agnes. She had told him this, and he knew it was true. He had become hers, both body and soul, because he had purchased the refuge of her mother-arms.

On this mild winter Thursday, Paddy was casting about for the leaves under the hedge with a wire rake. He knew it was late in the year to rake leaves but it was something to do. The tines of the rake caught in the roots of the hedge and Paddy cursed under his breath. As he cursed, he glanced instinctively at the

house even though he knew that Agnes had gone to
the hairdresser's. Agnes didn't like cursing. She didn't
like cursing or sleeping in church or drinking beer in
the parlor, and when Paddy violated any of these
rules he looked over his shoulder.

The rake jammed into a root and was caught there.
Paddy said "shit." He looked behind at the house and
shrugged his shoulders. Then he heard laughter from
the backyard across the split-log fence. It was from
either the Blake place or the one where the Earbrows
used to live.

"Oh, honey," the voice said, "you don't want to let
some little thing get you all in an uproar. Don't let a
little thing like leaves goose you."

Paddy took his time finding the voice. Women em-
barrassed him, and women who talked like bartenders
frightened him. He knew what Agnes said about
women like that and she was right. Agnes was always
right. Finally he saw the her of the voice. She was
leaning against a birch tree. She was wearing a cape
she'd had made from a Peruvian blanket and it didn't
button in the front. It was loose and Paddy looked
at her and wondered what held her breasts up that
way. They lolled and swayed in the loose, low jersey
she wore under the blanket jacket.

Paddy gulped and started to sweat. He looked up
at the house again. Agnes would kill him. He had to
do something. But he just stood there and wondered
about the breasts. He was dressed in blue jeans,
sneakers and an undershirt that allowed his muscles
the rippling freedom they needed. It was much too
cold for an undershirt and Agnes would talk to
him about that, but still it felt nice, nice and cool.
The breeze softly stirred the gray reddish hair on his
arms, chest and shoulders but inside he was stirring as
if his viscera were caught in the eye of a hurricane.

"You're Mrs. Blake," Paddy said.

"Call me Gilly," she said. She was laughing, laughing at the way he talked—it was like Red Skelton

talked at a show they once did together. But Red Skelton had been kidding and Paddy Madigan was not kidding.

Gillian cut the laugh short. She had assumed that the rough, tough approach would be best with Paddy but now she was not so sure. She had mentally slotted Paddy Madigan beside Ernie Miklos, the late Ernie Miklos, in a category she thought of as, simply, Musclemen. But now, for the moment, she was not so sure.

Paddy couldn't take his eyes off her breasts. They bounced when she laughed, and when she stopped they ended up pointing up. He thought of the girl he had seen in *Playboy* Magazine once; she had breasts that pointed up. Agnes had found the magazine and burned it. Paddy's mind saw through the fabric and he could see molded pink flesh and sturdy nipples and he dropped his rake. He hoped he wouldn't get a hard-on.

"I've been dying to meet you," Gillian said. Her eyes turned brilliant and brindle like a feline in cat-nip and she planted a small lie. "I've wanted so much to meet you. You were always my hero."

Paddy stopped gulping. He understood the word "hero." There was a time—and the boys in any bar in Mineola would remember it—when he had been a hero. Paddy Madigan had been the pride of the gin mills, the man announcer Johnnie Addie always mentioned after the magic words: "And the stellar attraction." Paddy Madigan had been the white image on the Thursday night fights televised from St. Aloysius Arena; the man who fought his way to a fight with the light-heavyweight champion of the world. He was the crinkly-haired left-handed fighter who carried almost all before him—until the desperation that worked so long failed when it had to fail.

Paddy preened. The muscles on his shoulders stiffened into chunks and he unconsciously drew in his stomach, drew up his buttocks and inhaled. Mentally, he whomped a left hook into a body bag.

"Don't overdo it, honey," Gillian said. "Don't waste all that muscle until I get there, will you?"

She settled then on the direct approach. Subtlety, she knew, would be a waste. She scampered to the fence, and, hurtling it, tripped. It was a sprawling fall and it carried her to Paddy's feet. He looked down at her numbly and didn't move.

"For Christ's sake!" she exploded—then changed the snarl to smiling Arpège. "Please, hon, give me your hand."

Paddy, at that moment, would have given her the loving cup from the mantel, the one that the President of Argentina handed to him when he won his division championship in the Pan-American Games. That was just before Paddy was old enough to vote. He gave her his hand and she took it. As he pulled Gillian to her feet, her free hand traveled lazily up his forearm and the skin there exploded in goosebumps.

"Are you hurt, missus?"

There was pain in Paddy's voice as he asked the question. When she didn't answer—when all she did was stroke his arm and smile, he asked the question again—the same words with precisely the same intonation.

"Good God, you're strong," she said. "Touching you gives me shocks."

Her palms rubbed up his arms and over his shoulders and down his chest. Paddy looked over his shoulder at the house. He reminded himself that Agnes was at the hairdresser's. Gillian was talking some more about Paddy's muscles, but he couldn't hear a word she said. What he heard was a gentle purring sound and the sound stirred him. He reached both hands behind Gillian, caught her by the globes of her rump and pulled her a foot off the ground. Then he kissed her hurriedly, catching only the last quarter of an inch of her lips on the right side. Gillian clenched her teeth and then, before opening her eyes, managed a smile.

"You certainly sweep a girl right off her feet," she said.

"Oh, missus. . . ."

Paddy was gulping again. He wanted to tell her he was sorry but the words wouldn't come. He stammered. And she cut off his misery with another smile and a light lingering touch that brushed over his chest and made a wide circular movement just above his belt buckle.

"Maybe it's not right," Gillian said—she tried spacing the words neatly between manufactured heavy breaths. "Maybe it's not right but I could keep my hands on you all day."

Oh you sexpot, she thought, you incorrigible sexpot. Her eyes closed and her head rolled against Paddy's chest. Paddy was gulping hard when Gillian slumped and cried out a feeble "Oh!" Paddy grabbed her.

"Whatsamatta, missus?" he choked. "I do somethin' to you?"

"My ankle"—Gillian tried her best Bette Davis look —"I think I'm going to faint. Maybe you had better . . . take me inside."

Paddy hadn't seen the movie. He tenderly gathered her up to him and minced his steps across the yard, up the back steps, through the kitchen and into the living room. He held her out in his arms and looked at her. She seemed in pain and there were tears in Paddy's eyes. Then he knelt in front of the couch and deposited her carefully among Agnes's doilies and antimacassars.

"Jesus, you're strong," Gillian said.

For the moment Bette Davis was forgotten. Paddy was squatting in front of her, and her hand roamed up his thigh. She hoped her eyes were properly glassy.

"I didn't know you were so strong," she said—trying to get a grip on his thigh. "I didn't know."

Paddy wanted to look at her and he fought against it. His eyes roamed over the room. There were the lamps that Agnes had bought when they were first married; the bookends her brother had given them at the same time; the prints, The Ruins of Pompeii and Blue Boy; the wallpaper with the violets on it— Paddy had found that wallpaper difficult to live with but Agnes told him it was "refined." And on the opposite wall was the crucifix, four feet high, that Agnes had bought from the Sisters of the Poor. Behind him— he knew without looking—was the tinted picture of Agnes that she had been sold years ago in Kresge's.

Paddy's inattention annoyed Gillian. What was *his* hangup? She squirmed and went into her kitten stretch. When even this didn't get his attention, she sighed. With the sigh she brought his hands together in front of her and allowed the knuckles to rest against her breasts. Paddy stopped thinking of the room.

"I can feel your strength going through me," she said, pressing his hands harder against her breasts.

"Oh, missus, Agnes. . . ."

"More," she said, unfolding his hands and placing the palms against her breasts. "More."

His hands were gnarled and stumpy, hands that had been broken and repaired countless times. She rubbed her long fingers over the twisted hands, and Paddy gently rubbed his hands against her breasts. Finally. Gillian sat up.

"I have to feel free." she said. "Undo me."

She lifted the top of her jersey and pointed out the three clips that held the bra in place. Paddy loosened two of them, but the third was more than a match for fingers that had grown thick and suddenly clumsy. Finally he put his hand between her back and the elastic and gave a short tug. The bra was in his hand then and he looked at it wonderingly.

"Not too fast, honey," Gillian said.

But the hands that had seemed so inexpressive a moment earlier were now strong and full of purpose. The protest died in her throat. Paddy lifted her. His left hand grabbed out, covered all of her right breast and part of the other and his right hand grabbed at the top of her beige slacks and ripped them down in one yank. He pulled them off and left them in a tired wad at the foot of the couch.

Then he lifted her up. He looked down at his possession for a moment, and Gillian assumed the glance was one of admiration. However, there were no words to reinforce her belief. Paddy carried her across the room and with his foot pushed open the bedroom door. This time there was no gentleness. He threw her body onto the large double bed. Gillian's initial fear was being replaced by another emotion, an emotion that was becoming increasingly familiar to her. Anticipation of the inevitable. And now she felt a need to hurry it along, to help him get where he wanted to be. To her small surprise, she found herself more than ready for him, eager for him, eager for him to pack some of that muscle into her.

Gillian reached up to his belt and tried to undo it, but he slapped her hand away. Wild-eyed now, Paddy tore his clothes off and fell upon Gillian, hardly giving her time to raise her legs and receive him in comfort. Paddy snorted and gasped. His body strained and convulsed. Then, in seconds, he subsided and, as he subsided, he breathed a low groan from his diaphragm and fell prostrate upon her.

"Oh, come on lover, come *on*." Gillian could wait no longer. She felt she might climax before he even entered her if he delayed much longer. "Put it in. For Christ's sake, put it in."

Paddy was weeping.

"It *was* in," he whimpered. "It's all over. It's . . . all over now."

Gillian sat up and touched herself and discovered that Paddy was as good as his word. He had been in and, dammit, it was all over. She shook her head in disbelief.

"Let me look," Gillian said. She grabbed at Paddy, at the shriveled remnant of his brief passion. She found it and held it firmly between her thumb and forefinger. Nothing in her past experience, even her recent past experience, had prepared her for the object which she now encountered. Her first reaction was near to awe.

"Someone short-changed you," she said. "You're muscle everywhere, everywhere but here."

Paddy looked away then, and tears rolled down his face onto the embroidered coverlet. Gillian was in an experimental mood. She stretched the tiny member to its full length, and it seemed to shrink even more in embarrassment. She toyed with it, coaxed it, managed to extend it as much as it could be extended—and even then it would have fit nicely into a . . . what? A thimble, she decided.

The humor of the moment finally overcame her frustration. And she laughed. How could one hope to destroy a marriage that was held together by such a fragile link? She couldn't control the laughter then, and she threw back her head and her body was heaving and her breasts were undulating with each round of laughter.

But Paddy was still crying.

"Please don't laugh," he said finally. "Don't you laugh. Agnes was the only one, she never laughed. Agnes says that fucking is dirty and you shouldn't do it but only once a month. Only when you have to. Fucking is the curse God gave us because of Mother Eve. Only Agnes never laughs."

"I won't laugh, honey," Gillian said.

But composure was difficult, especially with Paddy going on about Agnes. Then he was telling her how his name was really Walter, Walter Madigan, and that Paddy was given to him by his manager. And how it somehow seemed to fit with Agnes because her name really was Bridget Murphy before they were married and that she had changed her name to Agnes because her cousins told her that Bridget was too old-fashioned and too Irish. Then he told her about being in the Seabees during World War II, just a kid, and when he heard his outfit was going to Guam, he began wetting his bed, even though Guam was secured.

His tiny penis had made him shy of girls, he told her. There was a slut in San Francisco who said he was the only guy she had ever met who drove a tack with a sledge hammer. He had beaten that girl black and blue, and his manager had to pay her a thousand dollars just to keep her big mouth shut. And there was a girl in the Bronx who said it was so small she couldn't even bite it, and he had knocked out her two upper front teeth and that had cost $500.

Paddy began crying again.

Gillian's hand stroked his shoulder and then once again the ludicrousness of the situation struck home. She tried to hold back the giggle, but most of it escaped.

Paddy reached up then and slapped her across the face. That did it. Gillian's head made an arch to the pillow and she started to cry then. It was the first time she had ever been struck by a man. It wasn't the humiliation, though, that prompted the tears. It was the pain. Paddy had caught her a good one.

"Please don't cry," he was saying. "Please don't, missus."

It was no use. His words were almost a prayer, but they ran together and they seemed to come from a great distance. Gillian tried to look up at Paddy but his face appeared blurred, the face seen through a window in a rainstorm.

"Please, please, please," he was saying. "I'll make it right."

She felt him then, reaching under her and slowly massaging her buttocks. Wondering what the point of all this was, she didn't resist. She allowed Paddy to spread her legs, and his fingers found the dampness there and he stroked and crooned and she spread the legs even farther. Then, with a last quick cry, Paddy's face lowered itself into the darkness and Gillian crooned. She found herself holding onto the back of his head, guiding it, pressing it, and the tears went away.

It was nearly dark. Paddy felt as though he were waking from a long sleep but his eyes hadn't closed once. The time had gone somewhere and he hadn't been aware of its passing. Gillian had gone, too, and he hadn't known that either.

His manager had known the truth about Paddy. Maybe he was the only one besides Paddy to discover it. They both knew that Paddy Madigan fought out of desperation alone. "He's got a heart the size of a pea," the manager had told Agnes after that last fight, "but he's so scared that he fights like hell—that's what he's always had going for him."

Agnes had accepted this truth without comment. Her one reaction was to purchase a small Japanese pistol for self-protection. Paddy thought of that pistol as he struggled from the bed and smoothed it with faltering fingers. He could feel his desperation come to life again. He stumbled into the living room and groped through the closet under the stairs where Agnes kept her pistol.

Paddy was shaking then, saying words that only he and his God could understand. He grabbed at a chair, then threw it away from him and knelt down before the crucifix. He stared at the image of Christ on the cross for more than a minute, and then he turned away from it and faced the tinted picture of Agnes. He blessed himself with the right hand, forgetting that the pistol was clasped within that hand.

"Bless me, Agnes, for I have sinned," he began.

The wind, which bore only a tinge of its Canadian origin, had blown the loose leaves from the backyard toward the porch, and they swirled about the feet of

Agnes Madigan as she climbed the back stairs. She had just put her key into the lock when she heard the shot. She told the police she couldn't imagine why her husband killed himself. They had always been so happy.

EXCERPT FROM "THE BILLY & GILLY SHOW," FEBRUARY 27TH

Gilly: Your back seems to be bothering you again today, Billy.

Billy: Yes, it's that old sprain. It's probably age creeping up on me.

Gilly: That's a shame. And just a few weeks ago, we were talking about physical conditioning.

Billy: Right. No more squash and tennis for Billy Blake for a while.

Gilly: Well, you do have to be careful. You wouldn't want your condition to be any worse.

Billy: Actually, I feel buffeted from all sides. Not only is my back acting up, but did you read this morning's Times?

Gilly: You mean the radio column?

Billy: Yes. I'm afraid that man doesn't like us, dear.

Gilly: Wasn't it awful?

Billy: Pure vitriol.

Gilly: I'll tell you, I'm not even going to dignify what he had to say by discussing it on the air. I think that the wonderful people who listen to us can judge our show for themselves. They certainly don't need any nasty little man to tell them whether they like us or not.

Billy: I must say, darling, you're especially beautiful when you're angry.

Gilly: Thanks, sweetheart, I don't know what I'd do without you.

Billy: And I don't know what I'd do without you.

Gilly: I swear, Billy, you could pass for a southern gentleman, you're so courtly.

Billy: And I'm not even southern.

Gilly: But you are courtly.

Billy: *Seriously, that does seem to be a southern trait, doesn't it?*

Gilly: *Oh, absolutely. To tell you the truth, I think southern men are quite sexy. You know, like the character Marlon Brando played in* Sayonara.

Billy: *What do you think it is—the accent?*

Gilly: *That's probably part of it. But it's their whole approach. They know how to make a woman feel like a queen.*

Billy. *Ah do declare, Miz Blake. Ah've nevah seen you-all look more lovely.*

Gilly: *Oh Billy, you're too much.*

TAYLOR HAWKES

From where he sat, looking out over Research and Accounting, Taylor Hawkes could see in all directions, except behind him. Behind him was wall, gun-metal gray wall, like the side of a battleship. Taylor Hawkes had wished for a long time that the wall was cyprus paneling, or leather, or maybe even burlap like some of the offices in the city, but he was a little uneasy about asking the Baron for that. Glass to his left and two secretaries; glass to his right and three secretaries; glass in front of him and the vast secretarial pool; long straight rows of girls with adding machines; rows of girls with typewriters; the alcoves housing two dozen account executives; the department switchboard girl with the fine round bottom.

Taylor Hawkes could see in all directions, all right, except behind him on this day, February 27th, at 4:20 in the afternoon, with four Beefeater martinis and three vodka and tonics under his belt. Taylor Hawkes was looking down, his sunglasses still on, looking down at his desk, picking through the papers and memos, picking at the spike with the yellow message forms, the forms that showed who had called while he was at lunch, the time of the call, the degree of urgency and, when possible, the message. Ringold (Research) 2:10 p.m. . . . "Screw him," Taylor said out loud, "he didn't think I've got to eat?" Leonard (The Smellwell Account) 3:20 p.m. "Screw him, too." Mrs. Grace Belcher (a close friend of the Baron's, wanting some free advertising advice for Planned Parenthood in Roslyn) 12:50 p.m., 2:15 p.m., 3:55 p.m. "Well, the hell with you, Mrs. Belcher," Taylor said, wadding up the message form.

The message forms were the real pain in the ass, the worst thing when you just got back. Who was trouble? And who wasn't trouble? At the sound of the buzzer on his desk, Taylor Hawkes picked up the phone. He looked as he always did, to his right, watching Emily, good lady, talk to him while he was listening to her voice on the phone.

"Taylor, there's a Mrs. Gillian Blake in the lobby."

"Bring her in, Emily."

As he said it, Taylor swung the swivel chair around, looking out over Research and Accounting, and Emily must have looked, too. She didn't buzz this time; instead, she came to the glass door of his office and opened it.

"The Baron, Taylor."

"I see him, Emily."

"He's rolling fast," Emily said. "Real fast."

"He sure to God is," Taylor said. He felt perspiration at the back of his neck. "That ol' bastard can really roll."

"Mrs. Gillian Blake?" Emily said.

"Yeh," Taylor said. "Hold her, Emily. Get her some coffee. Show her the new computer setup or something. Hold her until I get the Baron out of here."

The Baron was about a third of the way through the huge room, rolling now, as Emily said, fast, real fast. He spun the wheelchair deftly down the narrow lane between the account executives' alcoves and the

adding machine girls, picking up speed in the wide
stretch between Taylor's office and the first row of
girls.

"He ain't stopping," Taylor said to himself. "He's
coming on."

Trouble now. Copy of the *Ladies Home Journal* on
the Baron's lap, bouncing on his lap, while he rolled
with both hands in his wheel chair. The old skinny
arms, pumping, pumping in his black suit, and the
little silver round head pointed right straight at Taylor's office, and rolling on, the old skinny arms and
the old little silver round head, rolling on.

"Old sonofabitch," Taylor said.

Can't get to my coat, he thought, no use trying to
put it on. Straightening tie, smoothing papers on the
desk. Take off the sunglasses, he see my eyes. Leave
sunglasses on, he think I'm drunk? Phone buzzing.

"Yeh?"

"Taylor"—it was Emily—"Mrs. Blake doesn't want
coffee. Doesn't want to see the computers. She wants
to see you. She. . . ."

"Jesus, Emily, tell her . . . tell her. . . ." The Baron
fifteen feet out now, slackening speed, rolling for
Taylor's glass door. "Just hold her, Emily."

"Taylor, she. . . . "

Then, another voice, this one in Taylor's ear.

"Taylor," Gillian said, "I'm not just another ordi-
nary, dissatisfied customer. You know, dear. . . ."

And another voice, in front of Taylor.

"You've seen this, Taylor?" The Baron was holding
up the magazine. "This is your idea of a small joke?"

The Baron's voice, very sharp. And on the phone,
Gillian—

"Taylor, if I want to see a computer deck, I'd go
over to IBM."

"No sir, Baron." Taylor said. "I haven't seen the
magazine yet. However, if it's the Honest ad, I can
explain—" He had the phone out in front of him,

shoulder high, it was breaking his arm, he could feel his hand clamped on it, knuckles splitting. "Gillian, please look at the computers. . . . I'm sorry, Baron, but the Cigaret Advertising Board said that business about the microfilters couldn't go. . . . Mrs. Blake, yes, you'll find the computers fascinating. . . ." Knuckles splitting and the phone hanging out there like a big black airplane between him and the Baron. "Gillian . . . Mrs. Blake . . . please look at the computers. Call you right back." Phone down, finally, and hand still cramped, knuckles going to split wide open.

"Mrs. William Blake?" the Baron said.

"Yes, sir," Taylor Hawkes said. "Lives out there in King's Neck."

"I *know*," the Baron said. "You seem to forget, the Blakes are my customers. *My* customers."

"Yes, sir," Taylor said.

"And I haven't even seen the Honest ad yet," the Baron said. "I'm talking about the Smellwell ad. Two pages in color, Taylor, and what do I see? Well?"

"You see the Smellwell research laboratories," Taylor said.

"That is what I see," the Baron said. "I see six men in white robes fussing, Taylor, fussing with test tubes. What I do not see is Vivian. I do not see Vivian Garland on a gondola in Venice. I do not see the slogan that I take personal credit for—'Tonight's the night, Vivian, with Smellwell.' Perhaps this refreshes your memory."

"Yes, sir," Taylor said. "We photographed that, just as you suggested. It was all ready to go and it was killed."

"And who may I ask had the temerity . . . ?"

"The old lady," Taylor said. "She said she thought the other one, the 'Tonight's-the-night' business, was . . . she said it was sinful. That was her word, Baron. She said we should bear in mind that Smellwell was a

product of modern science, a scientifically manufactured deodorant, and not some aphrodisiac used by
Italians."

"She said *that,* Taylor?"

"You were down on the ranch," Taylor was relaxing now, "and we didn't think you should be bothered
by something that could be fixed on the spot."

"In the future," the Baron said, "call me. If anyone
ever changes something I've assumed creative responsibility for, you call me. And if, by any chance, you cannot reach me, you tell the lady—or any client—that we
don't need their business."

"Yes, sir," Taylor said.

"And Taylor, while you're at it," the Baron went
on, "I want you to draft a letter to Vivian. To Vivian
Garland. I want you to explain to her why this happened. You may tell her, just as you told me, that
the decision was yours and that I was not consulted.
The letter will be on my desk, with your signature,
by tomorrow morning."

"Yes, Baron, of course."

"Taylor, how long have you been back from lunch?"

"Oh, some time now," he said. "Although, it was a
long lunch. I had a meeting at lunch with . . ."—he
tried to think of a name, any name—"with Mrs.
Belcher, Mrs. Grace Belcher of Roslyn. Planned Parenthood. Fine woman. They're planning big things
over there."

"A fine woman," the Baron said. "I suggested she
call you. But anything you do for them, Taylor, you're
on your own time." He rolled his wheelchair a foot
backward, then a foot forward, warming up for the
takeoff. "And at the conference tomorrow morning,
Taylor, be prepared to tell me about the Honest ad.
I will find time tonight to examine it. Be prepared
to defend whatever action you decided to take. Good
evening, Taylor."

A spin on the left wheel turned the chair around,

a thrust with the right hand sent it forward. And now, both hands pumping, the Baron was headed through Taylor Hawkes's glass door and out into the arena of business machines, picking up speed. Taylor watched the back of the Baron's little silver round head.

"Godamighty," Taylor said, "won't that old bastard ever die?"

Actually, he liked the Baron, got along with him well many days, respected the sharpness of the old man's mind, even when he was wrong, Baron Edward Osborne Morgan . . . one hundred and four years old . . . in a wheelchair since he was thrown playing polo at age seventy-one . . . fifty times, and more, a millionaire from investments and full owner of Morgan Advertising . . . but . . . but, and this was the part that always got Taylor Hawkes: Taylor's wife, Sarah, was the Baron's great-grandniece, his only living relative, and would Taylor be executive vice president of the agency today, if this was not the case?

Taylor didn't know. He thought so. He always told himself he would have made it anyway. He had beaten his way up through a string of southern agencies, had entered a Madison Avenue firm and made his way up through copy editing to account executive and, hell, all this was *before* he married Sarah, great-grandniece and the favorite person in all the world of Baron Edward Osborne Morgan. Hell, he had made it that far, he would have made it to the top, to a partnership, because he understood advertising. He understood the business and he understood the bullshit. You're damn right he would have. But executive vice president? If he hadn't married Sarah, would he . . . ?

Taylor Hawkes watched the little round silver head nearing the far end of the room, then saw the hard pump of the right hand and the wheelchair turning out into the corridor that would take the Baron to his own office at the end of the building.

The buzzer. He reached for the phone.

"Taylor, I'm coming in right now," Gillian said, "ready or not."

"Sure, Gillian," he said. "I've been waiting for you."

Taylor lifted the sunglasses from the bridge of his nose, squinted, rubbed his eyes, put the glasses on again. He wouldn't put on his coat. Standing, he sucked in his stomach and waited, watching as Emily guided Gillian Blake into the room.

She looks damn good, he thought. Not the greatest body in the world, but something there. Like she was proud of it. Would make you know it, too . . . crack your back with those good legs.

What does she want? Last week at the station's cocktail party, Taylor hadn't been sure. She had touched his hand when he lighted her cigarette, steadying his hand with her own, but a lot of women do that. And later she had backed that nice round behind against his forearm, hadn't hurried to move it either, he thought, but maybe that was because he had put his arm in a good place to get it backed into.

Still. . . .

Well, Taylor hadn't been sure. If he'd been sure, he would have thought of a way before now to see her. He'd been considering a casual way, safe, where if he had been wrong it would only look like the courtesy an ad man might show one of the people he was responsible for sponsoring. And the fact that they were neighbors in King's Neck was almost enough reason in itself. But, hell, who would believe that?

She was at the glass door, coming in, Emily stepping back.

"Hello, Gilly," he said.

"God, don't call me that," she said. "It sounds like some Lake Michigan fish."

"You use it on the radio," Taylor said.

"Well, *you* don't have to use it," she said. "You pay me pretty well to use a name like that on the radio. I'm on my own time now."

On your own time, Taylor. . . .

"Sit down," he said. "You want some coffee?"

Still standing, Gillian reached into her bag and pulled out a copy of the *New York Times*. She thrust it at him in much the manner of the Baron with the *Ladies Home Journal*.

"Have you read this?" she said.

"Sure," Taylor said. "Sure I've read it. What part?"

"*This* part," she said. "This part where their smart-assed critic rips me up."

"I didn't get that far," Taylor said.

"Pablum for breakfast," she said. "The worst show on morning radio. Makes you strangle on your coffee it's so bad."

"Hmmmm." Taylor said.

"Hmmmmm hell," Gillian said. "Do you advertise in this paper?"

"Gillian, everyone advertises in this paper."

"No more," she said. "I don't want you to put any more advertising in the *Times* until that critic loses his job."

"Well, now," Taylor said. "That may not be too easy. No one tells the critics what to write."

"Then, I suppose"—Gillian was still standing—"I'd better go see Baron Morgan directly."

"Well, now," Taylor said. "There's no need to bother him today. Why don't you just sit down and have some coffee? Let's us talk about it."

Gillian sat down, crossing her legs, her sand-colored dress riding up, showing Taylor a nice three inches above those good knees.

"I've been meaning to call you," Taylor Hawkes said.

"You should have," Gillian said.

"About tennis . . . about playing tennis. I couldn't remember whether your husband played."

"No," Gillian said. "No, he's stopped. A bad back . . . or a bad knee or a bad wrist or a bad something. I forget exactly which. He's stopped almost everything." She looked directly at Taylor. "But I still play."

"Fine," Taylor said. "We'll play."

"Fine," Gillian said.

Her eyes left Taylor. She was looking over his shoulder, through the secretaries' office and toward the front driveway.

"What *are* they doing?" she asked. "That car, the back. . . ."

Taylor looked out. "Oh, they're rollin' him in. You've never seen the Baron's car?"

Taylor had watched it a hundred times; hell, a thousand times; he'd watched it so many times he wasn't even aware any more that he was watching it. Louie, the Baron's chauffeur, was out there now, the same as always, letting down the back of the custom-built car. It dropped down just like the tailgate of a truck, except that it reached the pavement, making a ramp. The Baron, in his wheelchair, was back about twenty feet, getting ready to roll, getting ready to build up the speed that would take him into the car. And Old Lady Minnie, the Baron's secretary for forty-one years, was out there, same as always, her arms waving like an out-of-control kite, trying to help roll the Baron and he was waving back, same as always, saying, if you were out there so you could hear him, "Get back, Minnie! Get back, Louie!" Nobody rolled Baron Edward Osborne Morgan; he could make it himself.

"My God," Gillian said. "He almost sailed through the front seat."

"Naw," Taylor said. "He can stop it on a dime. That old bastard can really roll. He's just got to get up that speed to make the ramp. That's his special big-wheeled, high-speed chair."

"God," Gillian said.

"He's got about five wheelchairs," Taylor said. "Got a black one over at the estate. And a silver one for parties. And a couple around here. Got a little business wheelchair . . . comes down here in it. . . . I swear to God that's the fastest little wheelchair I ever saw in my whole life."

Gillian tapped a cigarette on her long left thumb-nail and Taylor stood up. As he extended a match, she cupped her hand on his, letting her hand linger, he thought, after he had blown out the flame. He looked out into the big room and saw that three of the girls had turned around and were watching him.

"You're kin to the Baron, aren't you?" Gillian said.

"No," Taylor said. He looked out again at the room. "No, it's my wife. She's his great-grandniece."

"Oh, yes," Gillian said. "I remember that. I met your wife at the station. . . . I can't remember her name."

"Sarah."

"Oh, yes," Gillian said. "I knew it was something from the Bible. She seemed nice."

"Thanks," Taylor said.

"Yes, I remember all of it now," Gillian said. "Some-body . . . a woman . . . she'd been drinking an awful lot . . . said the Baron just adores Sarah and that you wouldn't be where you are unless. . . ."

"Well, that's a bunch of . . .," Taylor cut himself off. "I . . . ah, the hell with those bitches."

"Why, it made you mad," Gillian said. "I'm sorry. I thought it was funny."

"Yeah," Taylor said. "Funny."

Gillian stood up and walked around Taylor's desk. Her arm coming up slowly, her fingertips brushing across Taylor's jaw.

"I *am* sorry," she said. "It did make you mad." She stepped back and looked at him. "Well, I've done enough. I won't bother anyone about this smart-assed critic. Call me."

"No," Taylor said. "I mean, no, don't go. We'll talk about it." He stood, fumbling for a cigarette, try-ing to think of something. "Gillian, could we . . . Gil-lian . . . walk down to the Baron's office?" He indicated his own three walls of glass. "Quieter there. Great pictures, too. The Baron in the Spanish-American War and World War I and playing polo. And some of his most successful campaigns."

"Fine," Gillian said. "Only I have the strangest feeling you're going to show me those computers before we're finished."

They walked through the door of Taylor's office. Taylor paused at Emily's desk.

"I'm not expecting any calls, Emily," he said.

"Yes, Mr. Hawkes"—she always called him Mr. Hawkes in front of outsiders.

Not a way in the damn world except to go right through the middle of the room, Taylor thought. Together they started. Pointing to the adding machines, Taylor said, "The adding machines." And, further on, "Account executives' offices." Trying to walk not fast, but not slow, and make it casual. Feeling eyes fixed on his back as they passed girl after girl, and seeing the ones still in front of them and knowing that they were waiting for him to pass with Gillian Blake so they could stare, too. And the account executives peering out of their cubbyholes. Those eyes must be eating up the backs of Gillian's calves and eating up those good muscles of hers under the sand-colored skirt, rolling a little, flexing gently, as Taylor knew those muscles would be.

"Lots of various campaigns being mapped out here," Taylor said. "Lots of various campaigns." He motioned. "This way." They were out of the room and into the hallway and now were standing, together, in front of the locked doors to the Baron's office.

Reaching into his pocket, Taylor brought out a chain and fumbled through the keys to every part of his life: front door of home, ignition key of station wagon, office key, trunk key of Buick, garage door, office desk, safe deposit box, ignition key of Buick. . . . Somehow, he was afraid that Gillian Blake was going

to say, Ah, the hell with it, Taylor, don't bother . . .
and then he found, and inserted into the lock, the key
to the Baron's office.

"There you go," he said, opening the door, stepping
aside, then quickly shutting the door behind them. He
pointed. "Those are the pictures I told you about."

"Yes," Gillian Blake said. "And that's a wall and
that's a chair and that's a rug." She looked at him.
"My, you're nervous, Taylor."

"Well, I wanted you to see the pictures," Taylor
said. "There's the Baron in the Spanish-American
War . . . and there he is on his hundredth birthday,
when we shot off a cannon on the front lawn . . . and
there's . . . well, there're lots of them. And the big
campaigns."

He reached over her, pointing, his arm across her
shoulders.

"My, God, you're a countryman," Gillian said, turning, facing him, standing so close that her breasts
touched his chest. "Isn't there anything else you wanted
to show me, Taylor?"

He pulled her against him, feeling her stomach and
thighs press into him. His right hand was on her back,
his left at the curve of her waist-buttocks, and his
mouth was starting at her neck.

"You'll rumple my dress, Taylor."

"Sweet Jesus, Gillian, I've got. . . ."

"But I'll take it off," she said.

With her right hand she ran down the zipper and
in one motion, it seemed, she pulled the dress over
her head. She stood before him in a half slip and a
bra. Now, looking at him she unhooked the bra, bringing it free in her hand, standing erect, her breasts not
large, but firm and white and straight out.

"Why don't you loosen your tie, Taylor?"

Taylor stopped staring and pulled at his tie as she
walked across the room. She stopped beside the Baron's glass-topped desk, and on the desk she laid her
dress, smoothing it out full length. She put the bra

on top of the dress. And then the half slip. She was standing nude when she picked up the twin pictures in the single frame.

"This is the Baron," she said, "and your wife?"

"Yes," Taylor said. "Yes."

Gillian put the pictures back on the desk, placing them at an angle that left the Baron and Taylor's wife looking out across the room. Looking out at Gillian and Taylor.

"Taylor," she said, "do you love your wife?"

"Good God, Gillian, how do I know?"

He was undressed now. And he was moving across the room to her, sucking in his stomach and wishing he still had the old suntan. Gillian wasn't even looking at him.

"And this is the Baron's . . . what did you call it? . . . *business* wheelchair? The fast one?" Naked, she stood as easily as if she were in Lord and Taylor's at 11:30 in the morning, trying on a new dress. She picked her bra from the desk and hung it across the left shoulder of the Baron's fast wheelchair. "Wear it with honor," she said.

"Don't forget that goddam thing," Taylor said, "and leave it hanging there."

"Taylor, are you *afraid* of the Baron?"

"Ah, hell, Gillian, just remember to get the thing. I've got to be back here in the morning to explain something the Baron'll be madder'n hell about, and it's going to be bad enough without a goddam brassiere hanging on his fast wheelchair."

Gillian picked her panties from the desk and hung them on the right shoulder of the wheelchair. Taylor caught her from the side and pulled her around, feeling her body against his. Walking her backward, he moved her in front of him. "If you're so interested in the Baron's chair, Gillian, I'll show you something else." With three steps, he maneuvered her and then pressed her over and came down on top of her, feeling her legs come up.

"This is the Baron's vibrating chair," he said. "When he's not sitting in that goddam fast wheelchair, he sits in this one and . . . vibrates."

It was also a reclining chair, tufted brown, with a footrest, and Taylor dug at Gillian's breasts with his face and mouth.

"Start it up," Gillian said.

"Godawmighty," Taylor said. "Are you talking about the chair?"

"If it vibrates, then start it," she said. "Or do you want me to get up and do it?"

Taylor leaned over the side, feeling for the buttons and gears. With his right hand, he pushed a lever and he felt them start, he and Gillian and the tiny wire-nerves in the chair that made it vibrate. And he was inside of Gillian, too, now, warm. And it was Gillian and he and the tiny wire-nerves and he and Gillian and Gillian and the tiny wire nerves and he and Gillian and he and he and he and Gillian and He and He and GILLIAN and HE and GILLIAN and HE . . . and HE. . . . and he . . . and he and Gillian . . . and gillian. And gillian.

The chair, its fabric crinkly against Taylor's side as he rolled over, was still vibrating. He reached over, feeling for the lever.

"Leave it alone," Gillian said quietly. "It feels good."

As they lay there, with the left side of Taylor's body against Gillian, he could feel the vibrations of the tiny wire-nerves. On his right side, the vibrations were direct. On his left, coming first through Gillian, they were soft.

"You're good, Taylor," she said. Gillian realized, with a start, that it was the first sincere compliment she had paid a man since the beginning. She was quiet, reflective, the lines on her face easy. "Did you like me?"

"Damn knows," Taylor said. "You're something *else*, Gillian. How do I tell you? How do you describe it?"

Unconsciously, his hand went toward his chest for a cigarette and then over the arm of the chair, as if he were reaching out toward the lamp table at home, the lamp table that separated Sarah's bed from his own.

"Why do men want to smoke afterward?" Gillian said.

"I don't know," Taylor said. "But you sure to God do. I guess if you didn't smoke, you wouldn't want to. But if you smoke, you sure to God want to."

Taylor got up, going across to his coat to get a cigarette, and wondering how he looked to her from the back, naked. He brought her a cigarette, too, and they lay there together in the vibrating chair, smoking and not talking.

Lightly, Gillian kissed Taylor on the neck and then on his chest.

"You're good, Taylor."

"I'll tell you one thing," Taylor said. "I've never felt so good in this office, not in the past fourteen years."

Again Gillian kissed Taylor on the chest and then, pushing with her hands, she was standing, walking toward her clothes. Taylor followed her. On the desk he could see the pictures of his wife and the Baron, both watching him, and they both seemed angry. He wondered how they liked him naked.

Gillian picked her bra from the left shoulder of the Baron's wheelchair, started to stretch her arms through the straps, but Taylor pulled her to him. She held the bra now in her right hand and, as her arms went around him, Taylor felt the bra skid once, gently, against his back as it slipped to the floor. Carefully, he lowered her back into the wheelchair.

With Gillian's arms around him, her body there just below him, Taylor Hawkes spun the wheelchair away from the wall. In the open room, on the deep green carpet, he gave a push with his foot and tried

to jump aboard, as he'd jumped as a child on a rolling scooter.

"The old sonofabitch," he said.

They hit the brown leather couch and came to a
stop there.

"My God, Taylor!"

He came down on her, pressing her legs apart,
against the arms of the chair, and feeling his knees
driving against the wheels. Almost. His knees off the
wheels, closer, and he was there now, there, but they
were rolling again.

"Goddam!"

"Make it stop rolling, Taylor!"

With his foot, he drove the chair into the angle
between the couch and the wall and lunged. "Taylor!
Oh, Taylor!" Gently, rhythmically, the chair skidded,
forward, backward, gently rhythmically.

Taylor heard it, didn't hear it, thought he heard
it, thought he didn't hear it—the click of the lock at
his back. The click of the lock and no other sound
as the rubber tires of another wheelchair moved silently across the deep green carpet. Glancing up,
Taylor saw him, saw the Baron, rolling toward them.
And now braking.

"Well, Taylor." The Baron.

"God, Taylor, don't stop!" Gillian.

And now all of them the three of them!

"Taylor! Taylor!" This was Gillian.

"Dammit, Taylor, if you break my chair. . . ."

"Now, Gillian! NOW! Gillian, oh, Gillian!"

For a moment Taylor lay there. And then, slowly,
they rose from the wheelchair, he and Gillian.

She made no effort to hurry or to cover herself. She
walked to the spot where she had dropped her bra on
the floor and bent to pick it up. The Baron, in his
black suit, with his round, silver head cocked slightly,
turned the chair an inch or two, Taylor thought, to
watch her walk.

And then the chair and the black suit and the round silver head were directed again at Taylor.

"In a wheelchair," the Baron said softly. "That's *something*, Taylor." He rolled his own chair six inches backward and six inches forward. "Well, Taylor, you won't have to explain the Honest ad tomorrow. I'll mail you your check." His voice was still even, quiet. "And I'll have a car pick up Sarah tonight."

"Baron," Taylor began, "if you. . . ."

"Good evening, Taylor." The Baron was starting to roll. Then he paused, a last look at Gillian. She had picked up the bra but she hadn't put it on. In her right hand, it swung at her knees.

"You have a fine body, young lady," the Baron said.

"Thank you, Baron Morgan," Gillian Blake replied. Stretching, she put her arms through the brassiere straps. The Baron made no effort to leave. "You don't live in King's Neck, do you, Baron?"

"Old Brookville," he said.

"Too bad," Gillian said. "I was going to ask why don't you roll over and see me sometime."

Gilly: *Did you ever stop to realize how everything
has become sexier these days, Billy? You know, movies, books, magazines.*

Billy: *I know what you mean. And without being
a prude, I think it's something we have to watch carefully. Because in some cases, it borders on, well, smut.*

Gilly: *Exactly.*

ANSEL VARTH

Ansel Varth walked as though he should have had a
staff in his hand and a tribe of Israelites trailing him.
It was, Gilly thought, bizarre in a man in his early
thirties. There was a grotesque quality about him that
had aroused Gilly's curiosity—and, concomitantly, her
libido. She needed something different. Ernie Miklos's
ice cubes, Paddy Madigan's mini-member, Arthur
Franhop's aberrant innocence, Joshua Turnbull's
flying leap—all these encounters had left Gilly jaded.
She was looking for a pick-me-up.

She had noticed Ansel Varth about the streets of
King's Neck. She had seen him standing beside the
gasoline pump in the Shell station, seemingly ab-
sorbed in the roll of the high-test meter. She had
glimpsed him leaving his home on Frigate Lane with
his plump little wife beside him. And she had seen
him sometimes at the post office. She had heard that
Varth was an accountant who worked out of his home,

and he apparently conducted much of his business by mail. It was at the post office that Varth was at his most grotesque. When he approached the slots, he had the furtive quality of a small boy who had dirtied himself and had decided to brazen it out by walking as if the lump in his trousers did not exist.

They reached the slots at the same time, and Gilly made contact. "Excuse me," she said, brushing against him. "I want to send this to Manhattan. Do I use the out-of-town slot, or the local slot?"

"The out-of-town slot," Varth answered, speaking with the careful enunciation of a second-rate comedian attempting to imitate a Harvard homosexual. "The out-of-town slot is for all mail not to be delivered within the unincorporated area of King's Neck. Any mail that is to be delivered within King's Neck goes into the local slot. I usually use the out-of-town slot."

Bingo! The voice was unmistakable. There was simply no question about it. Gillian knew immediately where she had heard it before. Gotcha you bastard, she thought. Then she started laughing. Of all people, she thought, Ansel Varth. Why he even wore a homburg.

"Well, I'll tell you one thing," she said. "I never thought it would be you."

"I beg your pardon," Varth said.

"Come on, you know who I am. I'm Gillian Blake. God knows you've spoken to me enough times."

"I don't believe I've had the pleasure, Mrs. Blake. I'm Ansel Varth from Frigate Lane."

Gillian stared at Varth and trapped his eyes. She smiled her sweetest smile. "Oh, we've had the pleasure," she said. "I've got a pair of big ones, and you're Jack the Fucker."

Varth's mail bag plopped to the floor. He looked as if he were going to cry.

"What was it you told me the last time you called?" said Gilly. "Oh yes, you came to a point. And you said I was a whore.

Now Varth looked as if he might be sick.

"Don't worry," Gillian said. "It was kind of nice, having a crank caller, all my own. Besides, you've heard of Madame Pompadour. Well, I'm her cousin, Lady Asshole."

"Please . . . ," said Varth.

"Don't worry," she said.

"You mean you're not. . . ."

"No," said Gillian. "Actually, it interests me."

Ansel Varth took off his eyeglasses. "Holy shit!" he said.

"That's better," Gilly said. "Why didn't you tell me it was you making all those phone calls? We would have met long before this."

"Son of a bitch!" said Varth.

Varth hastily stuffed his mail into the slots, and asked if they could go somewhere. Gillian suggested a motel. She was having a marvelous time. Ansel Varth might be just the tonic she was looking for. She was going to have this coitus-crazed accountant make an entry. Maybe even a double entry.

Varth loosened up during the drive to the motel. He was still talking as they entered the room. His conversation was full of words like cunt and snatch. Gilly was enchanted. Nobody had ever talked dirty that way to her before.

"I'll tell you one thing," she said. "You certainly don't sound like an accountant."

"What do you mean?"

"Oh, you can enunciate like one, but you'll have to admit that your conversation isn't what you'd expect from an accountant."

"What do I sound like?" he asked.

Gillian laughed. "Like a crank-caller," she said. "Or like someone who writes dirty books."

Varth, who had just shucked off his topcoat, dropped on the bed and stared at her.

"Cocksucker!"

"What's the matter?" she said.

"You're fantastic. You must be psychic or something."

"I don't understand you, lover."

"Well that's what I do, don't you see?"

"I'm afraid you're losing me."

"That's what I do. I write dirty books."

"You what!"

"I write dirty books! I mean, that's it. That's how I really make a living."

Now it was Gillian's turn to drop to the bed. "You're putting me on."

"No, no. Honestly. I really do."

"Son of a bitch!" This time it was Gillian. She shook her head. She had the look of a woman whose bra had just been snapped open. What a tonic, she thought.

Gillian had never met a professional pornographer before, and she questioned Varth almost as if she were doing an interview. For his part, Varth seemed genuinely relieved that somebody knew his secret. For the first time in his life, he was telling a stranger about his hidden life, and his voice filled with pride. "No one suspects," he said. "No one. Not even that idiotic wife of mine. She really thinks I'm an accountant, that I take care of all my work through the mails. Actually, I haven't been an accountant for years. I don't keep books. I write them."

Gilly sat close to him and nibbled his ear. "An honest-to-goodness pornographer," she said.

Ansel Varth shrugged with pride. "The best in the business," he said.

"It's a pleasure to meet you," said Gillian. "Listen, you'll have to autograph one of your books for me."

"Certainly," said Varth. "With my prick."

Gillian laughed. "Beautiful," she said.

"You're some piece of ass," Varth said, as he watched Gilly's blouse come off.

"It must be fascinating work," Gillian said, slipping

unconsciously into her radio style. "I mean, where do you get all your ideas?"

"Nature," said Varth. "From nature. Like any other writer, I draw from the human condition."

"I should have guessed," Gilly said.

"My pen never runs dry," said Varth.

"I can imagine," said Gilly. "But what started you? I mean, what was the catalyst?"

"An interesting question," said Varth. "I would have to say that it was my wife."

"Your wife?" said Gillian, as she took off her skirt.

"Yes. See, when I first married Astrid, that's my wife, I was in the Navy, and I used to bang the hell out of her when I was home on leave. And when I first got out of the service, she still gave me all I wanted. We even did it in a night club once, with her sitting on my lap. You know, in rhythm to the music—as I remember, it was a rhumba. Another time we did it in a rocking chair, and once we even did it in a snowbank."

"Mmmm," said Gilly. "All I've ever done in the snow is ski."

"You didn't have the right poles," said Varth.

"But I still don't see how your wife inspired your career," said Gilly.

"Oh, yes. Well, the thing was that, after a few years, she started turning me off. I guess she never really liked it that much, if you know what I mean. And when she did screw, she was like a cold clam. It was like playing with myself. In fact, I did start playing with myself, and that was better than Astrid. That's when I wrote my first dirty poetry. It was a four-line poem that went: 'I don't care if I go crazy/ long as I can beat my daisy/ four times eight is thirty-two/ three more pulls and I'll be through.'"

"That's got a nice rhythm," said Gilly.

"Yes," said Varth. "It's a beater's meter. But that still didn't satisfy me. As a matter of fact, I never was really satisfied. The thing is that even when I was

banging Astrid all the time, I wasn't necessarily enjoy-
ing it that much. Before Astrid, there were just a
Negro woman in Port-au-Prince who looked at me
as if I were a flea, and an old lady in a West Side
hotel who had a breast missing. And I guess you would
have to count Mr. Bagadello, my home room teacher
in junior high school."

"Yes," said Gilly. "I think early sex experiences are
especially rewarding."

"It's amazing how you understand these things,"
said Varth. "Well, to keep from drawing it out, I became bored with masturbation. And I found that I
had become quite shy in terms of personal contact. I
was all right on the telephone, but I never really did
anything. Anyway, I started writing stories for kicks.
Then I got the idea of selling them. I put ads in the
right magazines, and began building up a mailing
list. One thing led to another, and I met Solly Madchen."

Gillian had hooked a hand under Varth's trouser
cuff and was caressing his left calf. My God, she
thought, he wears garters. Then the name brought her
up short.

"Who?" she said.

"Solly Madchen."

"You mean the Solly Madchen?"

"That's him," said Varth.

"No kidding," said Gillian. "He's the pervert the
police are looking for."

"I know," said Varth. "But they'll never find him.
Old Solly. What a character! You know where he is?
He's hiding out in a kibbutz in Israel. No fooling.
Old Solly bought his own kibbutz, and for all I know
he's back in business. He's probably trying to sell cola-
flavored hormones to the Arabs."

"I forget the whole case now," said Gilly. "Why
was it the police were after him?"

"It was the LSD thing," said Varth. "That was
strictly Solly's operation. He mixed LSD with Span-

ish Fly. We were netting close to $10,000 a week on it, but I always told him there would be trouble. That's dynamite. The thing blew apart when a woman in Corpus Christi impaled herself on a fire hydrant, and a kid in upstate New York mutilated himself in a milking machine. Luckily, the police only got Solly's name."

Gilly was up now, removing her pants, and Varth's eyes fastened on her golden triangle. "Now the business is all mine," he said. "I have outlets in thirty cities. But I stick to books and movies. My first book was called *The Captain's Wife*. It was a classic. The captain is a sea captain who gives his wife a German shepherd pup just before he leaves on a long voyage. By the time the pup is eight months old, he is getting down on her. You can imagine what the pup is doing to her when he's full grown. And then I wrote a book about a wandering gypsy who travels around the countryside with six earrings in his foreskin."

Gilly was on the bed now, stretched out, her naked body beginning the motions that had become second nature to her.

"Another book I wrote," said Varth, "it was about this squirrel monkey who had an enormous dick. This monkey's keeper used to take him around to bridge clubs and charge the housewives for his services."

"Shhh," said Gilly. "That's enough for now."

Varth slowly took his clothes off, folding each garment neatly on a chair. Then he stood nude alongside the bed.

"Come on," said Gilly.

Ansel Varth, pornographer, never moved. Suddenly, he turned his head away.

"Come on," Gilly said again.

Varth shivered. "I can't," he whispered. "I can't."

"You're Jack the Fucker and I'm Lady Asshole," she said.

"No," he said. "I'm Jack the Phony. I can't. Don't you understand? I haven't had a woman since I stopped doing it with Astrid. All I do is write books and make phone calls. I can't get it up any other way."

Gilly made a brief visual examination. He was telling the truth. The poor bastard was positively flaccid. "Come to Gilly," she said reaching for it.

Nothing.

"Poor Jack the Fucker," Gilly said.

"Oh God!" Varth yelled. He leaped away, ran to a dresser and furiously started opening drawers.

"What's the matter?" Gilly cried.

"I'm looking for a pencil," he said. "Pencil and paper. I told you, all I can do is write books."

"Look," Gillian said, holding out her nipples. "I got a pair of big ones."

"I can't," Varth screamed. "I can't get the goddamn thing up!" He was still looking through the drawers.

Gilly tried to trigger him with words. "Cunt!" she yelled.

"Pecker!"

"Dick!"

"Suck!"

Varth had found a pencil and was jabbing at the air with it. "Paper!" he screamed. "Where's the hell's the paper?"

Just like that, the answer hit Gillian. "Ansel!" she shouted. "There's a way."

"What?"

"I know how to do it."

"No. No. I can't get it up."

"You can, Ansel. You can. We'll act out a story." Varth looked at her.

"Yes," she said. "We'll act out a story."

"How?"

"Well," Gillian was thinking fast. "Let's make believe that I'm a lady chimpanzee and you're a big horny camel."

Varth dropped his pencil.

"See," shouted Gilly. "I'm a chimpanzee." She

scratched herself under the arm and chattered. "See."

Varth saw. He leaned over and loped toward her as if he were indeed a desert beast. "I'm a camel!" he shouted. "I'm a camel."

Gilly hopped around chattering.

"I'm getting it up!" Varth yelled. "I'm getting it up."

Gilly chattered faster.

"I'm a camel!" Varth screamed. "I'm a camel!"

"Hump me!" Gilly shrieked. "Hump me!"

Varth was on her, grunting, gasping, humping. They heaved together on the white sheets faster and faster and harder and harder. Ansel turned to thunder, and the surf broke warm and dark on Gilly's beach. Again, it broke. And again.

Two hours later, Ansel Varth dropped off Gillian Blake at her parked car near the King's Neck Post Office. He told her that he was mad about her, that he couldn't wait to see her again, that she had changed his whole life. He said that Gilly had given him fresh inspiration. He was a real man. This time, he would surely write the great American dirty novel.

"I'll call you tomorrow," he said.

"Sure," Gilly said. "Sure."

As he drove away, Varth affectionately made an obscene gesture at Gilly. She laughed, and then she turned away from her car and walked into the post office, where she slipped into a telephone booth. "Hello," she said in a disguised falsetto voice after she had reached her party. "Is this police headquarters? Fine. Are you still looking for Solly Madchen's partner?"

EXCERPT FROM "THE BILLY & GILLY SHOW," MAY 4TH

Gilly: I'd have to agree with you, Billy. Fidelity is the key to a successful marriage.

Billy: Yes, it may sound corny, but when I read about all these wife-swapping clubs and such, I wonder what the world's coming to.

Gilly: I know, and the ideas some of our young people have about, well, sex. I mean, it's almost as if they advocate promiscuity.

Billy: I suspect that there are more moral people around than you think. It's just that the others get all the publicity.

Gilly: You may have something there. And I'll tell you something else. The men who do philander, well they're the ones with problems. I think they doubt their own virility.

Billy: My wife, the psychiatrist.

Gilly: No, really. Actually, I don't think there's anything more attractive than a truly moral man.

MELVIN CORBY

The afternoon sun caressed his face, drawing its golden fingers across his neck. In his mind, Melvin Corby was bronzed, muscled, a man-God behind the wheel of a Lotus-Climax at Le Mans. The Formula One motor throbbed and roared with loin-tingling power as he dominated the turns, conquered the straightaways. Women watched with excitement—the sun glinting on their tanned shoulders and the down-curves of their full breasts. Gillian Blake was in the front row, stretched forward on the tiptoes of her nylon-clad legs; her bust and behind snugly sheathed in white, her face eager, her pink tongue peeking out of her parted lips.

RRRRRR. RRRR. RRR. ROWR. ROWP. His power mower stalled, and the daydream disappeared in a kaleidoscope of splintered images. Gillian, he thought. Gillian. Gillian. Gil-li-an. Gilly. Oh, Gilly, Gilly, Gilly. He was still excited as he got off the power mower and faced the fact that he was out of gas. Melvin Corby paid a gardener to take care of most of the landscaping, but running the ride-on mower was a treat he reserved for himself. It was one of Melvin's special joys; the power mower represented a pleasure he could revel in openly. Sitting astride the mower, Melvin Corby—myopic, curly-haired, thin-shouldered, soft-bellied—was somebody. The power mower symbolized his material, if heavily mortgaged, achievement—the front-to-back split-level home and the half-acre that went with it. The house had cost $32,850—about $6,000 more than it was worth, but he was paying for the address. King's Neck. 69 Selma Lane, King's Neck. The builder had named the street after a daughter; probably, thought Melvin, in honor of her bathmitzvah. He wondered if it bothered the goyim who dominated King's Neck that the builder was a Jew.

It was some address, all right. King's Neck. It meant something. Last winter Melvin and his wife, Myrna, had followed the sun to Miami Beach. They had spent two weeks in that fabled land of papaya juice and potato knishes. Well, it had been worth every cent they had spent on the house to be able to say, "Yes, we live on the Island. King's Neck." When you said King's Neck, people looked up. People paid attention. They figured you were somebody. It didn't matter that Melvin lived in the southern section of King's Neck, that his property had once been part of a potato field, that there was a Negro slum strip on the edge of town less than two miles away. It was still King's Neck. An address like that, it was instant status. It was something you did for your children. In his case, for your child. David was only seven years old, and already he was going to a place where they taught horseback riding. Imagine, his son riding a horse. Only in America. My boy takes horseback-riding lessons.

It annoyed Melvin that his mother wasn't impressed by this. "Fancy, schmancy," his mother had said during one of their phone conversations. "Who needs it? Better he should get good marks." His mother still lived in the four-room apartment in Brooklyn in which he had grown up. Melvin was a good son; he called her every few weeks. He had even offered to come and get her one weekend and bring her out to see the house and David, but she had refused. "So what'll you tell the fancy neighbors? My name is Corby, and this is my mother, Mrs. Korbinsky?"

"Don't be ridiculous, ma," he had said, relieved by her refusal.

"Don't worry," she had answered. "I wouldn't embarrass you or Miss High and Mighty. Sadie Korbinsky don't go where she's not wanted. You could give me a million dollars, I wouldn't come."

Miss High and Mighty was Myrna. His mother and Myrna had never gotten along. "A Jewish girl who don't know enough to save chicken fat," was the way Mrs. Korbinsky had characterized her daughter-in-law. Whereas Myrna said that Mrs. Korbinsky, despite living in Brooklyn, was the "most East Side person" she had ever met.

"After all, Melvin," Myrna had once explained. "she simply refuses to change. You know I'm not class conscious. I mean how could I be? Doesn't my own

mother play mah-jongg? So it's not that. It's just that
your mother refuses to fit in. She acts sort of—well let's
face it, she acts kikey."

Myrna, of course, didn't play mah-jongg. She played
bridge. She also belonged to the PTA, she was in a
volleyball league at adult education, and she was a
member of the King's Neck Garden Club. Melvin was
extremely proud of the way she was active in the civic
life of King's Neck. She was making sure that they
fitted into the community.

You had to hand it to Myrna, thought Melvin.
Myrna Gold from Forest Hills, the dentist's daughter
whom Melvin had drilled at Grossinger's. The first
night, before they had even finished the peach soup,
they had discovered their mutual interests—books,
music, the fact that they were both Democrats. Later,
they had cha-chaed together and that was it. Her
parents were fine people; oh, maybe her mother was a
little overbearing, but after all Myrna's father was a
dentist. And the Golds had helped out financially in
a number of ways; they had even helped with the
house. And he loved Myrna, he owed her a lot. Besides, after nine years of marriage you know that nothing is perfect, that the thing is to do the best you can.
Myrna was dark, intense, skinny; she was a good host-
ess and she could talk about Dostoevsky and Camus.
At first, it had been her very nervousness that had attracted him—all that tension. It had held the promise
of explosion, but that had never happened. Still, you
kept trying. Even after nine years. He'd had great
hopes for the two weeks in Miami Beach. A second
honeymoon, he'd told Myrna. Just the two of them.
But it hadn't worked out. Maybe it had been Myrna's
bathing suit. A bikini, but she had looked bony in it,
she had looked—well, neuter. And there was a string-
iness about her hair. It hadn't helped the way she
looked that there had been a couple of real good-look-
ers at the hotel. There had been one who had looked
a little like Gillian Blake—a slim blonde with a good

bust. He had watched her at the pool, at the beach, and in the dining room. In Melvin's daydreams, she had seduced him in her cabana—he imagined that she wore black lace lingerie and used alluring perfume. And, also, that she was incredibly skilled in sex. When he was on top of Myrna in their hotel room, he had tried to visualize the blonde. One night, the fiction had succeeded and he had functioned well. But usually it had been the same as at home—no good. The body beneath him was neither soft nor firm, and they achieved little that was mutual except perspiration. Afterward, when he was in the bathroom with a men's magazine that he had hidden in his luggage, he thought he heard Myrna crying. But he didn't let on. Nothing was perfect. And it wasn't his fault. And anyway, they had so much together that was good—the house, David, common interests. Besides, sex was overrated. It wasn't everything. And there were always the men's magazines—a harmless preoccupation.

He had read about men with worse fetishes than men's magazines. Whips, fruit jars, all sorts of things. He was no nut. He was a professional man. A lawyer. A junior member of a New York law firm who specialized in real estate work. At the garden club's party the previous weekend, Gillian Blake—oh Gilly, Gilly, Gilly!—had asked him about it. "It must take a great deal of intelligence," she had said. Imagine. Gillian Blake! The Gillian Blake who was on the radio, and whose picture turned up in the newspapers. He and Myrna had seen the Blakes around King's Neck, but they had rarely talked to them. After all, the Blakes were celebrities. You couldn't just walk up and talk to them.

But at the party, Gillian had been very nice. She had seemed very natural to Melvin. Of course, her husband, William Blake, had been a little snobbish. But then he had been a little high. "Corby?" he had said. "That's not a Jewish name, is it?" Melvin had blushed. He had tried to stammer a reply, but Gillian had simply taken his arm and walked him away.

"Don't mind Billy," she said said. "That's the Princeton in him. I mean, he still sends to some silly store there for his sports jackets."

Myrna had smiled at him from across the room, obviously pleased that he was talking to Gillian Blake. Other people had noticed, also. Melvin remembered how self-conscious he had been. In heels, Gillian Blake was about an inch taller than he was. He had found himself staring at her breasts, which had seemed to be beckoning to him through that low-backed green dress. She had leaned in front of him to put down a drink, and her hair, tawny and sweet-smelling, had brushed his face. He had been able to see that she was wearing a strapless white bra. Just talking to her, he had gotten excited. There had been a smile at the edge of her lips as if she knew. She was the most provocative woman he had ever seen. And she was very intelligent, she knew all about existentialism. She said she had majored in Far Eastern religions and existentialism at Bard. After she had left him, it had taken a while before Melvin was able to walk across the room.

Now, as he got the gas can and filled his power mower tank, Melvin felt himself becoming excited just thinking about her. What a woman! And those breasts! Melvin shivered as he imagined how she would be in bed. There was nothing wrong with thinking about it; hell, he was only human. And the important thing was that, in nine years of marriage, he had never cheated on his wife. Never. Not once. Unless, of course, you counted the men's magazines in the bathroom, but that wasn't, well, with a person or anything. Besides, he loved Myrna. It was a fact of which he frequently reminded himself. You live with somebody for nine years, and you build something together. He had once heard Gillian Blake say something similar on her radio show; something about the good and bad of everyday life building a solid foundation for marriage. But it was hard to believe that there was anything everyday about Gillian.

Gillian Blake?" said Charlie Rider, when Melvin mentioned that she lived in King's Neck. "Yeah, I've seen pictures of her. Now that's what I'd call a piece of ass. And I bet she throws it around, too." It was Charlie's frequently cited belief that Melvin's faithfulness was doing him a great deal of harm. "What you need," he told Melvin, "is a good piece of ass."

"I never even think about things like that," Melvin had said on one occasion.

"Bullshit," said Charlie. "You think about it, but you're afraid. It's your upbringing. You're a victim of Judeo-Hebraic morality."

"That's nonsensical, besides being redundant," Melvin had said.

"No guts," said Charlie.

"I just don't believe in the double standard," Melvin answered. "I think fidelity should be a part of marriage."

"For chrissakes," Charlie said, "you knock something off and your wife'll respect you a lot more than she does now."

"Listen, I love my wife," said Melvin.

"What the hell has that got to do with it?" said Charlie.

"You don't understand," Melvin had said.

"Love!" said Charlie, and he had practically snorted. "Hey, you don't have to love a woman to bang her. In fact. if you love her you're in trouble. You have to be cool. You never love 'em. You just screw 'em."

"That's disgusting," Melvin had said.

"Bullshit," said Charlie. He said Melvin should get blown. "I bet you never had a good blow job," he said. "What the hell, that's not being unfaithful. It's not like you're getting laid."

Melvin didn't say so, but the idea fascinated him. Sometimes, when he was eyeing women, he stared at their lips and tried to visualize a good blow job. Myrna's lips were thin, and she had a faint mustache. Gillian Blake had firm, mobile lips. They were very sensual.

Melvin filled the power mower's gas tank and started to get back on the seat when the unbelievable happened.

"Hi there, home owner," she called. It was her! It was Gillian Blake!

Melvin got back off the mower. He felt as if he were in a dream. He trembled with excitement as he watched her coming up the walk. She was wearing a clinging white jersey, and white, tapered slacks. The slacks were sufficiently tight to afford him an impression of her love triangle as she came toward him. He just stood there admiring every inch of her.

"Do I really look that good?" she said.

"What?"

"The way you're looking at me. Do I really look that good?"

"Oh, uh. . . . Excuse me." Melvin was stammering.

"Don't apologize," she said. "You're just what the ego ordered."

"Well, uh, you do look very attractive, Mrs. Blake."

"Oh come on," she said, "call me Gilly."

"Gi-Gi-Gilly."

"Mmm, that's better. So, why am I here? Well, I must tell you that I'm being very civic today. I'm absolutely up to my you-know-what in good works. I'm collecting for dementia praecox."

Melvin gaped.

"Hey," she said, "that's a joke, son. Actually, I'm collecting for the National Parapsychology Association."

"Oh," he said. "Well, Myrna, uh my wife, she's not in right now. She's at the beauty parlor."

"We don't need her, do we? You can give me the donation."

"Right. Yes. Sure. Uh. . . , " he said. "Uh, you'll have to pardon me, I just don't seem to be organized today.

I mean, I was getting gas for the mower and everything."

"It's okay," she said. "I understand."

She probably did understand, thought Melvin. She probably understood everything there was to understand. She was wonderful.

Gillian smiled at him, and then started for the house. Melvin walked behind her. It was almost as if her rear end had a mind of its own, the way it moved in the tight, white stretch fabric.

Melvin wondered what reality was, as the object of most of his sex fantasies settled herself on a couch in his living room while he got out the checkbook. "My," she said. "you have a lovely home."

"You and your husband should come over sometime socially," Melvin said.

"Oh, let's not talk about him," she said. "My, isn't that nice." Melvin had given her a check for $25. He rarely gave more than a few dollars to causes but, after all, this was such a worthwhile charity.

"Listen, I'm glad to help," he said.

She leaned back, smiling at him.

"Uh, it certainly was nice talking to you at the Garden Club party," he said.

"Aren't you going to offer me a drink?" she said.

"Yes," he said. "Certainly. I was just about to ask." His voice almost cracked with excitement. "What would you like?"

"A martini. Very dry. Nine to one. Lemon peel."

Melvin bustled about the kitchen making the drinks. Thank God, he and Myrna had started having an occasional martini at home. Of course, he usually made his two to one. Holy Christ! Nine to one! He made enough for a couple of drinks.

Gillian plumped the couch, and motioned to him to sit next to her. "Cheers," she said. Then she laughed. "No. L'Chaim."

They touched glasses. The first swallow brought tears to Melvin's eyes, but he stuck with it. Thank

God, they had Beefeater gin in the house. He had been told that it was the best. He was sure someone as sophisticated as Gillian Blake could tell the difference.

"Really," he said, "you and Mr. Blake should come over some time."

"Please," she said. "I meant what I said before. Let's not talk about him. That would be much too dreary."

"But your husband does seem like an impressive guy."

"Believe me, Mel, you're twice as interesting."

The drink had hit Melvin almost immediately. "You're kidding me," he said.

"No, honestly," she said. She put her hand on his wrist. "I should have married someone like you. What is it they say, a nice Jewish boy?"

"That's right," said Melvin, thinking that nine to one was a perfect ratio. "A nice Jewish boy. Nice Jewish boys make great husbands."

"Ummm, I'll bet they do," she said. "I'll bet they make great lovers, too."

Melvin tried for what he hoped was a nonchalant grin.

She winked. "You know, Mel," she said, "you're a very attractive man."

"Listen," he said, overcome by her nearness and the nine-to-one ratio. "You're the best-looking woman I ever saw."

"Billy never tells me anything like that," she said.

"Well, he should," said Melvin, wondering what a woman like her had ever seen in a jerk like Blake. "You're terrific."

"You're a doll," she said. And now her hand was caressing his wrist. "You're really very nice."

"Not half as nice as you."

"Mel," she said as she stroked his wrist, "I wonder if I could ask you something personal?"

"Ask me anything."

"Have you ever been unfaithful to your wife?"

Melvin blushed. "Well, uh. . . ."

"No, really. Have you?"

He blurted out the truth. "No!"

"Honestly?"

"I haven't. Not ever."

"Really?"

"I'm telling you, it's the truth."

"You honestly never cheated on your wife?"

"No," he said. "I love my wife."

"Sure," she said. "But have you ever cheated on her?"

"No. I told you. No!"

"Isn't that amazing?" she said.

"I guess I sound like a real idiot to you."

"Not at all, Mel. You're a doll. But tell me, why not? Are you afraid?"

"No, it's not that. I mean, I'm not a prude or anything. I just don't think it's right. I don't believe in the double standard."

"Ummm," she said. "You are a challenge."

The martini had anesthetized Melvin; it was as if what was happening couldn't touch him. Or at least, he couldn't feel shock. But his physical feelings were intact. He'd had a stiff one ever since she'd put her hand on his wrist.

"Take your glasses off," she commanded.

He obeyed instantly.

"You have very sensitive eyes," she said. "I'll bet you're a very sensitive man."

RRRRR. "That's Myrna!" Melvin yelled in alarm as he heard the car come up the driveway outside.

"How nice," said Gillian Blake, and suddenly she was pressing herself against him. Melvin responded to her kiss, and she pushed his hand against her breast, and there was all the softness he had ever dreamed of. "Gilly, Gilly," he groaned.

Gillian gently pushed him away as Myrna reached the front door. "You're a sweetie," she said.

How he ever got through the next half hour was a

mystery to Melvin. Gillian told Myrna that she had been canvassing, and that Melvin had offered her a drink. As it turned out, Myrna's major reaction was one of excitement because Gillian Blake had been in her house. "I'm amazed that you had the sense to offer her a drink," Myrna told Melvin afterwards. She laughed. "Although I think you're a little potted. You should be careful, you know you're not much of a drinker."

She asked Melvin what he had talked to Gillian Blake about. He said they had discussed King's Neck and the Blakes's radio program.

"She's a very sexy woman," Myrna said. "But I'm lucky. I know I don't have to worry about you."

That night, Gillian Blake filled Melvin's mind as he huffed over his wife. But Myrna just lay there, a broomstick. He tried to feign orgasm. "I love you," he said. Then he went into the bathroom with a copy of a new men's magazine called *Modern Mammaries*.

Myrna was still awake when he came back to bed. "You made believe," she said.

"No," he said. "I love you." But he was thinking about Gilly, about how she would be in bed. Christ, the way her breasts had felt beneath the jersey. Only he couldn't. It was bad enough that he had gone as far as he had. It was the martini that had made him lose control. And the fact that Gillian, for some reason, was attracted to him. But the way she had felt. And the way she had kissed. He had practically been unfaithful just kissing her.

It was a sleepless night for Melvin as his mind raced and plunged with thoughts of Gillian Blake. Gilly in a bra and panties. Gilly nude. Gilly undulating in front of him. He and Gilly on a tiger skin, with her on top of him. Oh, Gilly, Gilly, Gilly. They were on a balcony overlooking a moon-dappled sea, and she was touching his bare chest with her fingertips. They were in a rickshaw making love as they were pulled through the streets of Shanghai. They were aboard a train rushing through the silent night. They were on a white sand beach with breakers roaring in the distance. Gillian was whispering in his ear. "The trouble with you, Melvin," she was saying, "is that you've never been laid."

"But I have," he was saying. "Ask Myrna."

"Myrna!" The Gillian Blake dominating his imagination was laughing. "Myrna doesn't count."

The next day was Sunday. Melvin was guilt-stricken about what had happened between him and Gillian Blake, but he knew he could never tell Myrna about it. It was something he would always have to live with. It gnawed at him. Usually, he told Myrna everything. The slightest guilt bore him down. He was miserable. He wanted to be nice to Myrna, and he knew he was being nasty. There was no softness to her, no grace. She was annoying. Skinny, nervous, darting, bugging him all the time. He snapped at her, and she told him to watch himself in front of the boy. "I don't know what's gotten into you," she said.

They were sitting on the patio, and the May sun was giving Melvin a headache. He wondered what Gillian Blake was doing, and he thought about what it would be like with her on a patio. Gilly, Gilly. He looked at Myrna and tried to smile. "You're right," he said. "I apologize."

"I'm sorry I yelled at you," she answered.

"It's okay," he said. Damn her. She was wearing an outfit like the one Gillian Blake had worn the day before, but on Myrna it just hung. Melvin got up and went into the house. "I have to go to the bathroom," he said.

He was at his desk the following day, when Gillian Blake called him. Just like that. "Hi sweetie, this is Gilly." Wow!

"Look," he said. "Uh, about what happened Saturday. I, well, I. . . ."

"You enjoyed it," she said.

"Yes, but what I have to say is that, um, well is, uh. . . ."

"Don't say anything. Or better still, tell me at lunch."

"No," he said. "I couldn't, I mean. . . ."

"Don't tease a girl, Mel. I said lunch and I mean lunch." She named a place in the East Fifties. "One o'clock," she said.

They had lunch. It was a French place. Even the vegetables were fancy. Sitting at a table with her, Melvin felt like a million dollars. He could feel the other men in the room looking at him enviously. He found himself drinking a Bloody Mary.

"We can't see each other any more," Melvin said.

"Nonsense," she said.

"You don't understand. I mean, you're the most exciting woman I've ever known."

"Well, what's wrong with that?"

"I know this sounds silly, but I just can't do something like that to my wife."

"I don't want you to do it to your wife," she said. "I want you to do it to me."

Melvin was shaking. He ordered lobster tails, but he was never conscious of tasting them. All he was conscious of was Gillian, who was sensational in a simple black dress with a strand of pearls. He had another Bloody Mary, and lapsed into half-stammers. He couldn't stop looking at her. She had ordered snails, and was popping them into her mouth.

In the taxi on the way back to her office, Melvin told Gillian once more that he couldn't see her again. She smiled. Then she took his hand and stuck it beneath her skirt, moving it up her leg to where the nylon ended and the flesh began. Then she kissed him, and their tongues were inside each other's mouths. Melvin remembered thinking that, if it wasn't for the Bloody Marys, he probably would have come.

"Jeez," the cabbie said afterward, as he dropped

Melvin off at his office. "that was Gillian Blake, wasn't it?"

"Yes," said Melvin.

The cabbie kept staring at him.

"Uh, she's a neighbor," Melvin explained.

That night was worse than the one before. Gilly never left his mind. Myrna had spent a difficult day: She had lost a garden club election, the cleaning girl had gotten sick and David had misbehaved in school. "You've got to deal with him," Myrna said.

"What's wrong with you?"

"You're the father."

"Look, I've had a hard day at the office."

"And what about me? That damn girl. You see how you like cleaning this house."

"Maybe you need a little work. Maybe then you won't be such a goddamn nervous wreck."

"Oh, is that what I am? And what about you? I don't thing you've heard a word I said in the last three days."

"Dammit, Myrna, leave me alone, will you?"

"You really are upset, aren't you?" Myrna said as she looked at him. "All right, I'm sorry I snapped at you. So what's the matter?"

"For crying out loud," Melvin screamed. "Get off my back, will you!"

"Melvin, what is it?"

"Aw, shut the hell up, you skinny bitch!"

Myrna ran upstairs crying. That night, Melvin slept on the playroom couch. Gilly, Gilly. God, but he wanted to make love to her. But he couldn't. He just couldn't. It was wrong. Wrong. It was against everything that mattered. It was, well, immoral. He just hadn't been brought up that way. He was no crazy Gentile. He just couldn't.

Poor Myrna, he thought. He did love her. They had so much else together, so much that was meaningful. But, oh Gilly—the feel of your body, the warmth of your flesh. Oh Gilly, Gil-leeeee.

He called her the following morning from work. "I've got to see you," he said. "I've got to explain to you why it has to end."

"You don't have to explain anything, Mel," she said. "You just have to do what you know you want to do."

"No," he said. "That's just it. I can't. I can't be unfaithful to my wife."

"Sweetie," she said, and her voice was purring into the phone. "Why don't you just shut up?"

"Gilly," Melvin moaned. "Gilly."

"Look," she said, "I'm leaving for King's Neck in an hour." She told Melvin to take an early train and come straight to her house. "And face it, baby," she said. "You're going to get laid."

Melvin Corby was like a somnambulist all the way to King's Neck. When he got into his car at the station, the trance turned into tension. He drove seventy miles an hour all the way to the Blake home. She was waiting in the living room for him—the very incarnation of desire in a diaphanous peignoir, with her hair falling in loose waves to her shoulders, her perfume scenting the room. She was sex, excitement, eternal woman. She was all of Melvin Corby's daydreams rolled into one incredible bundle. She was all the men's magazines he had ever read, all the pieces of ass Charlie Rider had ever talked about. She was Gillian.

Melvin stared wildly at her, his face burning, his hands shaking. No! his mind screamed inside itself. No!

"I can't," he said. "I can't. Don't your understand?"

She was breathing rapidly, her breasts rising and falling beneath the silken gown, her eyes burning into him, her tongue caressing her lips. "Sweetie," she said in a voice that was pure provocation, "do it to me."

"No!" and he was shouting it out loud. "No!"

Slowly, softly, her eyes never leaving him, she undid her robe and let it fall to the floor.

She simply stood there, the embodiment of Melvin's

fantasies—a sex goddess in a black lace bra and panties, bikini-style underthings that overwhelmed Melvin with loin-swelling desire.

"I won't do it!" he shouted. "I won't do it!"

Gillian Blake stood in the center of the room, lithe and soft, the ultimate in ecstasy on a fluffy blue carpet. Then she started moving. First the bra, then slowly, ever so slowly—Oh Christ!—the panties.

"Please," Melvin cried. "Please!"

Her eyes were half closed, her body was alive as she moved toward him, twisting and undulating.

"I won't!" Melvin yelped. "You can't make me!"

She was directly in front of him now, her hands cupping her rose-tipped, thrusting breasts, her thighs and belly moving back and forth, her soft golden muff pulsing to take him.

"No!" Melvin screamed.

She reached out and unzipped him. "Now," she whispered, as her hands stroked and massaged his treacherous organ.

"No!" Melvin yelled. "I love my wife!" He pulled away and ran for the door. He was groaning and sobbing as he galloped down the walk to his car. Somehow he got inside and started the motor. Gunning the car home, he was without coherent thought—his mind was a twisting, turbulent whirlpool. He was still moaning as he rushed into his house. He was a nightmare apparition, his hair wild and his jacket open.

Myrna was at the stove. "Is that you?" she called. "I hope you're in a better mood. The girl is still sick. And David hurt his knee, and. . . ."

Then she saw him. "What in the world?"

Melvin Corby stopped for a moment, and stared at his wife. She was perspiring from the heat of the stove, her hair was in curlers, her eyes bugged at him from behind her glasses, her body was an obstacle course of sharp angles, and the thought of going to bed with her made him sick.

"My God, Melvin," she said. "Zip your pants up!"

Snap! Something broke inside his head, and it seemed to Melvin that the sound must have filled the house. "Goddamn you to hell!" he screamed. Bang! His first punch caught her in the mouth.

Neighbors on Selma Lane heard the shrieking and called the police. They stood outside their houses in groups and watched the police car drive up. Then they watched the ambulance. The ambulances—two of them. One for a battered, bewildered Myrna Corby, the second for the screaming strait-jacketed figure of Melvin Corby.

Gilly: Did you notice the article in Time *this week about homosexuality, Billy?*

Billy: Yes, I did, dear, and it was shocking to find out how rapidly the number of homosexuals in our country is increasing.

Gilly: It certainly makes you wonder about the way we're bringing up our children. I mean, that's when it starts.

Billy: Well obviously, it's an illness, and it should be treated as such.

Gilly: I think the trouble is they haven't found the right way to treat it, yet.

WILLOUGHBY MARTIN

The day was sultry and oppressive. Under the low, thick blanket of clouds, one felt pressed down, glued to the boards of the ferry lollygagging through the Great South Bay. Willoughby Martin uncrossed his legs and lit a cigaret. He held the cigaret daintily between index and middle finger. Darn! The humidity would ruin his make-up.

He brushed a hand over his ash blond hair and wondered how to go about making up with Hank. A weekend at Fire Island with an angry Hank would be intolerable. They'd had a silly lovers' quarrel; Willoughby wasn't even sure what had triggered it. The whole thing was ridiculous because it wasn't as if

they were newlyweds. Hank—tall, angular, beaknosed
Hank—had been Willoughby's mate for two years. New
York's gay set knew them as an ideal couple. And
their neighbors in King's Neck had accepted them
into the area. They were the community's pet homosexuals.

They had met at Fire Island. Both of them had
come to Cherry Grove for a weekend of pleasure and
relaxation. It was a grand place for meeting people,
and it didn't matter that some of the men were married because the emphasis was on chance sex rather
than permanent liaison. Actually married men had
never done much for Willoughby: Either they were
AC-DC or they were wholly gay but had married hoping to fool the straight world. Willoughby felt sorry for
them. His own sexuality was devoid of ambivalence.
He couldn't understand any man who preferred
women. As far as he was concerned, women simply
were not sexy. You might go out with a woman, but
you certainly wouldn't want to sleep with one. And
all the noise about homosexuality being a sickness
absolutely drove Willoughby up the wall. That was
just something else the psychiatrists had made up to
swell their practices. Willoughby had never been sick
a day in his life. He was gay because he preferred it
that way. And it was perfectly healthy. After all, you
could go back to the Greek philosophers.

In any case, he and Hank had met in a bar where
they were doing the Madison, a group dance that had
been popular back then. As he remembered, they
were doing it with about twenty other men and three
dykes. The Madison's major advantage was that it
permitted men to dance with each other without risk-
ing arrest. That was important because the mainland
police who patrolled the area had adopted a live-and-
let-live policy toward Cherry Grove. As long as there
was no public flouting of the law, they left the in-
habitants pretty much alone. Anyway, it had been a
marvelous night. Willoughby still remembered the

fluffy orange sweater he had worn, and the tight chinos that had bulged with the kapok he had inserted in his jock. Hank had worn a plain white sport shirt and gray slacks; his lank ruggedness had excited Willoughby immediately. It turned out that Willoughby, an interior decorator, and Hank, a computer programmer, had a great deal in common besides their subscriptions to Mattachine Society literature. They both were interested in art, the theater, books, cooking, riding and music. That same night, they went to bed together, and it was beautiful. It had a depth and meaning transcending anything either had ever experienced. It was far above the meaningless physical contact available at the "meat rack"—a clearing at the end of a boardwalk that was used for hit-or-miss, night-shrouded sex encounters.

Soon afterward, they began living together. At first, they had shared a Manhattan apartment. Then, like many other young couples, they had decided to move to the suburbs. King's Neck had been especially attractive. It was countrified and yet close-in. Their being gay had never constituted a problem. Hank and Willoughby sometimes joked that their residence in King's Neck represented token integration. In fact, Willoughby believed that many of their neighbors boasted to friends about having a pair of homosexuals domiciled in the area. It gave King's Neck a certain sophistication. They were frequently invited to dinner parties in the community, and Willoughby and Hank had given a few parties of their own in return. Lately, Willoughby had been considering joining the garden club.

As the ferry neared Davis Park, to which they had been invited by some straight friends, Willoughby looked around. Hank was somewhere at the other end of the boat. As for Willoughby, he was surrounded by jauntily dressed young men with dark horn-rimmed glasses and by girls equipped for the weekend with hemp baskets, canvas suitcases, and paper shopping bags. The bags were crammed, for the most part with cornflakes and gin. The girls were mostly career women from East Side apartments; uniformly frantic-faced and dressed in tight white pants or patterned bell-bottoms. As a matter of fact, it was their very uniformity that made him spot Gillian Blake. She stood out. Willoughby knew Gillian on a small-talk basis: She and her husband had attended a few parties both in the city and in King's Neck where he and Hank had also been guests. Blake was an abysmal square, but Willoughby found Gillian likable. For a woman, he thought, Gillian wasn't bad-looking. There was a certain . . . litheness about her.

Gillian saw him and motioned for him to join her.

"Well," he said. "It's good to see you. I mean, most of these people are so utterly depressing."

"Yes," she said, "Mad Ave. on the make. But what are you doing here?"

"Hank and I are staying with some friends," Willoughby explained. "And we're looking forward to it ever so much. You know, we haven't been to a six-ish in such a long time."

"I feel the same way," she said. "Everybody needs a sixish now and then."

Willoughby laughed. Actually, the sixish was a rather charming custom. It was practically a tribal rite for the single people of Fire Island, especially Davis Park. The sixish was an evening cocktail party to which each guest brought his own drink. Some brought mayonnaise jars full of martinis, while others carried measuring cups filled with bourbon, and they all gathered where the noise was. They crowded onto the porch of one of the stilt-supported houses and jammed into one another and made social contacts. Most of the guests only gave their first names and occupations. Frequently they lied about their jobs, saying they were copy writers or television producers when they actually were clerks or stenographers. Eventually they paired for the evening. One of the rules was that you never selected anyone from the house at which you were staying. The people who stayed at a house usually were chipping in to rent it for the summer. They also shared expenses and cooking and housekeeping duties. Sleeping with somebody in your own house could lead to all sorts of complications within the group. The principle of exogamy had a very practical basis, Willoughby reflected.

As a whole, he thought, Fire Island was an anthropologist's delight. Each community was, to some extent, different. There was Ocean Beach, which was solidly built up and even had a small year-round community that necessitated a school. Ocean Beach was famous for summer residents who were prominent in the arts and in the entertainment world. There was Kismet, a middle-class community that included some interestingly built homes, a bar and a tennis court. There was Fire Island Pines, which was beginning to turn gay around the edges, and there was Cherry Grove, which was the loveliest community on Fire Island. Cherry Grove included a good hotel, gourmet-level restaurants, and a cornucopia of artistically decorated and beautifully kept summer homes. There was also Davis Park, which once had been a quiet beach for young marrieds in search of low rentals and solitude, and which now was a popular meeting ground for singles—most of them weekend refugees from such East Side hangouts as Friday's and Maxwell's Plum. They ranged in age from their early twenties into their late thirties, and there were a few men in their early forties. On weekends, they thundered herdlike off the Long Island Railroad trains at Bay Shore and Sayville and piled into taxis for mad dashes to the ferry docks.

Willoughby smiled at Gillian. "You'll have to look us up," he said.

"Without fail," said Gillian. "But where's Hank?"

"Oh, we're having a silly quarrel," Willoughby said. "How about you? Where's your husband?"

"He's not here," Gillian said. She added a tone of mock melodrama to her voice. "I'm on my own."

"Marvelous," said Willoughby. "That should be some sixish."

"Which one?"

"Whichever one you're at."

"Willy," said Gillian, "you're a real doll."

"I try to be," he said, simpering, and they both laughed.

The ferry backed into the slip with a jolt, and the weekenders scrambled for their cargoes of liquor, food and clever hats. From now until they got on the 7:00 p.m. ferry Sunday, they would be carefree vacationers. At least they would try to think of themselves that way. They would do their best to make merry and each other. And each of them would feel—or at least he'd pretend he felt that way—that he was really living. Heterosexuals, thought Willoughby, you had to feel sorry for them.

Gillian said she would look up him and Hank later on, and joined a group of friends waiting on the dock for her. Willoughby waited for Hank. When he saw him, Willoughby felt as if he were choking. There was a stab of pain in his very heart. Hank was with a young man—a slim, dark-haired young man in his early twenties. The young man was obviously gay, and he was looking adoringly at Hank.

Willoughby fought for control of himself. He tried to strike a casual note. "Hi there," he said.

"Hello, Willoughby." Hank's voice was cold, impersonal. He could have been talking to a stranger. Then he turned to the young man. "See you later, Vince," he said. The note of anticipation was obvious in his voice, and Willoughby knew they had already made an arrangement to meet that night.

"You bet, Hank," the young man answered. He grinned impudently at Willoughby.

A few minutes later, Willoughby and Hank were

arguing in their room. "See you later, Vince," Willoughby mimicked.

"Don't kid me," Hank said. "You only wish you saw him first."

"You bitch!" said Willoughby.

"You ought to know," Hank said. "When it comes to bitches, you wrote the book."

"And to think I loved you," said Willoughby.

Hank laughed derisively. "Oh come off it, Willoughby. You don't know what love is."

"Do you think Vince or whatever his name is knows?"

"You know something, Willoughby? You're getting to be an absolute bore."

"I suppose you're meeting him some place."

"As a matter of fact, we're going to take a beach buggy to Cherry Grove."

"You bitch!" Willoughby screamed. "You dirty bitch!" He threw a shoe at Hank's departing figure. Then he fell sobbing on the bed. How could Hank do a thing like that? He was giving Hank the best years of his life. The bitch! Willoughby thought his heart would break.

By sixish time, Willoughby was feeling considerably better. He couldn't believe that Hank would remain angry at him. After all, that Vince was just a boy. And he was cheap and flashy; you might sleep with him but you wouldn't want to live with him. Besides, Hank had been faithful to Willoughby for a long time. Perhaps a little fling would be good for him. And Willoughby had his own secret. He had once cheated on Hank. There was a hairdresser whom he had met at a gay bar in the city. It had been just a single incident and it had really meant nothing. He had never told Hank about it.

Also, the sixish had set up Willoughby. It had been ages since he had been to a party on Fire Island. Davis Park was a pretty straight community, but then you never knew whom you might meet. Maybe he just might have an adventure of his own. More and more people were going gay these days. Maybe some day they would outnumber the straights. Then heterosexuality would be the deviation.

Willoughby checked his make-up, and put on sandals, tight blue slacks and a pink sweater. He filled a peanut butter jar, provided by his hosts, with martinis, and he was ready. Sixish, he thought, here I come! He wondered what Hank was doing. Oh tush, he thought, the hell with Hank. Willoughby looked in the mirror and ran a comb through his hair. He stood there preening for a moment. He wasn't over the hill yet, he thought. He wiggled his behind and walked out into the sea-rustled evening.

Gillian Blake was at the second place he tried; a weathered pine cottage with a crowd milling on the porch. There were noise and bustle and the informal flux and color that went with the seaside. Most of the guests were groupers—the word for people sharing summer rentals—and they all seemed to be straight. That was perfectly all right with Willoughby because most of the men seemed singularly unattractive—at least there was no one for whom he sensed instant chemistry. He decided that he might as well talk to Gillian, whose pantherish quality was enhanced by black pants and a black-ribbed sleeveless sweater.

"Fancy meeting you here," he said.

"Yes, isn't it a coincidence?" said Gillian, her tongue running across the roof of her mouth as she gave him a quick catlike grin. Her eyes were sparkling, and her hair was soft and lustrous as it caressed her shoulders. She actually was quite attractive. For a girl, that is.

"You look charming," he said.

"Thanks," said Gillian. "You look very nice, too. I just love your sweater."

"I bought it in the Village," Willoughby said, and he gave her the name of the shop. They sipped at their jars, and talked clothes and decorating. Finally, Gillian mentioned Hank's absence.

"I'm not his keeper," Willoughby said.

"That's very wise," said Gillian. "It's a sensible way to look at it. It's awful when somebody tries to push you, to put you in a box."

Willoughby looked at her with new respect. "You know, you really are very sensitive."

"You have no idea," she said.

"I'm beginning to," Willoughby said, and he thought that he had never enjoyed a woman's company so much before. She was an exceptional person, he thought. They sipped some more and looked around them. The aura was one of noise and nervousness. Couples were beginning to link arms and walk off to the beach and the embrace of the night.

"They're too much, aren't they?" said Gillian.

"Yes, they're so utterly frantic."

"Don't be hard on them," she said, laughing. "They're not as sophisticated as you are. They're just simple heterosexuals."

Willoughby grinned. "I know. It's just too terrible the way they carry on. They do such awful things to each other."

"Yes," said Gillian. "You have to pity them, the poor things. I mean, it's a sickness."

Willoughby giggled. She was absolutely charming, he thought. It was really too bad she wasn't a man.

"Well, so long as they don't try to pervert me," said Willoughby. "It's okay as long as they stick to their own kind."

"They are terrible."

"Frightful," said Willoughby. "I think it's perfectly scandalous the way they carry on."

Gillian's eyes suddenly bored into his. "Do you really, Willoughby?"

"Not really," he said. "But it's not my cup of tea."

"Honestly?"

"Absolutely not."

"Yes, but don't you ever think about it? About having sex with a woman?"

"Not ever."

"Why?"

"Come now, Gillian. I told you. It's not my cup of tea."

"That's hard to believe."

"Your ego's showing, dear."

"No, I mean it. Haven't you ever done it with a woman?"

"No."

"Not even as a kid?"

"No. Not even then."

"Well then, I don't see how you can criticize it."

"What do you mean?"

"You know what they say," said Gillian, and her eyes were laughing at him. "Don't knock it until you've tried it."

Willoughby felt flustered. He tried for a joking answer. "Oh *you!* If Hank were here, you wouldn't dare talk to me that way. You heterosexual, you!"

Gillian chuckled, and moved nearer. Her perfume was enchanting. "But after all, Willoughby," she said, "you are a man."

"Let's just say I'm a better man," said Willoughby.

"Tell me," she said, "don't you feel, oh I don't know—don't you feel like a disenfranchised Negro sometimes?"

"No. I feel more like an emancipated one."

"My, my," said Gillian, "such a sense of freedom. And I wouldn't have been surprised if you'd said a castrated one."

"You're being vulgar, sweetie."

"I am sorry," she said. She moved her face closer. Then, staring right at him the whole while, she leaned forward and kissed him on the lips.

For a moment, Willoughby stood stock-still. His face wore a quizzical look. It hadn't been unpleasant at all, he thought. As a matter of fact—and the realization almost dizzied him—it had been rather pleasurable.

"That wasn't so bad now, was it?" said Gillian.

"No," Willoughby conceded with characteristic honesty. "I'll admit it. It wasn't bad."

"You'll have to tell Hank," she said.

"I love Hank," he said.

"Sure you do," she said. She moved forward again, and this time—oh my God, thought Willoughby—this time her tongue met his, circling it teasingly and then sucking deep. Willoughby was breathless as he pushed her away. "My God!" he said. He couldn't believe his excitement.

"Face up to it, Willoughby," she said. "You're more straight than you thought you were."

"No," he said. "That's ridiculous."

"You just never met the right woman before, that's all."

"It's the liquor," he said.

"Oh, come off it, Willoughby."

"But Hank. . . ."

"What about Hank? Like what do you think he's doing right now?"

Hank, thought Willoughby. Damn him. Damn him to hell, the bitch. "Forget about Hank," he said.

"Yes," she said, "let's forget about him." And their tongues were touching once again.

Gillian moved back and smiled. The peanut butter jars were empty, and Gillian and Willoughby stared at each other. Gillian's expression was omniscient; Willoughby looked confused.

"Yes," she said.

"No," he said. "No."

"Don't look so sad, Willy. You'll love it."

"It's crazy," he said. "The whole idea is crazy."

"It's a perfectly marvelous idea."

"I can't. I just can't."

"You can, you can."

The martinis sloshed about inside Willoughby's head. He couldn't understand what was happening. No woman had ever attracted him before. Yet he

couldn't lie to himself. Gillian Blake had a certain
. . . well, a certain excitement. Only he loved Hank.
Still, there had been the hairdresser. And Hank. With
that stupid Vince. The bitch!

Gillian reached out and took his hand. Her fingers
played with the hairs on the back of his wrist. Then
she was tugging gently at him.

"Come on, Willy," she said. "When in Rome, do as
the groupers do. Or something. Let's take a walk."

Double damn Hank, Willoughby thought. "Yes," he
said. "Let's. I mean, why the hell not?" But he knew
nothing would happen. Not with a woman. He simply couldn't.

They walked alongside the dunes, Willoughby
sometimes hesitating, and then moving on. Gillian
kept pace—not leading, not following. They came to
a hollow in the dunes just beyond the cluster of
houses, and they stopped.

"This really is nonsensical, Gillian," Willoughby
said.

"You don't really believe that, do you, Willoughby?"
She snuggled against him.

"Yes, I do. Look, Gillian, I'm a homosexual because
I want to be. Women make me sick."

"But I don't make you sick, do I, Willoughby?" she
said, and she leaned forward and brushed her lips
against his.

"No," he said. "I guess you don't. But I couldn't. I
just couldn't."

"Sure you could." Now she was nibbling on his ear.

"No."

"Yes." Now she was kissing him with her tongue.
"Ummm," she murmured. "You do that very well."

Willoughby was beginning to feel good. "It's my
specialty," he said.

"What's Hank's specialty?"

"Can you guess?" said Willoughby.

Her hand was inside his trousers now, and Willoughby sat as if he was riveted to the sand. An in-

credible thing was happening. Something that had never happened before in his entire life. He was experiencing a physical reaction to a woman! A physical reaction!

Now Gillian was at him with her mouth—with her soft lips and her skilled tongue. Willoughby lay back with closed eyes. He was being transported out of himself. Christ, but she was good. She was better than Hank! Oh my God! Oh! Oh! Oh my *God!*

Gillian sat up. "Well," she said. "Do you still think Hank has a corner on the market?"

"Gillian," he said. "Oh, Gillian."

"I know," she said, and they reached for each other and found pleasure in gentle caresses.

They spent perhaps an hour touching each other, exploring each other; Willoughby making new discoveries all the time. Why, a woman's body was interesting! They were both naked now; lying in the cool sand near the breaking sea. Gillian cupped her breasts with her hands and offered them to him. The nipples were firm and erect. Willoughby stared at the proud breasts blossoming in the shadows. Breasts, he thought, breasts. There was something he should do. Breasts. He fastened his eyes on them, and then, with primeval instinct, he leaned forward. He sucked.

A little while later, Gillian gently pushed him away. Her hands were on him again, eliciting stiffness. He tried to push her mouth down to him.

"No," she said. "This time we do it my way."

"But I can't. I never have."

"Come to Gilly," she crooned, caressing him.

"I want to," he said. "I want to." And it was as if the confession gave him strength. He mounted her as she fell back on the sand.

Slowly, gently. Slowly, gently. Slowly, nicely. Oh lovely, lovely. Then faster, quicker, faster, needful. Willoughby was lost in immense, billowy softness and riotous colors and roaring winds; he was the sand and the sea and the star-pierced sky. Faster, faster, faster.

Oh, oh, oh . . . . ahhhhhhh. From far off he heard a faint cry that turned into a moan; it was Gillian, and then Willoughby realized he had been moaning, too.

Afterward, they smoked and talked.

"Was I really good?" he asked.

"One of the all-time greats," she said.

"I'll be a son of a bitch," said Willoughby. He got up and strode to the water. He felt manful as hell. He urinated. Then he dipped his hands into the cold surf. He reached up and washed the make-up from his face. He strode back to Gillian.

"What about Hank?" she said.

Willoughby Martin breathed in the night air. "If that son of a bitch ever bothers me again," he said, "I'll knock him on his ass."

They laughed. Willoughby thought his voice sounded deeper. By God, he was a man.

They spent the night on the beach. That Gillian. He couldn't get enough of her. And imagine all the women who were out there in the world waiting for him. Just wait till Hank tried to come crawling back. Hank! thought Willoughby, and he snorted to himself. That damn queer.

A few weeks later, King's Neck lost its pet homosexuals. They moved out shortly after neighbors reported hearing a terrible row. The day after the fight, someone saw Hank in town with a bandaged nose and blackened eyes. A month after that, one of the garden club officers reported meeting Willoughby in the city. She said she had hardly recognized him; he was wearing a sweatshirt, and he had gotten a crew-cut. And believe it or not, she said, he had tried to proposition her. Someone told Gillian about it. "Well," she said. "It's like they say. Don't knock it until you've tried it."

Billy: The man says he doesn't want any publicity, that's what the man says. And, speaking personally, I find that attitude a refreshing change from most of the authors we manage to lure onto the show.

Gilly: You'd think that out of sheer neighborliness. . . .

Billy: Neighborliness? That fellow moves about in much the way an astronaut does—except, from what I hear, at a lower level. And I have to admit I've always felt he was overrated as a writer, strictly a one-book author.

Gilly: You mean The Hard and the Moist?

Billy: What else?

Gilly: Well, how about Mountaintop?

Billy: Same book, different title. Look at him, honey. What is he—forty-four years old?—the world's oldest flower child.

Gilly: But still, still he's Caradoc.

ZOLTAN CARADOC

Gillian realized there was no legitimate reason to include Zoltan Caradoc on her list. He had been married four times—most recently to Paige Marchand, the dancer—but they were never marriages in the customary sense. It had been several years since he had allowed a woman to share his bayside castle for more than a night or two. In fact, for nine months of every year Caradoc was a virtual hermit, a professional loner, a man who spent long hours fashioning sentences while studying the sullen winter waters of Long Island Sound.

These were his working months, his caged-in months. Caradoc spent the time roaming from one room to another, one glass-fronted cubicle to another, always within sight of the water and always surrounded by the tape recorders and stereo sets and color television consoles and electric typewriters. He lived three-fourths of his life in an ultra-modern electronic womb. Cable umbilicals carried him regular progress reports from the outside world; sensitive microphones were always handy to transmit and preserve his thoughts and memories for posterity. And though only forty-four years old, Zoltan Caradoc had already strung together enough words to more than equal the lifetime output of Proust.

And every year, as the cold season came to an end, Caradoc once again ventured into the real world. Ventured . . . no, say rather, exploded. He would, in that three-month interval, be photographed stalking chamois in Bhutan, hunting wild boar in Bulgaria, pursuing teenyboppers in San Francisco.

Gillian, like most of the cognoscenti, kept up with the ever growing legend that was Zoltan Caradoc. She recalled the news account of his bloody encounter with a killer shark off Tanzania; Caradoc had lost three fingers of his left hand but had saved the life of a native oarsman. And she recalled another hair-raising adventure—his being arrested in his suite at the Beverly Hills Hotel in the company of three blonde call girls, an ancient Negro sculptress and a Shetland pony.

Gillian had first met Caradoc in early winter—midway between Morton Earbrow and Joshua Turnbull, as she now measured time. It was during the power failure, the electric blackout of King's Neck that lasted twenty-seven hours. Caradoc had endured the power failure as long as he could and then had deserted his

suddenly lifeless machinery for the candlelit warmth
of Moriarity's Shamrock Bar & Grill. Gillian, too,
had stopped in for a moment's warmth. She stood, her
back to an open fire, and she instantly recognized his
face—the face she had seen on the jacket of a book
called *Mountaintop*.

The photo, however, was no more than a sterile reproduction of the original. Never before had she seen
a man with such piercing blue eyes, diamonds blazing
out of a square face beneath a mop of coal-blue hair
that curled and roamed over head and neck. The
nose had been broken more than once, the jaw was
firm, the total effect was softened slightly by the full
and sensual lips. The author was still in his working
garb—jeans with ragged cuffs, a faded denim shirt
with rolled-up sleeves. His forearms were thick, power-
ful, corded with veins and bristling with hair. Gillian
noticed the absence of three fingers from his left
hand.

The stool beside Caradoc was empty and Gillian
walked to it.

"Martini," she said. "On the dry side."

The bartender looked momentarily bewildered and
Caradoc roared with laughter.

"Not here," he said. "Here, Mrs. Blake, you better
settle for a beer."

"A beer then," she said to the bartender before
turning to Caradoc. "My mistake. I didn't mean to be
so radical. How did you know my name?"

"The same way you know mine," Caradoc said. "I
read the papers, same as you do."

"You've got me there," Gillian said, smoothing her
sweater.

"You didn't have to do that."

"Didn't have to do what?"

"That bit of business with the sweater," he said. "I
noticed them without any assistance from you."

"I like your work," Gillian said. "I loved *Mountaintop*."

Mountaintop was the latest. The critics had described it as a bristling, earthy and not unpoetic story of girls on the loose and boys on the bum. Kids with flowers in their hair and fire in their loins, to quote the *Time* critic. In the novel they had demonstrated for peace, group marriage, male prostitution and free public toilets. In the memorable final scene they had all stripped, guzzled cheap wine and chewed peyote. There had been a wild dance in the firelight followed by the hero expressing his love to a twelve-year-old girl and a three-year-old ewe. Gillian had sensed then, sensed again now, that the author had lived the scene. And that was Caradoc's strong point. Even his harshest critics agreed that he wrote from life, that this was the literature of experience.

"It wasn't a bad book," the author said. "It wasn't as good as some, not as good as *Anteaters and Belly Dancers*, but it wasn't bad."

As he spoke, the overhead lights flickered once, twice, then remained on. The end of the power failure. Gillian was sorry in a way. The candles that had lined the long dark bar at Morarity's were extinguished one by one; the saloon could now be seen in all its 60-watt splendor. Sawdust on the floor, grime on the windows, glasses coated with dust. The six other patrons of the moment, the regulars, should have been swept out with sawdust; they wouldn't have noticed.

"My place or yours?"

"What?" she said.

"My place or yours?" he repeated. "I'm assuming you don't want this to end any more than I do."

"Yours," she said.

Her intentions were innocent enough. There was no reason to look on Caradoc as a prospect. There was no marriage to be tested. And so, humming gently to herself, she calmly followed the writer as he drove through downhill woodland toward the shore. The house, every window now ablaze with light, sat on a rock base in a protective cove. The tide was high and the bay water had risen above the foundation and lay flat below his living room windows.

The wide tile-floored entranceway to the house was dominated by a huge wire statue, a male nude with an erection. Indeed, the small placard proclaimed the title of the work to be "Male Nude With Erection." Each room held its own array of wonders. Gillian noticed the names—Cezanne, Picasso, Van Gogh, Pollock, Warhol, Rivers—and was suitably impressed. There was a huge portrait of Caradoc's left eye—no mistaking the brilliance of that blue. An oil of Paige Marchand in bra, panties and leather boots. Ivory tusks, a mounted stingray, loudspeakers on every wall.

In the main room Caradoc paused to depress a wall switch that simultaneously dimmed the lights and started the record player—jetting the raucous sounds of the Jefferson Airplane from every available wall.

There were none of the standard overtures. Caradoc simply stood in the center of the huge room and undressed. First his jacket and his shirt, then his trousers and his shorts. Though Gillian had done nothing, said nothing, the author was in a state of visible excitement. The sight was impressive enough. What was even more impressive was the realization that Caradoc had served as model for the wire sculpture beside the front door. There was no mistaking the likeness; Gillian found herself wondering how long he had been able to hold the pose.

"What do you think you're doing?" she said.

"It's the visuality," he explained. "Very important."

"I think you've misjudged me, Mr. Caradoc," she said.

"I don't think so, Mrs. Blake," he said. "And I want to be completely honest with you. Everything that you say from now on will be recorded."

"Will be what?"

"Taped," he said. "If I ever write about this experience, if there is anything here worth writing about —and that should be a challenge to you, Mrs. Blake—

I want to get it right, letter-perfect. I want to tell it like it is."

"You're wasting your time—there'll be nothing to tell." She backed slowly toward the door. Caradoc, crossing the room with surprising agility, stood between Gillian and her escape route. Still in a clear state of sexual excitement, he advanced toward her.

"Don't," she said. "Please don't."

"I won't do anything you don't want," he said.

"I don't want anything but out," she said.

"That's what you say," he replied. "Some day you'll thank me for what I'm going to do."

Gillian, paralyzed now, saw his right hand, his good hand, reach out, felt his fingers close slowly over the top of her sweater. And then in one swift sure move, he ripped the sweater away from her. Then he reached for the skirt, shredded that.

"This is rape," Gillian said.

"It may begin as rape," he said, "but that's not the way it generally winds up."

"Please don't," Gillian said. "I don't want this to happen, not this way. I'll come back some other time when we feel better. I'll. . . ."

The promise was interrupted as his hands, gentle now, reached around her and expertly unlatched the brassiere strap. As it fell to the floor, Gillian turned and ran toward the first door she saw. A mistake—it was the bedroom and it was too late to escape. Caradoc stood at the doorway to the room, then came toward her, forcing her to retreat back onto the most enormous bed she had ever seen.

He stood over her then and smiled down at her. She closed her eyes to shut out the sight of the man but there was no way to eliminate the other sensations.

Gillian felt cold. She shivered, braced herself for the attack that never came. What Gillian recalled later was the surprising gentleness of Caradoc as he applied himself to his task. For long moments he did not put a hand on her. There was only his mouth to reckon with—a mouth fastened itself to her throat, then moved down to her breasts. She could feel his tongue as it traced the outline of her rib cage, paused to explore her naval, continued to chart a downward course.

Despite herself, despite a fear she could not really explain, Gillian felt the warmth returning. The mouth kissing, pleading, cajoling, insisting. Gillian felt herself relaxing, felt the tension flowing from her legs, felt her body beginning to writhe, responding to the mouth with the harmonic precision of an orchestra responding to a conductor's baton. The tongue was alternatingly gentle and impertinent, loving and demanding—very much like Caradoc himself.

Gillian was aware of an argument raging within herself, a great debate between body and mind. She felt herself lose all control over her legs. The insistent tongue urged them open and they opened. She felt her back stiffen and arch. It was not what she wanted, not really, but she found her hands reaching down to Caradoc's head, holding tight to his long blue-black hair, encouraging him now, guiding him, directing him.

And then it ended.

"All right, Mrs. Blake," she heard him say: "You can go home now."

"What do you mean?" she said.

"I was just testing your reactions," he said. "I think I've got what I wanted."

"You mean this—all this—was just an experiment?"

"That's all, Mrs. Blake," he said. "You can go home now . . . if you really want to."

He stood before her still physically aroused, taunting her, waiting to hear her beg for him to continue. Waiting to record her pleadings for some future novel. She had an unholy desire to reach out and touch him, to hold him there, to make him plead for her. But she did nothing. She retrieved her panties from the foot of the bed and stepped into them. She found her brassiere in the living room and put it back in place. She found an overcoat in the hall closet and put it on. Caradoc watched all this in mute wonder, in a seeming state of shock.

"Amazing!" was all he said.

"What is truly amazing," she said, "is your ego."

"Hey," he said, "you'll come back, won't you? You'll come back and visit me, won't you?"

"I'll think about it," she promised—that and no more—and then she was gone.

She thought about it and she came back. There had never been a rationalization, a justification, a way to explain her repeated visits to the isolated house by the water's edge. But time and time again she returned. Possibly because Caradoc became such an effective antidote for the sordid little affairs as they ended, perhaps because he was a bracing tonic for the new affairs that were about to begin. Most likely, however, because in a sense they both were scientists, experimenters seeking life's more elusive truths. Even their interests were similar—while he explored love, she explored marriage.

It ended only because it had to end. Caradoc drained her of time and emotion. With Caradoc she had found more than a mutuality of interests, more than sex, more than the conversation that never grew stale or repetitive. There came a time, as winter gave way to spring, that she thought, not without alarm, that it might even be love. If it was love, it would ruin everything—the show, possibly herself. If not love, there was no reason to continue. And so, one day early in June, as Zoltan Caradoc was saying that this year, for some reason, he didn't feel like going out on one of his annual three-month hunting expeditions, Gillian calmly did what had to be done. She ended it.

After that there was just one bit of communication. One last letter to become a treasure beyond price for literary historians tracing the career of Zoltan Caradoc. The envelope carried a postmark from Haiti.

Dear Gilly,

You have left your mark on King's Neck. The mark of the cat. The claw-shaped scar splayed across a neighborhood of broken lives. And I, almost as well as you, know the toll (God knows you boasted about it to me often enough). The dead, the destroyed, the psychotic, the forever sad. The marriages that you snapped in two as if you were breaking straws.

And finally, me—in a sense the beginning and the end. The mirror you saw your victories within, now shattered. I hope you have your seven years' bad luck; it is the least I can wish you. This is my last message, my curtain call for the part you made me play. After all the writing, all the words I was creating for you, I end our communication with a properly prosaic letter. But do not wrinkle that aristocratic nose. I dare not bore you, even now.

This letter will be like English beer, short and bitter. It must be brief because I have two ladies waiting for me in the next room. One is a pretty little blonde virgin of sixteen with a maddening resemblance to the White Rock girl. The other is a wildcat black who is a virgin only in her left ear. Sharing a bed with the two of them and exploring their reactions to the same events shall be my modest entertainment this cool summer evening. It is a curiously refreshing diversion. I call it sin and tonic.

But hold. This letter is serious. I am writing to humble myself before you, to acknowledge in cold blood what I have only recently come to realize: That in the end it was I who was your greatest triumph— your masterpiece of creative destruction. Your master piece. (One day I shall be crucified on a cross of puns.) And did you know it all along? Did you, my sweet, cynical destroyer?

We had our moments. We did, dear Gilly, didn't

we, in those days? At least admit that. The priestess
and the poet. I knew your game. I knew all the tables
were rigged for the house. But I saw no reason not to
play. After all, unlike your other conquests, I had
nothing to lose. There was nothing you could take
from me, nothing you could separate me from, nothing
you could destroy. Or so I thought. And I accepted
your love for what it seemed to be. So I made you my
muse—all the muse that's fit to print, as your newspaper friends would say.

The others didn't matter. I saw you bowl them over
like tenpins, one after another. Down they went. The
muscleman, the abortionist, the gangster, the prize-
fighter, the poor Jewish husband, the mad pornographer—I don't remember their names. I can't tell the
losers without a score card. Did you keep a score card,
Gilly? I wouldn't be surprised. You cut them all down,
Gilly; you cut them all down with the sharp edge of
your sex as if they were saplings thirsting for the ax.
But not Caradoc—not the Shakespeare of Suburbia,
the Messiah of the Misbegotten Generation, the Non-
conformist of *Time's* cover.

I saw them come and go, saw you mark up the
scores. I watched, knowing that after each one you
would return for the real thing. We may not have
made the earth move, Gilly, but we made my mind
spin—and until now that has always been the same
thing. All those times before the fireplace, the flames
turning your skin to copper, your breasts to the
Spanish hills below Valencia at sunset, your hollows
to the textured porous shadows of sifting sand. And
I had a gypsy for a muse. Making love before that
fire, feeding the flames with our own fuel, lying there
gazing through the skylight, reaching the stars.

You would smoke then, and I would talk of the
future. I was going to be immortal, wasn't I? My work.
What a legacy for the world. What greater gift for
my fellow man? What greater dedication than to dis-
till in words the essence of life?

What bullshit.

Does that shock you? Not likely. After all, bullshit is what the *Billy & Gilly* shows are made of. I suppose nothing could shock you, not now. Not you, dear Gilly. I suppose you planned it all. I had miscalculated, over-estimated your longing for immortality. You were to be my blonde Dark Mistress, remember? Graduate students and scholars were going to pore over my works in the twenty-first century and write endless theses, complete with footnotes, on the identity of Zoltan Caradoc's golden goddess. Only now, now that you are gone, do I realize that you are quite content to be listed in the book of life as Mrs. William Blake, the round-heeled half of *Billy & Gilly*. Three cheers for Salinger's Fat Lady. Hip, hip, hurrah!

The point is that I have not written a line, Gilly, not a word, since the day you left. I have given up the words. I relinquish them to those who still believe in them. That was your greatest triumph, Gilly, greater than any of the marriages you wrecked, or the deaths you caused, or the pain you produced.

When I finish this letter, in a moment, I am going into the bedroom to make perverse love to my virgin and my whore. It will be recorded on film and tape, part of the research, *my* research. I will read the transcripts and study the pictures. But the words will not come. They do not come any more.

I had no mate, Gilly, so you separated me from myself. It was brilliant. I don't know how early in the game you planned it that way. But I want you to know how completely you succeeded. Macbeth hath murdered sleep but he is no match for Gilly. Dear Gilly hath murdered Art. Gilly hath murdered im-mortality.

Yours, alas—

Z.

EXCERPT FROM "THE BILLY & GILLY SHOW," JULY 18TH

Gilly: Well, Billy, I see we're coming to the end of our last show, our last show before our vacation. Four glorious weeks to ourselves. Just the two of us. Then, when we come back, well . . . shall we tell them?

Billy: I don't see why not, darling.

Gilly: I never could keep a secret—but you knew that when you married me. We're moving again! That's right, the next time you hear this program, we'll be right back where we belong, right back in a lovely new apartment here in midtown Manhattan.

Billy: That's right, darling. But don't you think we owe our listeners a little explanation? It seems only yesterday—golly, I guess it was just about a year ago— that we announced we were moving out of the city and into suburbia, into our new home in King's Neck.

Gilly: Yes, I suppose an explanation would be germane to—oh, don't frown, sweetheart, everyone knows that means relevant. And I suppose an explanation would be relevant here.

Billy: As our listeners must know by now—they certainly hear it often enough—the purpose of this show is to look at marriage "in the crucible of modern living."

Gilly: Well put, darling.

Billy: And what better crucible than suburbia? For us, and I hope for our listeners, it has been a valuable year, a year of experimentation, an opportunity to look at. . . .

Gilly: Yes, dear, all that is true enough, but we may as well admit it hasn't all been sweetness and light. In fact, just the other day we both seemed to notice at the same time what has been happening in King's Neck. One marriage after another has crumbled, just gone up in smoke. . . .

Billy: I think you're mixing your metaphors, darling. . . .

Gilly: Anyway, we both noticed that our neighborhood is beginning to look like a ghost town. It seems as though there's a FOR SALE *sign in front of every home.*

Billy: Not that we regret having lived in King's Neck. It was, as I was saying a moment ago, a splendid opportunity to examine some of the forces that tend to twist and pry apart marriages. And nowhere do you see these forces as clearly as in suburbia.

Gilly: The pressures are simply terrific. The husbands and wives of King's Neck are, in a sense, separated. Not legally separated—but they certainly go their separate ways from morning to night. I've had many talks with the housewives of King's Neck and I've never see so many frustrated females in one place. There is the constant striving for material goods—new cars, new swimming pools—and somewhere along the way they seem to have lost sight of spiritual values. The effect this can have on a marriage can be simply devastating.

Billy: I think we can count ourselves among the lucky ones. . . .

Gilly: In all fairness, Billy, it isn't just luck. To make a marriage work—and how often we've said this! —people have to work at it.

Billy: I couldn't agree with you more wholeheartedly, darling. And I think we might add something else here. The first thing a person notices about a suburb such as King's Neck is the rootlessness. And with that, the restlessness. People all too often tend to turn their backs on tradition, tend to forget the valuable lessons that have been carefully preserved and handed down by past generations.

Gilly: I hope you're not going to say something as, well, basic as, "The family that prays together stays together." . . .

Billy: But maybe. . . .

Gilly: Perhaps, after all, it is something basic and simple. But maybe it goes something like this: The family that stays together stays together. I realize many of our listeners will feel that togetherness is just a little on the corny side. But I think we can say that togetherness has always been important to us.

Billy: Indeed it has, darling. Well, I see our time is running out. . . .

Gilly: Remember, our address may be a new one, but we'll be back at this same spot in just four weeks.

Billy: So you be thinking about us because. . . .

Gilly: We'll be thinking about you.

How many of these Dell bestsellers have you read?

The Money Game by "Adam Smith" $1.25

The Madonna Complex by Norman Bogner $1.25

The Manor by Isaac Bashevis Singer $1.25

The Other Side by James A. Pike   95c

Soul On Ice (A Delta Edition) by Eldridge Cleaver $1.95

Tell Me How Long The Train's Been Gone
by James Baldwin $1.25

The Beastly Beatitudes of Balthazar B by J. P. Donleavy $1.25

The Doctor's Quick Weight Loss Diet
by I. Maxwell Stillman M.D., and S. Sinclair Baker   95c

The Secret of Santa Vittoria by Robert Crichton   95c

The Hundred Yard War by Gary Cartwright   95c

Bruno's Dream by Iris Murdoch   95c

The Movie Maker by Herbert Kastle $1.25

The Astrological Guide to Marriage and Family Relations
by Carroll Righter   95c

A novel of an erotic paradise
by the author of *Eternal Fire* . . .

PROVIDENCE ISLAND

by Calder Willingham

Three people stranded on a desert island. A man and
two women. An indefatigable satyr in a Brooks Brothers
suit. A young minister's wife with her enormous sexuality barely held in check. And a man-hating female with
a taste for her own kind.

Only the extraordinary imagination of Calder Willingham could have conceived of this situation. Only his
dazzling skills could have transformed it into one of the
most fascinating, provocative and important novels of
the year.

"Great . . . a priapic gusto that will have readers reel-
ing."   —*Publisher's Weekly*

"Willingham is perhaps the most outstanding talent of
the generation of Norman Mailer, William Styron,
James Jones . . . the most original innovator . . . the
one writer who has achieved mastery . . . his unique
ability to see modern character as an hilarious interplay
of hypocrisies is as strong as ever."   —*Newsweek*

"Calder Willingham's most accomplished and mature
work . . . if you are stranded on any island, *Providence
Island* is the book to be stranded with."
                                              —*Saturday Review*

A DELL BOOK $1.25

THE BEASTLY BEATITUDES OF BALTHAZAR B

J. P. Donleavy

"You'll want to read BALTHAZAR B. It'll make you laugh and cry. The story is simple. A wealthy young Frenchman of Irish ancestry is born in Paris, schooled in England and at Trinity College, Dublin, married and separated in London. He begins and remains shy and gentle. He seeks love. It proves elusive, even harder to keep than to find. Neither the meek nor the arrogant inherit the earth in Donleavy's cosmos. While all possess it, none can keep it. In laughing or weeping over this poor little rich boy we really laugh and weep not for Balthazar but for ourselves."

SATURDAY REVIEW

"Incident upon hilarious, marvellously invented incident—encounters, disportings, disappointments, scenes of domestic life and strife, sexual spectaculars, small joys and further sadnesses. It is Donleavy at his best . . ."

NEWSWEEK

"Revelatory, delightful and sometimes very poignant, this romp of a novel is lush and lovely, bawdy and sad . . . the stuff of the passions and dreams of being alive."

THE NEW YORK TIMES

"Donleavy is capable of making the heterosexual act seem as lyrical and as blessed as it sometimes is in reality."

LIFE MAGAZINE

"While the overall tone of the book is tragic and almost elegiac, the individual scenes are often hilarious . . . unmatched in literature for comic ferocity."

TIME MAGAZINE

"*Genuine and touching* . . . J. P. Donleavy is, I think, one of the most accomplished and original writers of our time, and BALTHAZAR B belongs with his best."

JOSEPH HELLER

"*Adjective to come* . . . Because it is so readable, THE BEASTLY BEATITUDES OF BALTHAZAR B is probably the novel for those as yet uninitiated into Donleavy's talent to begin with . . . one of the few really great writers we have."

THE NEW LEADER

In hardcover: A Seymour Lawrence/Delacorte Press Book $6.95
In paperback: A Dell Book $1.25

Dell Publishing Co., Inc.

The Bestselling New Novel by the Author of
Seventh Avenue

"A narrative gift . . . a sure hand with
character . . . convincing . . . impressive"
—*Saturday Review Syndicate*

The
Madonna
Complex

by Norman Bogner

The compelling and disturbingly beautiful love story of
a Wall Street tycoon and a seductive younger woman.
This is Norman Bogner's spellbinding new novel of
sexual obsession, betrayal, and final strange salvation.

"A sexy book . . . all the pathos, greed and grief, longing and impatience, holiness and obscenity, depravity
and creativity of human sexuality . . . an exquisite and
moving, terrifying and haunting multifaceted novel"
—*Chicago Sun-Times*

"Gripping . . . compulsive readability"
—*Saturday Review*

A DELL BOOK $1.25